7-15-20

ALSO BY JAN SURASKY

Rage Against the Dying Light

BACK

TO

JERUSALEM

BACK

TO

JERUSALEM

A NOVEL

JAN SURASKY

Published by Sandalwood Press
Victor, New York

Jacket design and Illustration by
Rob Wood, Wood Ronsaville Harlin, Inc.

Interior book design by Susan Surasky
Larkspur Design

Library of Congress Cataloging-in-Publication Card Number:
TXu1-754-985

To the kindness of strangers

To see a World in a Grain of Sand
And a Heaven in a Wild Flower...

-William Blake

Acknowledgments

I would like to thank Book1One for their attention to quality and their ready willingness to answer all those technical questions.

I would like to thank the firm of Wood Ronsaville Harlin, Inc. Rob Wood for his magical and consistently beautiful cover art, Pam Ronsaville for her brilliant art direction, and Kassie Wood for keeping it all together and making it run so smoothly.

I would like to thank Marcia Blitz for sharing her tremendous expertise in creating great flap and back cover copy and for her much cherished and always upbeat wisdom.

I would like to thank the many vendors of the Windmill Market in Penn Yan for sharing with me their stories of the origins of the market and showing me firsthand how people can put aside their differences and work together for a common good.

Finally, my thanks to those who critiqued this manuscript and provided encouragement and support in bringing this tale to the written page.

BACK

TO

JERUSALEM

Chapter One

Jenny Thompson looked out over the landscape that was the small town of Jerusalem, New York in the 1970s. A long blade of grass, newly plucked before her climb to her perch on the half-second floor of her family's run-down barn, hung from her mouth, a reminder of the ones she had used to force the rudimentary sounds of an instrument through as a child when she had finished her chores. Not that she had ever had many. As the child of a successful farmer and owner of a tire store in town, she had mostly helped Mother in the kitchen, putting up jams and jellies and pickles, and pitting the sour cherries they found down by the river.

Often, she had tagged behind Hiram the hired man who fed and watered the horses, and baled the hay while Father plowed the fields that grew feed corn for cattle on neighboring farms, beans and oats, soy beans and sunflowers, and whatever cash crops he found appealing in the new edition of the Farmer's Almanac. The land was lush and fertile, but the work was hard, and the county still the second poorest in the state.

Sometimes, as a small child, Father would boost her up on the seat of the tractor in front of him, rolling off to the fields to plow or fertilize or sow the seeds that would soon sprout with the rays of the sun and the gentle mists of rain, if they were lucky. It was then she felt protected and all-powerful, especially if the skies were blue and the sun was very hot and strong upon them.

As she sat, Jenny crossed her legs on the rickety floorboards to give herself some leverage. The landscape that lay before her was home to mostly subsistence farming, with a number of pockets of poverty scattered about. The neatly-kept homes and barns of the Mennonites who farmed without electricity intermingled with the farms of the townspeople known as the "English." Trailers and small, disintegrating homes, in need of paint, with shingles falling from the rooftops, took their place next to clotheslines of shabby, flapping clothes. But, rich in beauty, its flatlands and gentle, rolling hills brought out the rusts, the oranges and the yellows of autumn, the lush greens of summer, the pinks, the lavenders and blues of spring, and the pristine white expanse of winter, as they stretched toward the evergreen-covered mountains of neighboring Bristol.

As she mused, Jenny realized this was the last year she and her friends would be gossiping about school and boys in the meadows and along the lanes of her family's farm. Seniors, they would soon be scattering to pursue their dreams of the future. Serious Caroline Mackey to Cornell to become a teacher. Flighty, fun Dotty Thatcher to business school a few towns away to learn typing and stenography. Jenny was struck with a mixture of fear and excitement.

"A penny for your thoughts," shouted a voice from the floor below. Jake Martin looked up, his overalls dirty from farm work, his muscles fairly rippling through the thin shirt he wore beneath it. He was pretty nearly on time, almost always catching Jenny at around four in the afternoon, when he was sure she had finished her chores, and he had finished his. As he climbed the ladder toward the loft, his blond hair, uneven from years of home haircuts, glistened in the late afternoon sun.

He settled on the floorboards next to her, pulling an envelope from his overall pocket. To Jenny, it looked pretty important. An official looking seal on the envelope, and one to match at the top of the letter he pulled from it. "What's this," said Jenny, as she wriggled over to give his large frame more room.

"I've been accepted at Hobart," said Jake. "Pa doesn't know about it. I'm not even sure he'll want me to go. I know he needs me on the farm. And, I know he thinks higher education is an intrusion into the purity of living. He has strong Mennonite beliefs, and I don't like to go against his wishes."

Jenny looked at Jake, so changed from when he first came to Jerusalem, a skinny, twelve-year-old dressed in what she thought were funny clothes. The oldest of a family which came here to follow the cheap land prices, settling on a piece of land next to the Thompson farm that had lain fallow for nearly twenty years. And, they had strange ways. Farming without gas or electricity, traveling about in a strange, black buggy pulled by two lively horses.

At first, Jenny stared, never offering to share her few possessions, but as the months passed, and she saw how much fun they had together, in the few hours they had for playtime, she relented, reveling, as an only child, in the comfort of their companionship. It was then she shared her barrel hoops, laughing and rolling them along with Jake and his five younger brothers and sisters. And, the old, tire swing hanging from the red maple aside from the porch. She and Jake passed many hours pushing the little ones and talking about what they would do when they grew up. They made Jenny laugh, the girls lifting their long skirts on a hot summer's day to cool their feet in the Thompsons' shallow stream, the boys donning black hats and turning somber for a Sunday morning service.

But, today she could see that Jake's usually sunny countenance was lost in conflict. "Jenny," he said, "I so much want to help the poor. But, to give good help, I will need an education."

"Why the poor?" she asked.

"When Pa looked around for a place for us to settle," said Jake, "he had no money for help here. He had to keep going back to Pennsylvania for advice from his cousins who knew little more than he did so he wouldn't get cheated."

"When we went to school," he continued, "most of the boys either teased us or ignored us. Bud Anderson and his crowd chased us off the playground at recess every day, picking fights and getting us into trouble, getting the teachers to side with them because their fathers were rich and big in town. If it wasn't for Sammy Walker, who the other kids teased because his pants were too short and too worn, taking me into the grove of elm trees behind the playground and showing me how to fight, I never would have been able to stand up to any of them.

"But Bud got him back by keeping him off the football team, his only hope for college."

"How will you help the poor?" she asked.

"I am going to be a lawyer."

"Then you will be rich. Emily Watson's father is a lawyer. Father says he is one of the richest men in town."

"You don't get rich helping the poor. But, what are you going to be when I am a poor lawyer?" he asked.

"I am going to be an artist. My paintings will be hanging in all the rich people's homes in New York."

"Then, you will be famous. And, I can say I knew you when you were a farm girl canning pickles and cherry jam."

Jenny turned toward Jake, her long brown hair, its chestnut highlights glistening in the rays of the sun that streamed through the open barn door, bouncing along her shoulders as she moved. "Will it be bad for you when everyone goes to the prom?" she asked.

"It's only one day," he said. "And Pa and I will be unloading the buggy after a long day's work at the market. And," he added, "the little ones need me. If one gets into trouble, they blame the other one, and then they both come to me to plead their case to Pa."

"I hope I get asked."

Jake looked at Jenny, her thick chestnut hair the envy of every girl in the school, her eyes, now wide, the blue of the Jerusalem sky on a sunny day. The scent of the lavender soap she always used filled his nostrils. "Of course, you'll get asked. You're the most beautiful girl in the class."

"Oh, Jake." She threw her arms around him. As she withdrew, she stood up. "I guess it's time to go help Mother with supper. No sense my hanging around here till she pulls on the bell. She'll only scold me for sitting around dreaming when I could be useful."

As she climbed down the ladder, Jake clambered after her, walking as far as the path that led to her house. Then, he turned, taking the tree-lined lane that ran between the Thompson and Martin farms.

The scent of the lavender, still lingering in his nostrils, mingled with the scent of the dogwood. Oblivious to the orange, the mauve, and the brilliant red of the early sunset, his mind was far away on thoughts of the future. The few stray stones crunched beneath the cleats of his sturdy boots.

Chapter Two

Peeling potatoes for supper with Mother was always an ordeal. Not only was she fussy about where the peels landed in the sink, and how carefully the "eyes" were removed with the end of the peeler, she was very interested in how Jenny had spent her day, especially when it came to making herself attractive to the boys in her class at Dundee-Penn Yan Central.

"Jenny, I think you should wear a little blush," she would say. "Your cheeks are so pale." Or, "I think we should tweeze those eyebrows, they're way too thick in the middle."

Today, she felt more inclined to complain about Father. "Your father picked the wrong crop again this year. No rain. The beans are small and he'll lose most of them if it's dry all season." Then, she sighed. "That will mean longer hours in the tire shop."

And, then came the same old refrain. "You know I gave up a lot to marry your father. My family had money and social standing. Your grandfather was a first-class printer, with over sixty people working for him in his heyday. He had jobs as far away as Syracuse and Elmira, Rochester and Buffalo. He was one of the few printers around who had the equipment to do four-color printing. We belonged to the Hunt Club and the Auburn Country Club.

"Your father's family were nothing but poor dirt farmers. He swept me off my feet, he was so handsome. But, he had nothing but big dreams. We eloped against my father's wishes right out of high school."

"I know, Mother, I know," Jenny would murmur, as she hastened her potato peeling, perhaps to get to her room and her homework that much sooner.

"Jenny," Mother would stop the cooking to look directly at her, an expression both decisive and wistful crossing her usually noncommittal angular features, "you are my only hope. You must marry someone with money and social standing. Then, you will have an easier life. You will have all the things and the gaiety I had as a girl."

"Yes, Mother." Jenny always agreed, hoping assent would get Mother to change the subject. But, she persisted.

"Has anyone asked you to the prom yet?"

"Well, no. But, there's still time. Dotty and Caroline haven't been asked yet, either."

"Maybe you should mingle more. Get interested in a few more after-school activities, instead of always hanging out with that tattered neighbor boy."

Mother knew Jake's name as well as her own, but she always persisted in referring to him as "that neighbor boy."

"Jake's not tattered, Mother," she countered. "His mother is a seamstress. She takes in mending and makes beautiful quilts." But, she didn't want to fight with Mother today, so she added, "Well, maybe I could go out for girl's softball. Tryouts start in three weeks."

"And, what about your clothes. We should get you a few new things for spring. It will give you a lift to add a few things to your wardrobe."

"Bud asked me out for Saturday."

"He did?" Mother could hardly contain her excitement.

"Well, he's been asking practically every girl in the class out since he broke up with Janey Masters, so it doesn't mean anything."

"Maybe he'll ask you to the prom. We'd better get your hair done. Mayva owes me a favor since I filled in for her at the church supper. I'll see if I can get her to do your hair on Saturday at her shop."

"I can do my own hair, Mother." Jenny tried not to let annoyance creep into her voice. Finished with her peeling, she added, "I better get to my homework."

"Oh, I forgot to mention your Aunt Gertrude called. She wants you to help her plant those seedlings she sprouted in the greenhouse." A short pause. "That woman should have married years ago. She was responsible for my mother's misery in her old age. When that Rafe of hers was killed she should have looked for another man."

"I'll go over on Saturday."

"Make sure you come when I call you for supper."

Jenny turned silently toward the old, wooden staircase that

went to the second floor of the century old, brick-red farmhouse. As she climbed, she wondered what Aunt Gert would think about her dating Bud Anderson, or how she could convince Mother to let her apply to art school. As she reached the landing, she picked up speed, skipping every other stair toward the small, pink flowered room that was hers across from Mother's and Father's, humming in anticipation.

Chapter Three

Jenny chose to bicycle to Aunt Gert's on Saturday. The day was bright and sunny and she would avoid the tug-of-war and the lecture she knew she would get from Mother if she asked to use the Chevy.

As she bicycled past the Martin farm she waved. Jake's sisters, Anne and Sarah, waved back, tending the fields in their long, plain dresses whipping about their slender bodies, their gauze caps rippling in the breeze. Peter and Jonah, the littlest, never noticed, too busy chasing their dogs and each other, sending imaginary sticks over the high, gabled roof of the barn their family had raised with the help of their neighbors over a decade ago. Today, Jenny didn't stop but called hello. The word seemed to echo as it wafted through the breezes now picking up speed across the open fields.

Next, past the Walker place, an old, mobile home set back amidst rubble and a small grove of trees. Their place looked deserted. Their old jalopy was up on a board, two of its tires missing. No doubt they were off to get a few rabbits, or see if the blackberries were ripe along the hills above the stream.

Jenny pulled up at Aunt Gert's, throwing her bike on the lawn as she ran up the stairs to knock on the heavy, timber door. Before she could raise her hand, the door flew open, and Aunt Gert, in jeans and a light, cotton flowered shirt, her hair

12

done up in rollers, threw her arms around her niece, jumping the threshold to land on the wide, grey veranda.

"Jenny," she laughed, as she looked out over the expanse of green meadow, "I saw you coming on that old Schwinn. What a beautiful day to plant.

"Would you like some lemonade?"

"Thanks, Aunt Gert, but I just ate breakfast."

"Alright, then we'll save it to go with the oatmeal raison cookies I just baked for after our planting."

"What are we planting?"

"Well, I've seeded some delphinium and nasturtium and lilies. It's a little early, but if the weather holds we'll have good, strong plants by summer. And I bought some tulip and daffodil bulbs from John's nursery down the road. The rabbits got most of them last year.

"Okay, let's get to work," she laughed.

As they walked toward the greenhouse at the side of the large, white frame farmhouse, Gert looked at her niece. The little, pigtailed girl who had romped in her gardens, played hopscotch on the small sidewalk that led to the garage, and chased a mongrel puppy called Chaucer had grown into a lovely young woman poised on the threshold of life.

"How's Jake?"

"Oh, he's fine Aunt Gert, but Mother doesn't like me hanging out with him too much. She wants me to pay more attention to my future."

"But, you like him, Jenny. Nothing's more important than that."

She stopped short of going any further. If she crossed her sister, she knew Mattie would keep Jenny away. And, Jenny had been a joy to her since the girl had let out her newborn cries in the nursery of Penn Yan's Soldiers and Sailors Hospital. Growing up with the stern-faced Matilda had been a challenge for the fun-loving kid sister.

"Bud asked me out for tonight."

"Bud Anderson, Leland's son?"

"Yes. He said something about going to the basketball game tonight. Penn Yan plays Geneva."

"Well, that sounds like fun. What kind of boy is Bud?"

"Popular. He's the only boy who gets to borrow a Corvette for a Saturday night date."

"Well, Leland's had that agency for a long time. He built it out of nothing, a few Corvettes on a sand lot. Now he vies with an Elmira group for the number one spot along the southern tier. But, he's always working. No wonder he spoils his son. He's never home."

"Well, since he broke up with Janey Masters, he's been playing the field. I think he's asked everybody out on the cheerleading team but me."

"That's okay, Jenny. You should be playing the field yourself. You're too young to be attached to just one boy."

As they reached the greenhouse, Aunt Gert opened the door, letting Jenny in first. As Jenny entered, the scent of rose blossoms filled the air, the powerful aroma enveloping all her senses. The orchids, elegant in their pots, added a rare beauty to the sunlight sparkling along the panes.

"Aunt Gert, they are beautiful."

"Everyone should be surrounded by beauty, at least for a little while. But, between Mother's Day and prom night I shall have to part with most of them," she laughed.

"What should we do first?"

"I think we'll take the delphinium and the lilies and plant them in a small garden of their own near the bench and the rock garden. There's plenty of sun there, and they won't hide the annuals we'll plant in the big garden come summer."

"Okay, Aunt Gert, I'll take the pitchfork and the trowel."

"And, I'll take these flats. The colors should blend, the blues of the delphinium and the oranges, the red, and the yellows of the lilies."

"They'll be beautiful, Aunt Gert, as long as Chaucer doesn't dig in that garden."

"Oh, he's an old dog now, Jenny. He doesn't do much digging," she laughed.

"Jenny, maybe we can do your hair after we plant. How would you like to wear it up in a French twist? I have plenty of combs and bows and ribbons, and maybe we can add a fresh rose from the greenhouse."

"I'd like that, Aunt Gert. Show me where you need me to turn the dirt over, so I can get back before Mother starts to worry that I've stood up Bud."

Early afternoon saw the end of the planting and aunt and niece headed back to the old, frame farmhouse. "This house must be a hundred years old, Aunt Gert," said Jenny, as she hopped the stairs to pull open the old, bent screen door, which creaked though Aunt Gert oiled it on a regular basis.

"One hundred and forty years old, to be exact," she laughed. "I guess I'll have to get Hyman Phillips over to fix that screen door when I get to it."

Inside, Jenny saw what she had seen ever since she could remember. The couch with the plaid, cotton slipcover, the big, plush chair, and the rocker. A few paintings on the wall done by an old friend of Aunt Gert's, a floral still life, horses in a pasture with a red, wooden barn in the background, and photographs everywhere. Old photographs. One of Mother and Aunt Gert in a formal pose, both in lacy dresses, another of their parents with Aunt Gert as a baby and Mother as a toddler. A number of Jenny, as an infant in a woolen cap, playing hopscotch, her hair in pigtails, jumping rope on Aunt Gert's front lawn with Chaucer nipping at the rope as it hit the dirt.

Then, there was a small, round table, covered with a lace tablecloth, devoted to photographs of Rafe. Rafe at the senior prom with a beaming and beautiful Gert, Rafe looking out of a fighter jet in Korea, his helmet and goggles covering most of his features, Rafe looking out of a Piper Cub on the runway he used over at the Tewksbury farm, the whistle-clean milk tanks and the twin silos in the background.

"What was Rafe like, Aunt Gert?"

Gert stopped, her feet rounding the corner toward the old, linoleum kitchen floor, her hand poised to raise the lid of the cookie jar. Her face took on a look of both sadness and joy. "Well," she said, "he was handsome. The handsomest boy I ever saw before or since. But, it was more than that, Jenny. He had heart, and sensitivity, and dreams. So many dreams. We were going to share a life together and we had it all planned.

"He always wanted to fly, ever since he was small. And, when he finally got his pilot's license, he was so excited. We would fly to Geneva, hitch a ride into town, and stroll the city streets. We even flew to Niagara Falls once. Flying was his sense of freedom. And, he wanted to show me the world.

"We planned a life together. We would buy this farm, put an airstrip on it, and Rafe would haul freight and maybe some passengers. I would rent out the land and teach the girls at Keuka College. We had a name for the farm. We were going to call it Windborne Acres. We even made a sign for it one night, one silly night, bright red paint on a piece of old barn timber. I still have it in the attic," she laughed.

"Now, we should drink our lemonade so we can do your hair up. First, we'll wash it in a lavender shampoo, then put you in a towel and let it dry while we search through the drawer for combs and bows. Oh, Jenny, you'll be the hit of the game."

"Thanks, Aunt Gert."

The afternoon flew, the two chatting and giggling as Gert fashioned Jenny's thick, chestnut mane into a perfect French twist, complete with the scent and the brilliance of a deep, red American Beauty rosebud, held by an antique tortoiseshell comb.

As she hugged her aunt goodbye, Jenny hopped on her bike, pedaling faster as she saw the sun quickly disappearing behind the horizon of the trees in the distance over the open fields. The Martin's fields were empty, a light in their kitchen as the family sat down to supper. She must hurry. Mother would be anxious.

Chapter Four

The Penn Yan Dundee Central gym was abuzz with excitement as the home team prepared to take on their biggest rival, Geneva Central. A city, Geneva had always had a larger pool of talent to pull from, and their part-time faculty coaches had access to Hobart College and the tips of a full-time coaching staff. But, Penn Yan had spirit. And, tonight's game would decide which team went to the sectional playoffs.

Jenny was glowing as she walked in with Bud Anderson, a pink carnation he had bought her for no particular reason adorning the light, blue sweater she had chosen to wear over a pale, pink blouse which topped her jeans, to ward off the chill of the evening.

They had driven to the game in a fire-engine red Corvette which Bud had chosen from his father's lot. He had arrived on the dot of seven to pick her up, a sign which Mother chose to interpret as an omen that the blond, muscular, local football hero favored Jenny.

As they entered the gym, people everywhere vied for Bud's attention, calling out a "hey, Bud" or a "how's it goin'" to attract a notice. The girls he dated either looked down demurely into their laps or called out a flirtatious "hi", either boldly or punctuated by a long, loud giggle. The boys, especially the jocks, hustled each other for a chance to come over and slap him on the back, give him a high five, or reach out for a manly handshake. Mr. Pritchard, the biology teacher and football coach, already seated in the bleachers with his new, young wife gave him a nod and a dazzling smile.

"Hey, Bud, what college you gonna play for?" or "You gonna make it to All-American?" followed him as he turned to Jenny, a grin still on his face, taking her hand to lead her up the stairway between the rows of bleachers. "How's this?" he asked, as he found an empty spot in the second last row, next to Dotty Thatcher and her date.

"This is great," she answered, as she climbed in ahead of him to take her place next to Dotty, relieved that she would have someone to talk to if Bud got engrossed in the plays with his buddies around them. Dotty introduced them to her date, a freshman from nearby Syracuse University College of Forestry named Jason, which interested Bud, because he was still deciding who he would play football for, and Syracuse was near the top of the list.

"You like basketball?" Bud asked.

"I like football better," said Jason. "But, where I come from, hoops is an in sport."

"Where you from?"

"Short Hills, New Jersey. We used to play Chatham. We were big rivals."

Immediately, Bud's ears perked up. He might be from a small, downstate town, but he knew wealth when he heard it. His father had dealt with a few Short Hills buyers hoping to get a better price from a dealer along the economically depressed southern tier.

"What say we go out for a burger and a malt or something after the game?"

"Great," said Jason, reaching over for a handshake.

As they chatted over the noise of the crowd, a cheer went up. The home team had run onto the court, their shiny royal blue and white tank top jerseys sporting the school colors, their jog onto the court a show of confidence. Quiet followed the entrance of the opposing team, the few boos sent up by an unruly few silenced by the glare of the principal, and a raucous set of cheers and whistles from the few Geneva students who had given up a Saturday night on the town to follow the team.

"Hey, Whit, go for it," yelled Bud, cupping his hands around his mouth for effect. Charles Whitfield, III, at nearly six feet four the Penn Yan center, son of one of the few wealthy entrepreneurs in Yates County, who had made his money first taking a gamble in the futures market and then selling produce and hogs wholesale to national chains, and one of Bud's best friends, was on the court to prove to his domineering father that he had the guts to be a Whitfield, too. His father sat in the back of the stands, squelching his obvious pride with an empty stare and a slight mocking curl of his lips. Bud had bet a pile on the game and Penn Yan's winning the pennant.

As the ref threw up the ball to signal the start of the game, Geneva's center, with an inch or two on Whitfield, raised his arm to send the ball flying over Whitfield's head and into the hands of the waiting Geneva forward, who swiveled to score for Geneva. Applause and wild whistling from the Geneva contingent. Silence from Penn Yan.

As the game progressed, Bud continued to take bets from his friends around him, raking in a lot of money for the team. Jenny and Dotty caught up on gossip in between cheering their school team and bending Jason's ear with the attractions of Penn Yan. Dotty had dated Bud in their junior year, but she had long ago lost interest and was obviously on to a more sophisticated and wealthier catch.

Bud turned to Jenny. "How about having a few of the guys on the team join us after the game? We could all go down to The Captain's for a burger and then maybe we could take my dad's boat out. It holds at least fourteen."

"Great," she answered, trying to feign enthusiasm. She didn't know what she would say to these boys, since they seemed to snub her in the halls, certain they were on to fame in college basketball. But, she thought Jason would enjoy it. She was more at home with the football team. They had been together since freshman year, her as a cheerleader, them just happy to be junior members of a team they aspired to be on since grade school, with college dreams way off into the future.

As they spoke, cheers went up making further conversation nearly impossible. Bud leaned forward, slapping his friend Dan Watson sitting in front of him squarely between the shoulder blades. Penn Yan had scored, bringing the now hefty score to a tie.

Whit now stood before the basket for two foul shots. The gym was hushed, the center eyeing the basket as he calculated the distance and the aim. The first, a rim shot, dropped in as the crowd collectively held their breath. The second, a clean shot, passed through the net to give Penn Yan the lead, giving the crowd another reason to scream. Then, half-time.

Bud took Jenny's hand as they made their way to the once polished gym floor, now filled with the scuffs of a very close game. "Would you like a coke, Jenny?" he asked, as he made his way from corner to corner to get commitments from buddies to meet at The Captain's following the game.

"Sure."

Standing by the coke machine as he handed her a can and went after his own, she wondered whether a boy like Bud had ambitions of his own.

"Bud, what will you do when we graduate?"

"Oh, I'll go to college, play football, then come back and

work in my father's dealership," he answered fairly quickly. "That's been the plan since I was probably two."

"Don't you have anything to say about it?"

"I don't mind," he laughed. "I kinda like it. I've been hanging out there since I've been nine. And, I think I'll own my own agency by the time I'm twenty-five. And, then, I'll branch out. Maybe into Elmira or Corning. By the time I'm my dad's age, I expect I'll be big in the southern tier car business.

"The car business has its perks. If you're big, you work hard, but you get to party hard, too. A lotta glad-handing in car sales. I expect to make a lotta contacts both on the football field and off. Did you ever think about that way of life, Jenny?" he asked.

"Not really, Bud," she said, the color creeping up around her cheeks as she penetrated his meaning, looking away as she tried to change the subject. "All I've wanted to do is go to art school."

"Just the same, you'd make a really good partner in the auto game. You dress well, you're a good looker, lotsa poise. That's what guys look for."

"Thanks, Bud, but I think I'll stick with my original plan," she laughed. "It looks like everyone's going back in for the second half," she said, choking down the last of her coke and throwing the can in the wastebasket as she headed back to the gym. Bud followed, greeted by a few "See ya at The Captain's" as they climbed the bleachers back to their seats.

The second half gave Geneva a second wind, and despite the slim Penn Yan lead, a chance to defeat a team they had always thought of as country bumpkins. The score was a disaster, 56-28, taking the city-bred team to the playoffs and a chance for possible national attention. Penn Yan was going to need a big morale boost in the hours following the game.

As Bud put his arm around Jenny's shoulders to lead her down the bleachers, his hand-picked group gravitated to the corner of the gym to choose up rides, the family sedans that needed to be back by eleven weeded out, and those without a place relegated to walking the streets in the balm of a moonlit spring evening. Dotty and Jason chose to ride with Bud, crammed in the tiny space of a double back seat.

As they neared the water, the moon cast an eerie light on the dock in front of The Captain's, the restaurant's excursion boat lashed securely to one of its posts, it's hull moving back and forth over the top of the gently rolling waves, the noise of the water slapping its sides a predictable rhythm against the stillness of the night.

"Okay, let's go for it," shouted Bud, as he squealed his tires rounding the corner to a parking space set out at the far end of the lot. Dotty and Jason piled out as Jenny pulled the front seat forward, Dotty's new bob a tangle of disheveled curls, confirming the gossip Jenny had heard that Syracuse boys are fast.

Bud put his arm around Jenny's waist as they walked to the entrance of the restaurant bathed in the moonlight of the early spring evening, the stars clear in the sky. The scent of dogwood wafted from the bushes along the back of the old, white building. Bud pulled open the screen door.

"Hey, Cap'n," he shouted, "how 'bout a keg?"

"How about a few pitchers?" returned Jack Harmon, muscular and tattooed owner of the establishment, and "captain" to all who ate there. "You're father will have my license if I break open a keg for you."

"Okay, okay, but wait till I get rich. I'll have you hauling out kegs for the whole town, especially on St. Patrick's Day."

"I'll get on it now. But, in the meantime, you kids get over to that table and pipe down. You're scaring my customers."

Bud parked himself at the large table at the far end of the restaurant reserved for after-game get togethers. A few kids were already there. He pulled Jenny down beside him.

"What'll it be, Jen? A burger? A pizza? How about a large pizza for the whole table with everything on it?"

Before Jenny could answer, he turned to the waitress, who was busy serving burgers to the next table. "Hey, Sue, the largest pizza you have with everything on it."

"Be right there, Bud," she shouted, wiping her greasy hands on her already soiled apron. "Only got two hands."

Bud poured Jenny some beer. "Drink up. We're gonna party," he said. "The team put up a good fight."

As he spoke, Whit and two other team members, along with the group Bud had gotten together, ambled in, the look of disappointment on their faces almost palpable.

"Hey, Whit, why the long face? You guys put up a good fight. You know those city slickers practically buy their players."

"My dad will come close to disowning me, Bud. Practically my whole college education was riding on this, plus his reputation in the national distribution industry."

"Oh, c'mon, Whit, sit down. He'll get over it. We're gonna party. You'll play for Cornell or Syracuse or Hobart or Buffalo. You're gonna put Penn Yan on the map."

As Whit and the group settled in, the more they drank, and the friendlier Bud got to Jenny. To Jason as well. Bud knew who to play to.

The boat ride was beautiful in the moonlight. But, Bud's love of speed changed his passengers' pleasure into near, sheer terror. Jason huddled below, close to seasickness on the fairly calm midnight waters of the small, forked lake that once supplied fish to the Native Americans who named it. Dotty stayed nearby to console him. The rest, filled with beer, silently prayed for land and the chance to throw the rope around a post at the Penn Yan-Dundee yacht club very soon.

Bud drove Jenny home, his arm around her as they walked the sidewalk to her door, without so much as an attempt at a goodnight kiss.

"Thanks so much for a very nice time, Bud," she offered, as she fished for the key in the side pocket of her jeans.

"Great time, Jen. Maybe we'll try it again sometime. See ya Monday."

As Jenny opened the door, she mentally reminded herself to close it as quietly as she could, putting off Mother's barrage of questions until the morning.

Chapter Five

Jenny was the talk of the school when she arrived on Monday morning. A date with Bud brought a girl to near-celebrity status.

"What was it like?" asked Caroline Mackey, sidling up to Jenny as they passed in the hall on their way to third period, a giggle barely suppressed behind a big grin.

"Caroline, you're one of my best friends. You're not supposed to get me in the halls."

"How can I keep my place in the gossip mills if I don't?"

"Okay, okay. We're due for a talk, anyway. How about 2:30 at Embrey's after school? I'm going to walk home today."

"Good. See you there. I could use a coke. But, don't let me eat those doughnuts. Gotta keep in shape for those college boys."

As Caroline sped to her third period class, all the way to the end of the hall and up one flight, Jenny ambled to hers, just two doors down from her second. She didn't want to be first in, because she knew Mrs. Ames would ask her about art school, and she didn't want to tell her she hadn't gotten permission yet. But, the fresh, spring air had kept the rest of the class around the open window at the far end of the hall, ready to sprint only at the sound of the bell. Despite her head bent over paperwork, the art teacher heard Jenny's attempt to slip quietly in.

"Jenny, I've been waiting to see you."

Jenny walked up the aisle and settled in the seat nearest Mrs. Ames' desk.

"I have what I think is good news. I've been talking to Mr. Richards to see if there wasn't a scholarship or some kind of grant we could use to help you go to art school. I know you've had a hard time convincing your parents. And, I know it's hard for your folks to face the cost."

"Well, it's not only that, Mrs. Ames. Mother would like me to go to business school like Dotty Thatcher. She would like me to do something useful, like learning to keep books."

"Art might not seem as useful as keeping books or typing, but it has its place. It brings beauty to the world and revives the spirit. You can't put a price on that. You have real talent, Jenny. Not everyone can portray the beauty of a rose on canvas so that you can almost feel the softness of its petals or sense the rapture of its fragrance as you did with the scene of your Aunt Gert's greenhouse. Or catch the antics of a cat knocking over a saucer of milk in pen and ink like your prize-winning sketch from last year's art show."

"Thank you, Mrs. Ames. I'll try to talk to Mother."

"This might help. Mr. Richards uncovered a scholarship that hasn't been used in years. It's not much, but it's given every college year for four years. It was given with the stipulation that it be awarded only if there is a deserving student to receive it. Mr. Richards and I think you are deserving of that award. So would Mrs. Tewksbury, I think, if she were still alive. She left it to us in memory of her son who was lost in the Korean War. He was a brilliant art student here."

"I know of him. He was engaged to my Aunt Gertrude."

"Then, I guess your Aunt Gert would be very pleased if you accepted that scholarship."

As Jenny rose to end the conversation, the quiet of the mid-morning interlude was ended by the jostling of a crowd trying to get through the door before the bell sounded. Its minute-long ring, its tone the same as it had been since Jenny entered high school, signaled the start of third period to the farthest corners of the school, even the annex. Jenny walked to her locker and pulled out her smock. As she set out her paintbrushes, she stared at the half-finished canvas set up on her easel. How would she make that snow look like real snow. How could she show its purity, the cold of the new fallen snow to the touch of a tongue. Or, did she want to take a snowflake, the brilliant facets of its design, and surround it with bursts of color. But, the assignment was a winter scene. With a sigh, Jenny lifted her paintbrush and set to work.

As she left school, Jenny looked down at the sidewalk on her way to Embrey's, avoiding the cracks and the bumps of the newly poured squares of repair cement. The daffodils and the tulips were in bloom highlighting the fronts of the small frame houses and bringing bursts of red and yellow to the bases of maple and sycamore tree trunks. Dandelions were sprouting everywhere, forming a golden yellow blanket over the lawns turned newly green after the dingy brown of winter. The slight drizzle of rain caused mists everywhere, bringing small rainbows to the gardens as she passed.

Caroline was already at Embrey's, seated in a slightly ripped red vinyl chair at a yellow formica and chrome table sipping a coke and reading a copy of *Mademoiselle*. Jenny slipped into the chair next to her.

"How's the celebrity?"

"Caroline, you know Bud's dated practically the whole school."

"He hasn't dated me. And, he never will. I'm not his type. How was it?"

"It wasn't like anything. He hardly talked to me at all. He was more interested in impressing his friends. But, I did get to see Dotty Thatcher's new interest."

"Once she gets her claws into him, he won't be able to get loose," laughed Caroline.

"But, I did hear the boys talking about you, though. A little different than they usually talk about Bud's latest conquest. I think he has respect for you, Jenny."

"All I know is that it gave Mother more of a thrill than it gave me. She wouldn't stop talking about it on Sunday. She insisted on getting to church early, and then she couldn't get rid of the smug look all morning."

"You shouldn't put it off, Jen. Bud's a good catch. His family's well connected, and there's money there."

"Did you decide what you're going to take in college?"

"I'd like to be a vet, but I lost out in the competition for those few places in pre-vet in the Ag School. I got into Hum Ec, though, so I think I might study nutrition."

Jenny knew what a disappointment that was. Caroline loved animals.

"Maybe you can switch when you get there."

"Maybe. I'll just be glad to be there. I've had my heart set on that school."

"I might visit you, depending on where I end up."

"That would be great, Jen. Maybe we could double date, if the boys aren't all dogs there."

"Well, how could they all be dogs, Caroline? There are thousands of them there."

"I hear from Sue who went there last year that a lot of them are from New York and pretty fast."

"Then you'll just have to find one from a small town like you." She sighed, "I think I will have to get going. Mother will throw a fit if I'm not there to set the table."

"I'll write to you, Jen. We have to be friends forever."

"I'll write back."

They embraced as they had done often on parting, picking up their books to go off in their respective directions. Today, Jenny's mind was everywhere but here. How would she get Mother and Father to agree to art school? And, where was Jake? She had missed him for a week at their usual meeting in the hayloft. She quickened her steps to see if she could catch him.

Chapter Six

Jenny checked the hayloft before she started to take the lane to the Martin farm. Mother didn't like her mixing with the Martins, and Mrs. Martin, small and meek, with wire-rimmed glasses, didn't want to cross her "English" neighbors.

As she approached, she heard the sound of a whippoorwill, the distinct whistle that she and Jake had learned to make as children in the first few months after he had moved to the southern tier, a call that became their signal. But, they hadn't used it since Jenny had entered high school. Out of practice, she called on every facial muscle to softly answer. The cheery, siren call of a bird, nearly invisible by day, the color of its shaggy feathers a blend of the woods it lives in, their softness a mark of silent, nocturnal flight.

As she entered the barn, she saw that Jake was already there, chewing on a piece of straw he had picked up out of the hayloft, his heavy-duty overalls stained with the sweat of planting.

"Hi, Jenny."

She climbed the ladder to settle next to him.

"I hear you went out with Bud Anderson Saturday."

She forgot how Jake might take it. He hated Bud. But, he seemed hurt as well. Not showing up for a week after she told

Bud yes. News travels fast in a small community. Even if you're homeschooled.

"Yeah. Well, you know, he's asked about every girl in the school out."

"But, you're not every girl, Jenny. You're special."

"It wasn't all that great. He paid more attention to his friends than he did to me.

"But, it sure was good for Mother. She hasn't lost a chance to brag to every one of her friends. And, she's glad I went out with somebody so respectable."

"I'm not sure he's so respectable."

Jenny didn't answer. She realized anything she might say to back up her statement might be thought of as a slight to Jake's family.

"You have a mind of your own, Jenny. You didn't have to go."

Jake perked up, changing the subject. "What're your father and Hiram planting this year?"

"He's trying soy beans along with his usual feed corn and beans and cabbage. He's heard it's a good crop."

"Pa puts in the same thing every year. Hay for the horses, feed corn for the few dairy cows, and peas, beans, cabbage and lettuce that we sell at the market. Ma tends her pickling cucumbers. We make a big profit on the dills and the sweets she puts up."

"Have you told your father about wanting to go to

Hobart?"

"Pa took it hard when I told him, barely speaking to me for over a week. But, when he recovered, he made me a deal. I could go, as long as I was there to help him with the crops. I think that hearing that I don't want to be a farmer like he is hit him the worst. Amos Pearson and Ethan Eldridge both went into the farms with their fathers this year. I think he's hoping that the fast pace of the school and its students will send me back to the fields.

"And you, Jenny? Have you thought about art school?"

"Mrs. Ames talked to me today. She found a scholarship if I study art. But, first I have to convince Mother. She thinks artists sit around studios growing their hair long, never earning a living. She would like me to take business so I can work a few years, marry a business executive and have an easier life than she's had."

"Well, it looks like she's got your whole life planned out. What do you think about it?"

"I think I'd like to study art. If I promise to take business along with it, I think she'll come around. Aunt Gert can get me into Keuka where I can take both. And, I'll still be close enough to help her with the greenhouse."

"I hope it works. You're great at art."

"Thanks, Jake." Jenny paused. "I hear you had a church social over the weekend. Did you meet any girls?"

"I'm not interested in girls right now. All my cousins got

married when they were eighteen, farming and making furniture and raising five kids by the time they were twenty-five. I don't want that kind of life."

"I bet there are a lot of girls after you already."

"I would take you out if I could. But, I know what a fuss it would cause with your folks. And, mine too, I guess. I never wanted to cause any trouble for you, Jenny."

Jenny looked at Jake. She had never considered him as a date. His background so different than hers, his beliefs a century away. But, she had always hoped that she'd find someone like Jake, with his kindness, his playfulness, and the special way he got serious when he voiced his convictions. But, whoever it was, he would have to fit the social mold set out for her from the beginning. Jenny was no rebel. She had always gotten her pleasures without making waves.

"I'd better go. I left the fields early to get here. Anne and Sarah took over my chores, but only if I promised to help them with their math and push Pa to let them go with us to the market on Saturday."

"I suppose I'd better go, too. I better butter Mother up so I can talk to her about art school."

As Jenny picked up her books, Jake glanced at her. He wondered why every boy in the school didn't date her, not just Bud Anderson. She had so much more spirit than the girls he knew, all them stuck in the beliefs of a religion that relied on the passivity of women, breeding large families, working long hours to care for and support them, and submitting to the uncontestable decisions of their husbands.

As he stood, he pulled Jenny up. Her hands were so soft, her hair the fresh scent of lavender. He carried her books down the ladder, handing them to her as they parted, each going off in opposite directions, heading toward home in time for an early supper, as they had done for years. But, this time they parted in silence.

Chapter Seven

Matilda Thompson added flour and milk to the sliced potatoes she had placed on top of the ham steak in the oblong Pyrex sitting on the wooden kitchen table. The tight waves of her permanent kept her light brown hair in a neat semi-circle about her firm face, her strands of grey covered by peroxide highlights. Jenny walked into the kitchen.

"Where have you been, Jenny? I had to peel the potatoes myself."

"I met Caroline at Embrey's after school. Then, I walked home."

"Bud's been calling you. He wants you to go out again. He'll call back this evening."

"I'll be here. Mrs. Fisher gave us enough history homework to keep us busy for at least two hours."

"I hope you'll say 'yes' to Bud. He's a good catch, Jenny. Someday his father will own a large part of the southern tier."

"He runs with a fast crowd, Mother."

"Well, that shouldn't bother you. You've had dancing lessons and piano lessons. You should learn to bowl, Jenny. It will make you more popular. Everyone knows how to bowl."

"The last time I bowled at the youth center I nearly knocked over the set up boys. And, my ball always wound up in the alley."

"Well, maybe you need a lighter ball. Or lessons. Mayva's good at bowling. Maybe she can teach you after she closes her shop on Saturdays."

"Mother, I wanted to talk to you about college."

"Later, Jenny. I'm already late with supper. You weren't here to peel the potatoes. We'll talk about it at the table. Your father should be back from the fields in ten minutes. Now, you can put salt and pepper on the casserole and put it into the oven. Then, you can set the table. And, remember to put out the blue patterned dishes I got at the market."

Jenny sighed, but obeyed. The earlier they ate, the earlier she could bring up art school.

"I'll go up and get a start on my homework."

"Okay. But, mind you come when I call you."

Jenny bounded up the stairs toward the haven of her pink, flowered room. If she finished her homework early, she could lie out under the stars for a short time before going to bed, or perhaps she could call softly to Jake along the lane to see if he had slipped out as well. Sometimes, in the summer, when Jenny had no homework, they would stay up late, watching the stars together. It was with Jake she had seen her first shooting star and wished upon it. They were both certain it was good luck.

As Jenny finished the last part of the chapter on the French Revolution, she closed the book. She would answer the questions after supper. She could hear Father's tired voice answering Mother's persistent questions, and now she could hear her summons. She walked slowly down the stairs, trying to be soft about it, but despite a change into sneakers from her school loafers, the creaks in the hundred-year-old stair treads announced her arrival as loudly as when she had left.

"Hurry, Jenny, it'll get cold."

Jenny sat, waiting for her turn after Father first, then Mother. Mother made it clear that Father should have the first helping, taking as much as he wanted. He needed his strength for the long days in the fields. Ham steak casserole was a staple. It was easy. Mother hated to cook, as she often told Jenny.

"What did you put in today, Lyman?"

"Just the beans, Mattie. We didn't get to planting the feed corn. Hiram could only stay half the day."

"Well, you better get busy. I hear Jed Thomas and John Stewart are adding feed corn to their usual crops. And, I don't see a lot of new cattle around here. In fact, Harold Neuberger is thinking of selling his herd and retiring."

Father sighed. "I'll look into it, Mattie."

"And who's minding the tire store?"

"Dick Putnam's youngest. His oldest is running errands for the grocery, so if Jackson needs help, his older brother just stops by on the way to a delivery. It works out just fine."

"Well, he doesn't sound too bright. You better finish the

fields and get down there. Memorial Day rush should start pretty soon."

"I hear you, Mother. Now, could I get a bite of this delicious ham? It's a mighty fine casserole, Mattie. "

Father was the only one who could shut Mother up, bringing a slight flush to her cheeks, and sometimes even a slight, shy look, even after twenty-two years of marriage.

"Mother, Mrs. Ames talked to me today. She mentioned a scholarship for art school. She said it's not given every year but she and Mr. Richards think I could get it."

"Oh, Jenny, not that art talk again. Your father's sister fancied herself an artist and closed herself up in her room she called a studio. After making no money, she finally got out and sold linens at Harold Potter's shop."

"But, Mother, Aunt Eileen paints beautifully. Her winter scenes are the talk of the town. She's even sold some at the art shows."

"But, not enough to put bread on the table. And goodness knows they need it. Andy has been sick on and off for years."

"Now, Mattie, you know Eileen has worked hard."

"Mother, I would really like to take art."

"Well, it won't get you a job. And, the only boys you'll meet will have long hair and sandals and talk nonsense. How will you meet a decent husband?"

"Well, now Mattie, maybe Jenny should take what she likes."

"I'll take business classes, I promise. Aunt Gert says they have typing and stenography just like Dotty Thatcher's school has."

"Well, alright. But, you'd better learn to type at least 140 words a minute. When I was in high school, I could type 160. I won the prize. Why, if I didn't marry right out of high school I could be a pretty fancy private secretary by now."

"Alright, it's settled. But, you'd better get your application in right away. Your Aunt Gert says the deadline is only two weeks away." Father kept his voice gentle, not to agitate Mother. He knew she liked to win.

"Let's get these dishes cleared. Jenny, you wash. As quickly as you can. You have homework and school tomorrow. I'll dry." Mother got up from the table, ending the discussion.

As Jenny filled the sink with water and added the soap suds, scraping the garbage into a plastic-lined pail, the phone rang. Mother jumped to answer it, her voice perking up as she got an answer to her very dramatic hello, a rhythm she had picked up in her high school drama club which she felt gave her the social poise to hold her own in Penn Yan society despite her financial position.

"Hello, Bud. Yes, I'm fine. How is your mother? She seemed kind of peaked in church last Sunday.

"Oh, I'm glad she saw Doc Masterson. If anyone can cure her, he can.

"Yes, Jenny's here. I'll get her away from the dishes."

As Mother handed the phone to Jenny, Bud's voice came over the lines loud and confident, as deep as if he were still yelling after a touchdown. "Hey, Jen, a bunch of us are getting together Saturday night to drive to Geneva. A couple of parties there. Maybe a softball game. Or, maybe a Hobart baseball game. Some of the guys have friends on the team. Would you like to go?"

"Yes, Bud. Sounds like fun."

"Okay. I'll pick you up at six. We'll grab a burger at Captain's and then we'll be off."

"See you then."

Jenny hung up the phone, making her way back to the dishes now soaking in the sink.

"Jenny, why didn't you carry on a conversation with him. He'll think you don't like him. You have to learn how to make small talk."

"I'm not interested in small talk. If a boy wants to take me out, he will. I'm not going to play up to him like Dotty Thatcher."

"You could learn a few more social graces. I saw a few good articles on how to make conversation at Mayva's shop on Saturday. Maybe she could lend them to you."

As Mother dried, she entertained Jenny on the art of catching a husband. "Boys don't like it if you act too smart, Jenny. You have to pretend that you don't know anything.

"And, never call a boy on the phone or ask him out. Mary Lou Anderson says the phone is ringing off the hook with girls calling Bud after school. They have no shame. You'll stand out Jenny if you're not forward."

"I think I'm finished now, Mother. I'm going upstairs to do my homework."

"Don't forget to go to bed early. Girls need their beauty sleep. Nothing scares boys away faster than dark circles under the eyes."

Jenny made an attempt to answer her social studies questions, but the draw of spring fever outweighed the spirit of the French Revolution. The light, spring air wafting through her open window confused nobles with peasants, Marie Antoinette and Louis with Josephine and Napoleon. They all blended together as she thought about Jake. How they had watched the stars together under a full moon, the fields softly lit by its eerie glow. Ursa Major and Minor, the Big Dipper, and sometimes the North Star on a very clear night. He with his arm about her to keep her from the chill of the evening, she with his threadbare jacket about her shoulders.

She decided against slipping out after her homework was done. She would get up early and ride her bike to school. She really wanted that scholarship and she knew a good work ethic would help. If she beat the school bus crowd, she could be sure of a spot on softball.

Chapter Eight

The sun streamed in through the windows of Aunt Gert's old farmhouse as Jenny tried to get the landscape right on the canvas set on the easel in front of her. Daubs of different greens brightened up the trees, but the newly planted fields still posed a problem. Depicting the delicate, young seedlings of the bean plants or the heartier sprouts of the feed corn was easy. But, the browns of the earth eluded her. She had always had trouble with brown. Should she add more burnt sienna? How could she get it to look like a fertile field without ruining it with too much yellow so that it looked like a field of mud?

She put down her paint brush, looking around the small room that was once a bedroom. The windows were still covered in the dotted swiss Aunt Gert had sewn into curtains when she first moved in. The room had been Jenny's playroom when she was small, but at ten Aunt Gert had turned it into her "studio", presenting her with a smock from the art store in Geneva, complete with her name embroidered on it in bright colors by the owner of the shop, and a table with a place for paints on it. Aunt Gert had watched her draw with the special pencils and papers she had bought her for her birthdays. At sixteen, she had bought her a beautiful wooden easel.

Aunt Gert knocked, pushing the warped door hard to get it to open. She surveyed the almost finished canvas. "Nice. It looks just like the bean field Charlie Potter put in. I don't know what I would do without him. Between his rental money and my green house, and what I make at the college, I just make ends meet.

"I suppose I could sell this place and move into town into one of those new places Carl and Lyman Andrews put up. But, I wouldn't be happy. This house has been my comfort and my salvation. When things get rough, I find peace in these old walls."

"I love this place, too, Aunt Gert."

"It's been Chaucer's home since he was a six-week-old puppy," laughed Aunt Gert, as she looked at the sleeping dog who had found a patch of shade for an afternoon nap. "I think he would miss it, too.

"How was your date with Bud?"

"He asked me to the prom, Aunt Gert."

"Are you going, Jenny?"

"I couldn't turn him down," Jenny laughed. "I think it's been Mother's dream since I've been in kindergarten."

"How do you feel about Bud, Jenny?"

"I like the attention a girl gets as Bud's date. But, he runs with such a fast crowd. Mother thinks I just need bowling lessons and some on how to make conversation."

"I can help you with the conversation. We do a section on ice breakers that gives the girls a chance to learn social poise and how to be a public speaker."

"Thanks, Aunt Gert."

Jenny paused before she spoke. "Aunt Gert, why did you never marry?"

Aunt Gert looked thoughtful, a wrinkle furrowing her usually sunny brow. "I dated in college," she said slowly. "I even dated men I met later on after I moved in here. I dated some nice men, some wild men. They were an interesting mix. But, none of it ever took. I never felt the same as I did when I was with Rafe.

"I had to make a decision. Rafe still had my heart. It wouldn't be fair to give someone only part of myself. I decided to live with the memory of someone I truly loved, rather than with someone I didn't.

"Jenny, did you get Mother to agree to art school?"

"Yes, Aunt Gert. She's not pleased. But, Father helped."

"Your father is a good man, Jenny. Your mother was lucky to get him. But, she hates that he has to farm for a living. Mattie always liked to put on airs.

"I'll talk to the registrar on Monday. I'm sure they can find a spot for you. And, maybe we can find a way for a double major in business and in art."

"I hate business, Aunt Gert. I made more mistakes in

typing class than anyone, and the only lesson I liked was when we could make hearts for Valentine's Day with X's."

"You might like shorthand, Jenny. It's like your own private language. And, if you're good at it, you can almost name your job.

"So, what should we have for supper? Mother said you could stay, as long as you're home early. Why don't you take Chaucer out for a run while I look in the fridge? He doesn't get too much exercise anymore."

Jenny rose, soaking her brushes in her can of turpentine and wiping up her splotches with a well-used rag. Then, she roused Chaucer, who was only too happy to follow her out the old screen door with memories of his puppyhood lingering in his brain as he picked up his pace to chase her to the barn. If she could get this canvas finished by summer, maybe she could enter it in the art show. Mrs. Ames had encouraged her with the still life she had done, a class exercise, but she favored the landscapes she did after school, especially in the spring when the dogwood bloomed and the evergreens, steady in the winter, looked greener among them. And, the tiny seedlings sprouting in the newly plowed fields. They had been a staple ever since Jenny remembered.

She would get Aunt Eileen to help her enter the show. But for now, she just wanted to run with Chaucer. He had been her companion since she was six, but he had never made any demands on her, settling for a gentle pat on the head or a hearty romp in the woods whenever she felt like it.

She wondered what Aunt Gert was cooking for supper. Sometimes it was elegant, a paella pan full of the fresh seafood Aunt Gert picked up at the big market in Geneva, or roasted duck with an orange-current sauce she had learned from a gourmet magazine she found at the college, with a scoop of French vanilla in a champagne glass topped with fresh cherries and a brandied sauce Aunt Gert flamed for a dramatic finale under dimmed lights and the brilliance of the stars shining through the open windows, the lace curtains sometimes flapping with the breeze.

Or, it could be a meatloaf, or a simple beef stew, or in summer, a tuna salad and cold, boiled potatoes. But always there was conversation. Aunt Gert asked Jenny what she thought. About world affairs, about the latest trends, about politics in Penn Yan and the country. Sometimes Aunt Gert would give her a historical or cultural perspective.

Jenny held out the tug-of-war rope length to Chaucer, inviting him to pull hard as he could. He grabbed it, shaking his head and making fierce noises, causing her to pull back with some strength to keep her balance. She laughed as they put the toy back in the barn.

As they walked toward the house, Chaucer panting but happy, the aroma of pot roast simmering in its juices greeted them through the open front door.

Chapter Nine

J enny looked up at the colored lights spinning and swirling above her. Put in by the prom committee the night before, they transformed the school gymnasium into a big-city disco. Music blared from the soundstage where a Hobart band shot out the latest sounds on two electric guitars, a great set of drums and a hot keyboard.

Bud had picked her up promptly at seven. Her limousine tonight had been a tiger-yellow corvette with black leather interior. Bud held the door, helping her in with an excitement she had rarely seen in him except on the football field.

"I've made reservations at Belham's Castle-on-the Lake. We're meeting Whit and his date and Dotty and Jason. "Tiger" Lewis will drop in on us later. He's picking his date up in Syracuse. Big city gal with lots of money, I hear."

The drive to the restaurant was quiet. Bud took the back roads. The sun was setting, and its fading light barely lit the cornfields, giving way to shadows.

"Have you decided on a college yet, Jenny?"

"I'll be going to Keuka, if I get in. My Aunt Gert will help."

"You'll get in. You've got everything going for you. That's great. You'll be near home."

"That's the plan. How about you?"

"I'm pretty close to picking Syracuse. They've got the best

offer, and I'd be close to the agency if I had to get back on weekends. And, I hear the contacts are great."

"Sounds good."

"There's only one problem. Studying. College football takes up most of your life. But, Jason said he could get me into his fraternity. Their old exam file is huge. And, sometimes guys will write your papers for you on the sly. It's their way of supporting the football team."

Jenny didn't answer. She only thought about Jake who worked the fields by day and stayed up late hours at night to study. Jake would never turn in someone else's paper.

"I don't think I will join a sorority. I'll have enough trouble keeping up with a double major."

"Sure you will, Jenny. You gotta have fun. That's what college is for."

As they rounded the corner, they came upon Route 14 where Belham's was, just down the road from Hobart, the college's beautifully kept large, white frame former homes turned offices lining the shore of deep, blue Seneca Lake.

As they drove the long, curved driveway that led to the former mansion turned restaurant, it's well kept blacktop shaded by enormous oaks and maples, Jenny felt a sense of awe, as if she could almost see guests promenading on the lawns in long dresses and parasols, the men in black tie, addressing each other in formal and elegant language.

Bud parked, turning off the ignition to jump out and help

her out of the car. As they walked toward the front door, set above a half-flight of carefully chiseled steps, the red of the lavish Medina stone, the gables and the turrets, added to the imposing turn-of-the-century aura.

"Looks like Whit is already here. That's his silver Jag at the end of the row.

"Have you ever been to the Castle before?"

"Not really."

"Then you should be in for a treat. Their chef is great. And, famous. Paul Newman has left his autograph here.

"The view is beautiful. That's why I chose it. My dad wanted us to go to the club, but there's no view. I wanted us to have a good time tonight, Jenny."

As they entered the restaurant, they spotted Whit and his date, already seated. Whit raised his martini glass in recognition. His date sat silent, somewhat stuffed into a very tight low-cut pink taffeta gown, shoes dyed to match.

Ushered to the table, Bud seated Jenny, taking care to leave her time to arrange the long skirt of the strapless, pale aqua chiffon and taffeta gown she had had her eye on since she had seen it unwrapped from the shipment at Martin's hardware and apparel four months ago. Mother had approved it only because she deemed it almost as fashionable as they could find in a trip to Syracuse and it would show off Jenny's figure to advantage. As Jenny arranged her dress, she took care not to disturb the delicate petals of the rare orchid wrist corsage

Bud had had made up in Geneva, its deep purple dots and misty striations vivid against the purity of a snow-white background.

Whit introduced his date. Jane Colson from Dundee. Jenny knew her vaguely from football. As they sat, Dotty and Jason walked in, arms wound around each other, tipsy from a previous celebration. Tiger Lewis breezed in last, a sophisticated Amanda Kathryn Johnson from Westchester County on his arm, here to visit a cousin and look over Syracuse University, her dress an off-the-shoulder pure silk jade green, her heavy makeup light years away from the powder and lipstick of the rest of the girls.

Dinner went fast, Bud urging Jenny to try the signature soup, a lobster bisque, purported to be Paul Newman's favorite. The boys talked college, football and basketball, but Amanda held the floor with her descriptions of her recent coming-out party, complete with an elite band no one had heard of that was booked at least four years in advance.

"Hey, Whit, have you decided on a college?" Bud shouted over the noise.

"I think I'll play for Rochester. They offered me a good deal even though we lost the sectionals."

"You better visit me often. I hear that school doesn't know how to party."

At the dance, as Jenny looked up at the lights, after a dinner that had gone all too fast, she realized that this would be the last time she would be part of a school event as a student. After the next few weeks, she would be an outsider, a visitor to these halls, an oddity to the regular students, a Martian-like intruder.

Bud touched her arm. "Would you like some punch? I hear it's spiked. We'd better get it before old Richards finds out."

"Sure."

As Bud left, Jenny looked around. The room was a swirl of pink and yellow and blue chiffon and taffeta, and rented prom suits.

As she stood, Whit ambled over, a bit unsteady on his feet. "Want to dance?"

"Where's your date?"

"Powdering her nose. I think she had a few too many martinis."

"Do you want me to see if she's okay?"

"Not necessary. She's got a school friend in with her. But thanks, Jenny."

"Bud will be back soon."

"He won't mind. It'll give him a chance to show off on the dance floor."

Whit talked while they danced. "Looking forward to going to college?"

"Yes and no. I'll miss this place."

"Me too. I'll miss Bud. We've been friends since the cradle. I love the guy."

"Hey, what are you trying to do, steal my girl?"

Bud cut in, steadying Whit as he tapped him on the shoulder.

"I hope your date's alright."

"She'll survive. I just have to get her back in one piece so her whiskey-swigging old man doesn't come after me riding shotgun."

As they whirled about the dance floor, Bud adeptly leading, the music, Bud's cheek smooth against hers, one arm securely around her, the other pulling her close, Jenny felt a feeling she had never felt before, but the moment ended. The band took a break.

"Let's drink our punch. I put it on that table I staked out over there."

As Jenny felt the warmth of the alcohol, a bitter taste over the sweetness of the fruit, Bud put his hand on hers. "What do you say we blow this place early? Whit's gonna take his date home and meet up with us after and Dotty and Jason will join us at some good haunts he knows in Geneva. Then, we can find a breakfast spot and watch the sun come up."

"Okay, if it doesn't involve a lot of alcohol. I promised Mother."

"I'll take care of you, Jenny. I won't get drunk."

As the band returned, Bud led Jenny back to the dance floor. As the music played, the glow of the earlier moment returned. Bud held her close or twirled her about with the skill of a dance master, earning nearly as much admiration from their classmates as he did on the football field. As the band neared "Good Night Ladies," the prom finale since the school had opened, Bud grabbed her hand, hastening her out the door as he picked up her wrap, a gift from Aunt Gert, the same white, crocheted shawl she had worn to her own prom.

"This way we won't have to listen to old Richard's speech."

The drive back to Geneva went quickly, the neon lights of the few bars on Route 20 still open heralding the city, now mostly dark. Bud stayed as sober as he could, the strong, black coffee of a diner which opened at five bringing him back to reality. They made it back to Penn Yan and the marina at six.

As they sat on the bow of the Anderson' thirty-two-foot boat, Bud put his arm around her. "Jenny, I'd like to ask you a question. I know we're going to be separated soon. But, I'd like you to be my girl."

"Bud, we've hardly dated."

"I know my own mind. And, I don't want to lose you."

"Yes. I think I'd like that."

"Good. That's settled. We can visit, and I know you'll be back here almost every weekend.

"Can we seal that with a kiss?" Without waiting for an answer, he took her in his arms. The warmth of his kiss, the scent of his after-shave, brought back the sensations of the earlier evening. Jenny scarcely noticed the sunrise which they had come to watch.

Chapter Ten

Graduation was finally here. The years of preparation seemed to have flown by. Jenny primped as she looked into the full-length mirror which hung on the back of her parents' bedroom closet, adjusting her cap with the tassel to the left, fixing the nearly-disposable white gown that had come boxed especially for her. She patted the pocket to make sure the short speech she was to give in acceptance of her art award was still there.

Mother was rushing them, worried that the seats among the elite would all be taken. "Hurry, Jenny, we'll be late and we'll have to sit with the Walkers or the Kendals. Now, finish up and come down here."

Jenny walked the stairs with a sigh, realizing this was the last time she would tread the winding, creaking staircase as a high school student. As she reached the landing, Mother fussed. "Jenny, I wish you had done this earlier. That gown could use another pressing. But, Father wants some pictures before we leave. Let's hurry."

As they all three stared into the camera, the sun full behind it, the camera set up on a tripod in the front yard with the timer set, with Mother urging them to all say "cheese," Jenny thought of Jake. It's true it was a day of rest for the Martins, but Jake would be sure to notice the stream of cars heading toward the school, the extra relatives chattering noisily through the open windows in their Sunday best scrunched together in all the back seats. She could see Anne and Sarah quietly sitting, or helping their mother with the midday meal, the little ones playing in the background.

"Time to go." Mother cut into her reverie with a snap-to attitude and orders to Father to pack up the camera and haul it along in the old Chevy which passed as the family car. Jenny piled in the back.

"Now, Jenny, don't forget to stand up straight and thank Mr. Richards when he hands you your diploma. Father wants to get a good shot.

"Look at those Walkers, all piled into that jalopy of a pick-up. You'd think they'd have a little more sense than to keep adding to that brood when they can hardly feed what they've got."

Jenny tried to ignore the Walkers as Father passed the old Ford truck she had often seen up on blocks in front of their trailer. The parents sat in the cab, while the rest of the Walkers sat along an old board set up to resemble a seat. They all waved as Father gunned the motor. Jenny couldn't help returning the sign with a smile.

"Just stare straight ahead and they will ignore you."

"Mattie, you can't be unfriendly. They're honest folk."

"Watch the road, Lyman. They're white trash. Mary Walker should have gotten a job a long time ago instead of staying home and chasing after a bunch of dirt-poor brats. It's true she takes in washing, but she could have been cleaning houses and making a few dollars more. There's plenty of people like the Andersons who can use good help."

As they arrived at the school, the parking lot was filling fast, cars coming in from all over, many of them with out-of-state plates. Father found a place in the back, off the asphalt and into the field behind. Jenny walked carefully, avoiding the dirt potholes to keep clean her new white pumps. Her dress, a pink cotton, lay carefully under her open gown, the heat wrinkling slightly the careful press she had given it.

Aunt Gert was already there, waiting in the hall outside the auditorium. "Jenny," she cried, as she hugged her niece, "I'm so proud of you."

"Oh Gert, let's not be so demonstrative."

"Aren't you proud, too, Mattie? I know you are. Hello, Lyman. How's my favorite brother-in-law?"

"How do, Gert. Long time no see. Don't be a stranger. And, let me know if Charlie Potter needs help with the harvest."

"I will, Lyman. He does pretty well with his brother Alfred. They got the planting done pretty much with that old tractor they keep in the barn."

"Let's go in. Hurry Lyman. Otherwise we'll have to sit in those old folding chairs along the side."

Jenny left to sit in the area roped off especially for the graduates, finding a seat near both Caroline and Dotty.

Mother sheparded Father and Aunt Gert to three seats along the aisle, Father sitting on the end so he could snap the appropriate photos. The Walkers sat nearby. Aunt Gert smiled at Mrs. Walker and waved to the children. Mother, looking annoyed, checked to see if Mary Lou Anderson had noticed.

The chatter was loud among the graduates. Bud sneaked over to give Jenny a kiss on the cheek. Jenny talked to Caroline, who was full of excitement and talk about the family reunion and graduation party in her honor taking place in her family's backyard. The tent was already set up and her mother and aunts had spent weeks freezing sandwiches and cookies, pies and cakes. Dotty talked of nothing but Jason, and Katt Johnson from Westchester County here to visit her cousin and get in some back woods graduation fun as her guest.

Mr. Richards walked on stage, quieting the chatter. As he stood by the microphone, he surveyed his twenty-fourth graduating class. "Good afternoon and welcome. We are here to honor the sixty-first graduating class of the Penn Yan Dundee Central School District. Many of you have had parents graduate from our district, and some of you even grandparents.

"I will try to keep my remarks short. It is a hot afternoon, and I know most of you are looking forward to celebrations.

"I would like to say to the graduates that this is not the end of a long journey, but the beginning. Or, at least a threshold of great opportunity. An opportunity to educate yourself further, even further than we have educated you here. An opportunity in what should be a life-long learning process. A chance to learn and give back. A chance to appreciate what your parents and teachers have given you. A chance to contribute to the world, to leave your mark upon it, to leave it a better place than you have found it, to take the good in it you have seen and propel it forward. May you all do so each in your own way.

"Now, the special awards.

"Leland Anderson, Jr., Athlete of the Year.

"Caroline Mackey, first prize, Westinghouse National Science Competition for high school seniors.

"Jennifer Thompson, Tewksbury Art Award, given only in years to a senior deemed deserving by the faculty."

Jenny shared her classmates' accomplishments as the list continued, each student standing as their name was called.

Then, the diploma ceremony. "Graduates, please form a line to the left. As your name is called, please rise to the top step.

"Jennifer Ruth Thompson." The formality gave Jenny a special thrill, and a pride she hadn't felt before. She smiled as Father beamed and snapped pictures.

As the auditorium emptied, the graduates beaming as they held their new diplomas, everyone congratulating everyone else, Jenny returned to her family. Aunt Gert gave her a special hug.

On the way to the car, Bud ran over for a last-minute hug. Mother's face nearly burst with pride.

As they reached the old farmhouse, Mother and Aunt Gert filed into the kitchen, their voices filling the air with reminiscences of their own graduations and recipes for sandwiches and cakes and pies and cookies for next week's family reunion and graduation party they had planned for months to hold out on the front lawn. Jenny slipped upstairs to change.

As she stored her gown and threw on an old pair of jeans, she suddenly felt an urge for the comfort of Jake. She slipped out to the barn and climbed the ladder to the hayloft. As she climbed, she noticed a package, brightly wrapped, sticking out from under the stray stalks of hay escaped from the last storage of autumn bales.

She pulled the card from the brightly colored wrap.

"Dear Jenny,

I would have liked to share your joy today, but I knew I couldn't. I would like to be friends forever. I have gotten you a book of poetry by William Blake. He was an artist like you and I thought you would like his work. He wrote a poem about Jerusalem. It's about England, where he lived, but I thought it might remind you of our Jerusalem. I hope you will read these poems when times are tough and when you need some time away from those fast college kids. I will be preparing to take my exams soon and will attend Hobart orientation in a month. I hope you will always remember our times together. I know I always will.

Jake

As she unwrapped the package, she noticed the bookmark, a plastic with the four leaf clover they had found together when Jake had first moved in, embedded between its two pieces. She opened the book to the page it marked. The title, *Auguries of Innocence*, was surrounded by the simple and airy faeries and angels of Blake's engravings. She read the first two lines.

> To see a World in a Grain of Sand
> And a Heaven in a Wild Flower,

She turned to climb down the rickety ladder to the barn floor. Mother was making a special pot roast, and Aunt Gert had brought a four-layer cake with raspberry filling and a French icing she had made specially at Brandinis in Geneva.

Chapter Eleven

J enny looked round her dorm room for her steno book. It was probably under her paint brushes or her oil rags. She finally found it under the scattered pile of clothes where she had left it two days ago. She gathered a few pencils, sharpened them to razor sharp quality, and took off for the class she liked the least.

Miss Ransom the instructor was a middle-aged type with light brown mousy hair cut in a page boy and bangs who insisted on being called Miss when almost everyone had adjusted to Ms. long ago, and who only wore tweed suits or starched white blouses with proper skirts. But, Miss Ransom was a whiz at shorthand, and it was rumored that she had worked as a high-priced steno and private secretary for some of the best ad agencies and law firms in New York before she was called home to care for her ill widowed mother.

Jenny left a note for her roommate Amanda, nicknamed "Sparky" for her ability to fix car motors in a flash, as well as vacuums, sewing machines, and sometimes even boom boxes, for a date for dinner and maybe a walk along the waterfront after their trip to the dining center. Amanda, from Westchester County, liked Jenny to show her the secrets of New York's southern tier, and Jenny enjoyed doing it when they had time.

Jenny walked across the campus, picking up her steps so she wouldn't be late for the one o'clock class, slipping into a seat in the second row when she arrived. Miss Ransom, busy shuffling papers and getting last week's tests together, called for order.

"Order is the most important thing you'll need. A clean desk, carefully organized files.

"Now, before I hand out the tests, which most of you failed, I am going to dictate a paragraph. Listen carefully. Listening is more important than handwriting. You can always correct your notes, but you won't get a second chance at listening to a letter."

Jenny tried to listen, her pencil flying across her steno book with shorthand symbols, but her mind was on her next class, the one she liked the best, Mr. Sigolowski's mixed media. The young mustachioed professor, on leave from a failed stint to become a great artist in New York, always tried to make the class fun and succeeded. Nevertheless, her hand went up before the other girls. Miss Ransom began to collect the papers.

The rest of the class was a blur, Miss Ransom delivering tirades on neat desks, secretarial proprieties, and the history of shorthand. To Miss Ransom, shorthand had a noble background, beginning with the Roman orator Cicero's secretary who invented the first known shorthand. To Jenny, the symbols made good fodder for graffiti on Roman stone walls by bored and angry students.

As the class ended, Miss Ransom called out her name. Jenny came up to the front instead of filing out with the other students who promptly cleared the room at the end of every class.

"Jennifer, I know you don't like shorthand, but it may come in handy for you someday, putting you into a corporation where you have an insider's view of the greatest opportunities that exist."

"I know, Miss Ransom. But, I'm here only to please my parents. And, that was a condition for college."

"You have an aptitude for the subject, particularly because you have the artistic ability to form the symbols both quickly and quite beautifully. It would help if you would set a better example for the other girls."

"I'll try, Miss Ransom."

"See you on Tuesday."

Jenny hiked across the campus to Roberts Hall, home of art and drama. Mr. Sigolowski, usually late, was in the midst of setting up a long, huge canvas.

"We're going to do a class project. We will be in competition with the Wednesday class. The best canvas will be sent to the Elmira Memorial Gallery for a month long exhibit. This will be your first juried show. Good luck."

As the students grappled with the heavier materials set out, Jenny decided on lengths of rope and beautiful shards of colored cut glass, set out to reflect the light pouring in from the large, open windows. She wondered what Chaucer would have thought of the random piles.

Vivian Stanton, known to all as "Viv" and straight from Manhattan, placed the first piece, a garbage can cover, off to the right, and a little above the center. After that, the buzz of excited chatter or the silence of concentrated thought filled the room and the next hour. Mr. Sigolowski had to shout to end the class.

As Jenny trudged the campus to Abbott Hall and her dorm room, she thought about Bud. Though he called her almost daily and picked her up almost every weekend to drive to the Syracuse campus, she still wondered what it was he had seen in her. His golden good looks and his spot on the football team must be making almost every Syracuse woman want to melt and fall at his feet. But, he and Jenny were pinned now, Bud having joined Psi U where the test and paper files stretched almost to the next frat house. Jenny dismissed these thoughts as the sun poured down upon her back and she looked upward at a nearly cloudless sky.

"Hi, Sparks." Her roommate lay on her perennially disheveled bed, clad in a torn pair of jeans and a fairly reputable tee shirt.

"Jen. I've been waiting. Got your note. What say we study for an hour, head for the dining center, and sneak our dinner out onto the beach."

"Great. That way we can study till the sun goes down, watch the fish jump, and be back here to study some more till we hear the sign off on WKCB."

"You are a good influence. I'm sure my mom is counting her blessings on a daily basis knowing I'm rooming with you."

"It's just that I have to make the most of the week. Weekends are losers for work. And, I promised my parents I'd work as hard as I can. They're paying half my tuition."

"Great, Jen. But, when are you going to do something for yourself?"

"You're a bad influence, Sparks. I'm not going to listen to you."

"May be. But, I know how to have fun. I'm not sure about you, Jenny.

"Okay, Jen, I won't talk to you if you don't talk to me. But, one hour and we're heading for the simple but upscale Lucretia Mott Dining Center."

As they studied, Jenny's thoughts kept wandering to Bud and the next Syracuse weekend. "Okay, time's up." Sparky slammed her thick, used engineering book shut. "Time to please the palate and the soul."

71

As they trudged to the dining hall, Jenny wondered if she could make it through four years. A world without families, groceries, or shops. Without fields of corn and hay. Without dogs or barn cats.

Sparky had their food into her backpack before Jenny could reach for a thing. They walked to the beach in silence.

As Jenny lay their blanket upon the sand, they threw their books on top of it and removed their sneakers. The sand felt good between their toes.

"I'll race you into the water." Sparky rolled up her jeans, splashing before Jenny had hers up to her knees.

"Do you realize, Sparks, this lake watered the Indians and their horses before us."

"It's Native Americans, and I can't relate because I come from a place where they sold the land for $24 in wampum that became home to eight million people with skyscrapers you wouldn't believe."

"Still, Sparks, we have a history here."

"Okay, quit mooning and let's get to work.

"Are you looking forward to the next Bud weekend and the exciting SU campus?"

"We're going to see a Broadway show at the Elgin theater in Syracuse. I'll be staying with Katt Johnson and she and her date will be going as well. Jason and his date, a Syracuse woman he just met, will be going along with us. Jason and Dotty broke up last week. Jason got Bud into Psi U."

"Well, you've got it made, Jenny. I have a hard time finding a date. And, there's not much to do if you find one."

"There's always Cornell and Syracuse. You know those boys are always looking for dates here. Maybe Bud could find you a nice Syracuse guy."

"Too fast for me. I'm not even sure what boys are doing in my classes. I spent too long at girls' schools."

"As soon as the guys around here figure out what a great woman you are, you'll be dating up a storm."

"I think I'm meant to be an old maid aunt."

"Oh, hush, Sparky. We'd better settle in before the sun goes down."

As the daylight faded, Sparky picked up the mechanical engineering books she loved. Jenny looked at her shorthand, but her mind was on Bud and the next Syracuse weekend.

As the sun began to set, Jenny looked up at the reds, the oranges, the mauves. She suddenly thought of Jake. It must have been hundreds of sunsets they watched together, his arm around her to shelter her from the cool evening breezes, their talk silly stuff, Jake's brothers and sisters, Jenny's job, school, the crickets they heard by day, the owls by night. She must write Jake a letter. She would find out how he was getting on.

As she watched the sun quickly sink into the haze of the cloudless gray sky, she was certain the sun set only over Jerusalem and the shores of the beautiful, blue lake it sat on.

Chapter Twelve

The day was bright and sunny. Bud whizzed them through Penn Yan in a bright, yellow Camarro. Another Syracuse weekend and activities from dawn to dusk. Jenny knew the shorthand homework must go until at least Monday.

The pace of college life was a drain for a girl from the farmlands of southern New York. Sodas on Saturdays at Embrey's Drug Store had been replaced by mixers at Holt Hall, the student union. Clubs galore had replaced the lazy afternoons out in the fields and in the barn with her school classmates. Even sailing, practiced by the wealthier students who could afford it, replaced the occasional ride in a Kris Kraft with Bud.

Jenny dreaded the Syracuse weekends. Endless activities with students who seemed only to know how to party. But, she liked the security of it. No dates to find among her own college classmates. No Saturday nights in the dorm alone while everyone partied.

"Hey, Jen. Did you bring a swimsuit?"

"I did."

"Great. We're gonna picnic at Taughannock over on Cayuga Lake where the Cornell Ivy League types hang out and the partiers from Ithaca College. I've already got a few six packs in the back to get us started.

"Did you get a bikini?"

"No, Bud, I didn't."

"You gotta get with it. The SU women are really cool. Besides, I like to show you off."

"I'm not sure Mother would approve."

"C'mon, Jen. You're in college now. You can do what you want.

"Do you wanna stop at Melroy's Department Store? They have better stuff than hardware and apparel."

"Maybe next time."

"Okay, we'll head for Katt's room. Drop your suitcase and get you settled. Then, we'd better take off for Taughannock before the sun goes down. Lotsa guys with sailfish and water skis."

Katt, heavy makeup intact, was waiting.

"Hey, Bud. Just put the suitcase over there."

"Hey, Katt."

"My date should be here soon. Then, we can get a move on."

"I think we'll head out now. Just bring yourselves. We've got extra food and brew."

"Jenny, make yourself at home. No roommate. Lucky number for the draw for singles."

"I hope your date can cook. The hamburger meat is raw."

"No problem. I turn a pretty mean burger myself when I'm in the mood."

"Don't take too long. You gotta join the bikini parade. I bet Long Island has a lot to offer."

"Bud, you're crazy! Take him away, Jenny."

Taughannock was beautiful as they searched for a spot to stake out.

"Hey, Jenny, over here!"

Jenny gratefully lay down her pile of blankets and towels on a fairly clean table as Bud lay the cooler on the ground.

"Well get the rest of the stuff later. Let's get changed.

"See you on the beach!"

Bud was out of the men's bath house and on the beach while she was still struggling with the latex of her swimsuit. But, the struggle was worth it. The cerise of her suit set off the chestnut of her hair. Her bare legs, clad only in a pair of rubber flip-flops, gave rise to a very slender figure.

Bud let out a long, slow whistle as she approached. "Score one for Keuka College. You're gonna knock 'em dead when we get you that bikini.

"Hey, what do you say I race you to that float? Last one in cooks the hamburgers."

His well-honed muscles fairly rippled as he moved through the waters with a perfect Australian crawl, his blond hair, wet and shaggy, still bleached from the summer sun. He beat Jenny to the raft by only a few strokes. As he pulled her up, his laughter echoed across the waves.

As they lay upon the bare wood, sunshine pouring down upon their backs, Bud rubbed Jenny with suntan lotion from a small bottle he had toted through the water in a zippered pocket of his swim trunks. Jenny basked in the coolness of the lotion and the warmth of his touch.

"Hey, Bud. Scott Wilson. Met you at your dad's cottage this summer. Auto meet. My dad sells Mercedes. Good to see you."

"Great to see you, too." Bud stood up to shake hands with a well-built swimmer in plaid swim trunks.

"How's it going at Syracuse?"

"Swell. Training's been keeping me busy. But, it looks like a good season."

"Great. We should get together sometime. I'm at Cornell. There are plenty of beer kegs and the gin flows like water at my frat house. I'll call you."

With that, the swimmer dove into the water and was out of sight before Bud could call an answer.

"Hey, Jen, we should get back and start the fire. I'm starving."

The swim back was leisurely and Bud was attentive, putting his arm around her waist as they reached the shore. Katt and Jason, dates in tow, were already setting the table when they reached their spot.

"Hey, Katt. Pretty fancy tablecloth."

"The best Long Island has to offer.

"Bud and Jenny, I'd like you to meet Jim Wentworth. He came all the way from Long Island to grace upstate New York."

"Welcome, Jim. What brings you to the hinterlands?"

"Katt, of course. She's hard to say no to."

"Not exactly. I've been begging him for weeks to get up here."

"And, I'd like you all to meet Brenda. She's a Wells College woman."

As Jenny took Brenda in, a wave of sympathy shot through her. A small town girl trying to make it with a fast-paced college crowd.

Wentworth was good with the hamburgers, and they were eating before sundown. Just in time to volley a few badminton birdies across the beach before dark. As the sun set, Katt and Jim took off for the campus. Jason and Brenda headed back toward Wells.

"Jen, how about getting a look at one of the highest falls around? Let's pack up and head across the road."

As they walked the trail, a generous, dirt path constructed by the CCC during the Great Depression, Jenny looked around. Beautiful mountains, evergreens dotting steep inclines, some uprooted by the storms of spring, tops pointed perilously toward the pathway. Rocks and boulders tumbling downward perpetuating the laws of gravity. Occasionally, the sound of a night bird. A stream rushing along a shale rock bed.

As they reached the moonlit falls, its height towering above them, Bud took Jenny's hand. He kissed her hard on the mouth. Then, he moved his hand toward her breasts.

"Bud, I don't want to."

"But, Jenny, you're in college now. Most girls put out."

"I want to wait."

"You're way too old fashioned. But, I will respect that.

"C'mon, let's get back. I've got a big game tomorrow, the first of the season. And, you need your beauty sleep."

As they drove, the moon lit the way for the yellow Camarro as it sped back to campus along the dark, narrow roads.

Chapter Thirteen

The summer following Jenny's freshman year was frantic. Bud had proposed, and Mother had convinced Jenny to set the wedding date for the next summer over her objections that she wanted to finish at Keuka College. Leaving Bud at such a large university with all those sophisticated women was just too big a risk according to Mother.

Jenny took a job at Embrey's Drugs to escape the fray and worked a lot of hours. She found peace only in trips to Aunt Gert's on the few Sunday afternoons she could get away to help set out the gardens and weed them.

Pedaling past the Martin farm brought no sight of Jake. Anne and Sarah were there, weeding the fields, cultivators in hand, their long dresses swaying in the breeze. Approaching the Walker trailer showed Sammy working on the perpetual wreck, this time a Chevy coupe.

"Hey, Sammy."

"Hey, Jenny." The rather lanky boy looked down, his scruffy overalls covered in grease. He knew the protocol, and he knew Mrs. Thompson's feelings on exchanging conversation.

"What have you been doing, Sammy?"

"Working for Mr. Anderson. Pay's pretty good. Pa's been sick, so I can help out."

"How's Etta? I always liked the cookies you brought to school she baked."

"Pretty good. She had to drop out of school to get married. She's expectin' in August."

"I'm sorry she had to drop out of school. I bet she could get a good job with Mr. Schneider down at his bakery. He's always looking for good help."

"Thanks, Jenny. I'll tell her."

"Sammy, have you seen Jake?"

"Not for a while. But, he stopped over the other day for a game of catch. He's got some kind of a scholarship so he's going to New York."

"New York?" Jenny tried to hide her disappointment. "But, that's so far away."

"Well, it's a good opportunity for Jake. It pays everything. All he has to do is to help some professor do some research.

"I hear you're getting married, Jenny. Congratulations."

"Well, it's not until next year, but thanks, Sammy."

"Guess I'll pedal on to Aunt Gert's. She's waiting for me to set out the new orchids and gardenias. See you, Sammy."

"See ya, Jenny."

Aunt Gert, decked out in a new pair of overalls and a bright, red polka dot scarf which held back her honey brown hair greeted her niece with the usual bear hug. Chaucer tagged behind.

"How's work, Jenny? Jim Barnes keeping you busy?"

"Mr. Barnes has me waiting tables, working the soda fountain, and sometimes helping the pharmacist package prescriptions. I'm worn out by the end of the day. But, it's good, Mother doesn't push me to choose a color for the bridesmaids' dresses or the flowers for the church."

"Mattie likes to do that herself. I'm surprised she's letting you have any say at all.

"Well, you've got a year to tie up the details, so take your time. You've got a lot to think about. Your studies, for instance. Have you decided what you're going to do about them?"

"Bud said he would get me a job on campus so I could support us. He needs to finish school. But, he promised he would get me a job that includes a free course or two."

"Good. That way you can keep up your art work.

"So, let's get to work. The new gardenias arrived yesterday and the new orchids today. They both could use a lot of sun and warmth. Let's head for the greenhouse.

"Why the long face, Jenny? I thought you liked digging in the greenhouse dirt."

"Jake is going to New York. I just found out about it from Sammy. He got a scholarship there."

"Well, I know it must be a disappointment for you. But, Jake is a smart boy. I'm not surprised. And, Hobart is good to its promising students."

"I know I don't have a right to expect Jake to stay here. But, I will miss him. He's been a part of my life since I was ten."

"Well, Jake has had a good upbringing. The Martins are good people. But, there was always a little restlessness in Jake. A desire to go beyond the simple, farm life he has been given. Jake is a hard worker, and he has a wisdom beyond his years. He'll do fine.

"And, you, Jenny. You'll be busy. What with work, and then school, and planning a wedding, you'll have little time to think about Jake. That will be a blessing. I know what it's like to miss someone who you've shared your innermost thoughts and feelings with for a very long time.

"Okay, let's get busy with those orchids and gardenias."

The new orchids were covered in the deepest purple striations, and the gardenias the purest white. Their beautiful, delicate perfume filled the nursery. Jenny repotted them to give them room to grow, digging in the lush ebon topsoil. Chaucer lay nearby, too old to dig holes in the bags of potting soil.

"How is Bud taking all this, Jenny?"

"He's busy helping his dad sell cars. He wants to stay as far away from the arrangements as he can."

"Well, that's normal. Guys don't always go in for all that. And, Bud is used to having everything done for him.

"Rafe was different, though. He was so artistic, and had such a spirit of adventure. It would not have done for him to have an ordinary wedding. He had ours all planned. He wanted lilies of the valley all over, for to him they represented beauty and peace. My dress would be the hues of the rainbow, his palette and his universe. Wild flowers in my hair, and soft earth beneath our feet. We would leave in his plane, from that landing strip over there, and leave the guests to dance the night away."

"It sounds beautiful, Aunt Gert. Is that why the lilies of the valley come up everywhere around here?"

"Yes, we planted them in the spring. Rafe wanted to make sure there were enough for my bouquet and for the tables and for the guests to take home. Their perfume is delicious."

"Mother is planning a traditional wedding for me. Formal floral arrangements for the church, red roses for my bouquet."

"Have you chosen a dress yet, Jenny?"

"Mother hasn't seen one she's liked. We've looked all over Syracuse and Rochester. She's hoping Mayva can make one. Mayva is a dressmaker besides running her hair salon on Saturdays."

"Yes. I've seen her work. Very delicate."

"Mother has clipped designs from all the European bridal magazines and Vogue. She has specifically mentioned that the fabric must come from New York, the dress of satin with a very long train, lots of tiny buttons, trim of bows and lace, with a bridal veil of special fabric she has heard about."

"Well, I hope Mayva is up to this. But, I know she's

determined. She once made a long dress for Mrs. Anderson when Leland held a political rally to support a candidate for governor which he held at the Penn Yan Country Club. It got a mention in *The New York Times*."

At that, Chaucer barked at a garter snake making its way toward a pile of clay pots. The snake was too fast for the dog, who was putting his paw lazily out to try and capture his prey. The snake wriggled under the pile, leaving him to whine a bit at the loss and plop down again at Jenny's feet. She laughed, setting down her trowel to pat him.

As Chaucer waggled his tail in response, the "sundial" clock in the corner struck four. "I'd better head home, Aunt Gert. I promised Mother I'd peel the potatoes and help put the meatloaf together. She invited Hiram and his wife to supper. It's her annual contribution to keeping what Father calls the best hired hand this side of the Rockies."

"See you the next Sunday Jim Barnes sets you free."

"I'll be here. It's the only peace I get from wedding plans and apartment hunting talk."

Jenny hugged Aunt Gert. She had come to appreciate these Sundays more and more as she knew they were getting scarcer.

As she pedaled back home, the sun began to set, signaling the shorter days of autumn. As she looked round, she could almost picture the leaves of Jerusalem turning.

Chapter Fourteen

Jenny moved quickly toward the barn. It was early evening and she hadn't had time to herself in weeks. As she went, she heard the long, low whistle of the whippoorwill. It was Jake. He hadn't forgotten their signal.

"Hi, Jenny."

"Hi, Jake."

"I've waited for you a lot of evenings. You haven't been around."

"I know. Mr. Barnes has kept me busy nearly seven days a week."

"I've been fairly busy myself. What with helping Pa and heading for Geneva three days a week, I've hardly had any sleep."

"I'm sorry, Jake. How're Anne and Sarah?"

"They're good. Sarah's getting engaged to Jesse Watson. He's apprenticed to his Pa since he was seven making furniture, so he's ready for his own place. That means they'll have a house of their own down the road."

"I bet your mother is pleased."

"She's glad Sarah will be so well settled."

"What are you working on in Geneva?'

"I'm doing some research for one of my professors. We're doing a paper on the political process."

"It sounds interesting."

"I wanted to include a part on checking to see if our representation benefits everyone, or just the monied crowd. So, he suggested I knock on doors, especially the poor, or people like Pa who don't have a regular job, and see what they think."

"What about New York?"

"You heard about that?"

"Yes. I saw Jimmy."

"Well, Professor Thornton has a friend who teaches at Columbia in New York. He suggested they work together on the paper and I could be their research assistant. His friend just got a big grant, so it would pay for most of my tuition to Columbia."

"That sounds great, Jake. But, what about your parents? What do they think?"

"Well, Pa was against it in the beginning. But Ma, though she didn't want me living in New York, finally convinced him that it was an opportunity. He doesn't like higher education. He thinks it corrupts people."

"I'm glad you got the scholarship, Jake. It'll make it easier."

"Yes. And, I'm glad to be working on something I have some say on. Professor Thornton says if we do it right, our findings could be published in a law journal. And, then, maybe it would change things for better representation for the poor."

"That sounds great, Jake. I know you'll do real well with it."

Jake was still in his overalls stained with dirt. "I hear you're getting married, Jenny."

"Yes. Next summer. Bud and I will live in Syracuse."

"Aren't you going to finish your studies at Keuka?"

"Well, I'll be able to take a course or two at SU. But, I'll have to drop out from full-time studies because I'll have to work full-time."

"What about your art?"

"I'll try to keep it up. But, between working and entertaining for Bud, who will be gathering future clients for his dad's car agency, I'm not sure how much time I'll have."

"Well, I hope you try and think of yourself as much as you can. I remember a girl who had dreams of becoming a great artist."

"I will, Jake. I'll have the whole Syracuse campus to paint in my spare time."

"I'll be leaving for New York in a few weeks. I'll probably be back next summer. Maybe I'll see you then."

"Maybe. After Bud graduates, we'll be moving back here."

"I'll bet your mother is pleased."

"She's ecstatic. She sees herself in the society column every other week."

"I have to go now, Jenny. Gotta help Pa gather up tools and make a plan to harvest. I wish you the best of everything."

"Me, too, Jake. I wish you the best as well. Be careful in New York."

As they stood, Jenny could see in the moonlight Jake had changed. Gone was the home haircut, and his stance was way more poised. But, the shy farm boy was still there beneath.

Jake took Jenny in his arms. "I will always remember our times together, Jenny. The spring nights with their gentle breezes. The song of the whippoorwill. And, the cold nights we huddled in the barn together away from the winter cold."

"And I will remember that you and Anne and Sarah shared your family with me, an only child.

"I'll write you, Jake."

"I'm not much of a letter writer, Jen. But, Anne and Sarah will always know where I am."

Jake released her and turned to head toward home. She watched until he disappeared into the shadows.

Chapter Fifteen

J enny looked round the old farmhouse she had grown up in. This would be the last day she would spend in it as a single woman.

The day of the wedding had finally arrived though she was hoping it would be farther off. Mother was alternately clucking and crowing as she bustled about the house tidying up and checking the last minute details.

"Lyman, get your tux on. I'll be in to tie your tie.

"Jenny, get your wedding dress together. Make sure your veil is in a separate box.

"I hope your suitcase is all packed. We need to put it in the trunk before we lay your dress in the back.

"Amanda called. She'll be at the church early with Aunt Gert to help you dress."

Jenny had almost forgotten Sparky's given name, but Mother was there to remind her, and to remind her that a nod to formality wouldn't hurt her status with the Andersons. After all, they had invited not only their relatives but business acquaintances from New York.

"Make sure you shake everyone's hand and thank them for coming."

Mother peeked in to Jenny's room, already clad in her long, red satin dress, smoothing an imaginary wrinkle.

"Mother, you look beautiful."

"Thank you, Jenny. I think Mayva outdid herself. I think she worked just as hard on this as she did on Mary Lou Anderson's dress for the governor's ball.

"You had better get ready, Jenny. We mustn't be late. The Andersons are arriving at the church by noon."

"Yes, Mother."

"Now, don't be nervous, Jenny. Getting married isn't all that bad. Especially to someone like Bud who can provide for you in a grander style than you've ever had."

"Yes, Mother." Jenny bit her lip. Now was no time to challenge Mother.

"Chariot's ready. All gassed up and ready to go." Father had pulled the old Chevy round the front.

"Let's go. Jenny, I'll help you with your dress. Lyman, make sure you put Jenny's suitcase in the trunk so we can switch it to the limo when it arrives."

"Here, Jenny. I'll take your bag and your shoes. No sense tripping before we get there."

"Thanks, Father."

The trip to the church was silent save for Mother's ever-present chatter which no one answered. Despite the rush, the Andersons' had already arrived. The long, black Lincoln Town car sat in front of the church's red door. Pastor Wycliff Lyndley had had it painted when he took over the parsonage not quite a year ago. Though a good deal of the congregation had thought it out of place on the whitewashed clapboard building, he had insisted.

"Hurry, Jenny. You go round the back. You mustn't see Bud. There's a back stairway to the changing room. Mayva will be there to see to last minute details."

The changing room was small with only one high placed window. But, the mirror was large and the dimly lit dressing table more than adequate. Jenny surveyed the lines on her face as she set out her makeup and lingerie.

"Hey, Jen. Let's get that look off your face. It's just nerves."

Sparky had arrived with Aunt Gert looking every bit the debutante she once was. Her long, deep blue velvet maid-of-honor gown was set off with a single strand of pearls, her makeup perfect, and the limp braid that usually hung down her back had been transformed into a very sophisticated updo.

"You look delicious, Sparky. I bet every male eye will be upon you."

"Nonsense, Jen. This is your show. Now hold still so I can get this makeup started."

As Sparky added soft, brown lines to Jenny's pale brows, Mother appeared with Mayva. "Hello, Mattie. I see you brought the dressmaker as well as the bride. Hey, Mayva."

"Hey, Gert. I don't see you at the shop on Saturdays lately."

"Busy season. How's the hairdressing going?"

"Good, but I'd like to expand the dressmaking. No overhead. I can do it in my basement."

"I'll see what I can do over at the college. And, of course, if your customers can use fresh flowers, I wouldn't mind you talking it up on the weekends."

"Will do. And, how's our bride coming."

Sparky had finished the makeup and was popping the dress over Jenny's unbrushed hair. As Mayva took over to fasten the many buttons a hush fell over the room. "And, now, the bridal coiffure. How's this, Jenny?"

Jenny stared at the photo of a model clipped from a bridal magazine. "It's beautiful, Mayva."

"Sit still, Jenny, so Mayva can work."

"She's fine, Mattie. She's a bride. She's nervous."

Armed with a curling iron and several brushes, the expert hairdresser transformed the mane of chestnut hair into several long curls, a partial upsweep, and soft, wisps of curls along her hairline. Jenny looked beautiful.

"And, now, for the final touch. I've made your bouquet out of my prize orchids, a few gardenias, and a cascade of baby white roses."

"It's beautiful, Aunt Gert."

"I'm going to call the photographer. Jenny, get some color in your cheeks. What will the Andersons think?"

As the photographer snapped and Sparky added blush to

Jenny's pale cheeks, the Reverend Wycliff Lyndley stuck his head in.

"Everybody ready? Are you ready, Jenny?"

"Ready, Pastor."

"Okay. I'll help you every step of the way. Just remember our rehearsal."

As they descended the stairs, Jenny took her place next to Father. The wedding party, except for Sparky, was already assembled in front of the flower bedecked altar. Caroline and Dotty, their pale blue organza bridesmaids gowns a perfect complement to Sparky's deep blue velvet, stood to one side, Whit, the best man looking for all like a prom date, stood to the other. Bud stood next to him.

After Sparky's march accompanied by an usher, Bud's cousin, the music signaled the bride. Father shook as he led her down the aisle. Jenny could see Mother scrutinizing her stance. Nevertheless, a hush fell over the congregation. Jenny was a beautiful bride.

"Dearly Beloved, We are gathered together…" The words became a blur.

"Will you, Jenny, take Leland "Bud" Anderson as your lawful wedded…"

"Will you, Leland "Bud" Anderson take…"

"Will the groom place the ring on the bride's finger."

"I now pronounce you husband and wife." At that, Bud looked at Jenny, beaming.

"You may kiss the bride." Bud obliged, and the congregation rose to its feet, following the bridal couple with its eyes.

"Hey, Jen, why the nerves? I thought you were going to faint and I'd have to catch you."

"Not a chance, Whit. See you at the reception."

Bud, a fire-engine red Corvette at his disposal, got them there in record time. Whit and his friends, horns blaring, trailed the bridal couple. The Andersons pulled alongside.

"George has the reception set up in the Fairway Room."

"Thanks, Dad, we'll find it."

The Penn Yan Country Club was bustling as Jenny and Bud made their way to the Fairway Ball Room. George was already signaling them to start the reception line.

Jenny shook hands with nearly two hundred guests, most of them friends of the Andersons. Sparky hugged her as she came through and Aunt Gert planted a congratulatory kiss on her already worn cheek.

After several rounds of hors d'oeuvres, from shrimp to puff pastries to cheeses from around the world, a sit down dinner was announced. Liver pate flown in from France and pheasant with hearty port wine sauce. The Andersons had outdone themselves. Jenny dutifully hopped from table to table to thank all the guests for coming.

"The band should be here soon, Jen. We get the first dance.

Or, at least, after I dance with my mother and you dance with your father. I think that's how it's done."

"George will tell us. He seems to be the coordinator. I hope there's somebody to dance with Aunt Gert. Or even Miss Ransom. She did me a favor to come."

"There's plenty of guys out there who will do the proper thing. We have a lot of business acquaintances here."

"How are you doing, darling?"

"Fine, Mom."

"Your father's looking for you. He's got a lot of business acquaintances to introduce you to."

"I'll catch him, Mom. I think I see him over there at the bar."

"Jennifer, I'd like to talk to you for a moment."

"Yes, Mrs. Anderson."

"First of all, I'd like to welcome you into the family. I hope you will do everything possible to keep the family name up. It is highly respected from here to New York and across the country as well. Bud's great great grandfather was a New York State senator."

"Yes, Mrs. Anderson."

"Jennifer, it is no secret that I was against this match from the first. So, I hope you will do your best to take care of all Bud's needs. His socks and his underwear need to be laundered on a regular basis and his suits need to be pressed weekly."

"I will see to it."

"I've enrolled you in an etiquette and charm school in the Syracuse area. I hope you will attend regularly."

"I'm not sure I'll have time. I have a full-time job and I'm signed up for two courses."

"Then, maybe you'd better drop one. The school goes for one semester."

"I'll do my best, Mrs. Anderson."

"Jenny, the first dance is ours. Mr. Bennett said the band will be here any minute."

"Thank you, Father. I'm ready."

"Have her back in time, Lyman. The bridal couple lead the next one."

"Will do, Mary. Lovely reception."

"Thank you, Lyman. I thought we could do this better than you. We have a lot of business clients to impress."

As Jenny whirled in Father's arms, all eyes upon them, she thought of the autumn and baling hay and helping Father and Hiram to pull in the latest cash crop.

"Jenny, I hope you'll come home now and then. We'll miss you."

"Of course, Father. I know you can use an extra hand to bale the hay."

"Your life will be with Bud, now. His needs will come first. But, if you ever need anything, you give Mother or me a call."

"Thanks, Father. I will."

"I think Bud will treat you right. He seems like a responsible lad. And, the Andersons have money and power. A little high and mighty, but they should do right by you.

"How's that Martin boy doing?"

"He's going to New York. Got a scholarship."

"I knew he was a smart boy. Seems a shame Josiah will lose his best hand. They're funny people, but they mind their own business and they don't hurt a soul."

"Anne and Sarah are staying on to help him."

"Well, the dance is ending. You enjoy yourself on that fancy island the Anderson
s picked for the honeymoon."

"I will, Father. I'll send you a postcard."

"Hey, Jen, you ready? It's our dance."

"Ready, Bud."

As she whirled in Bud's arms, all Jenny could think of was her trousseau. The new pants and skirts, the sweaters set for a Syracuse winter, and even a suit for more formal occasions. Especially the new, cerise bikini she planned to surprise Bud with on the exotic island of St. Martin.

"Hey, Jen, wake up. Let's give 'em a better show."

Bud changed his lead to add a few fancy steps to the tempo, whirling and twirling and adding a mix of samba and tango. Jenny caught up.

"Let's get outta here. We need to catch a plane."

"Right, Bud. I won't be long."

Jenny returned in a flouncy skirt and a simple white cotton blouse she had chosen for the occasion. The guests threw rose petals since rice had long ago been outlawed at the club.

As they drove away, Jenny had barely noticed the "just married" sign strung along the Corvette's rear bumper. The noise of the old boots and cans attached to its strings followed them to the airport.

Chapter Sixteen

T he honeymoon on the island of St. Martin was everything Jenny had hoped for. Long walks on the beach, kisses in the moonlight, candlelit dinners in tropical restaurants surrounded by lush tropical foliage. The native towns, the shops and the open air markets. The pure white sands surrounded by mountains looming out of the sea.

Bud had been a consummate lover, guiding Jenny at every turn. Except for his forays down to the beach where he surrounded himself with topless bathers, everything had been dreamy.

"Telephone, Jennifer."

Miss Lindstrom, her boss and the assistant dean of the Arts College, was interrupting her reverie. "Thanks, Miss Lindstrom, I'll take it in the back room."

"Hi, Sparky."

"Jen. Long time no see."

"I know. How would you like to come to dinner next week and try out my cooking?"

"I'd love it, Jen. I'll bring Chinese for backup."

"No need. I've been studying cookbooks."

"Okay. How about next Tuesday? That way my exams will be over and I'll be able to show you the new Chevy convertible my parents surprised me with this semester."

"Sounds great, Sparks. Maybe we can take in an art opening. Miss Lindstrom gave me two tickets to the latest exhibit. Maybe we can make some connections."

"See you next Tuesday. Don't fuss, Jen. I'm still used to the dorm way of life."

"How's your friend Amanda?"

"Good, Miss Lindstrom. Hitting the books. She's a serious student."

"That's good. We need women like her. Graduate and break that glass ceiling in this male-dominated work world."

"Yes, Miss Lindstrom. Do you need me to call the speakers now for inter-semester week?"

"Good, Jenny. See if you can get that English physicist what's-his-name. He's hot and we'd be the envy of every upstate school around."

"I'll try. And how about that photographer?"

"Well, I guess so. All he photographs is doors. But, I guess the architecture students would go out of their minds and the art students might get it as well."

"I'll get on it right now. Time's wasting. It's almost three o'clock."

"Good, Jenny. Help yourself to the chocolate chip cookies. Fresh baked last night. At almost three. I had to catch up on these reports."

"Thanks, Miss Lindstrom." As she moved to the back desk, Jenny surveyed her boss. Great legs. Prim and proper clothing. Dark thick hair perennially pulled back in a bun and clipped with an old diamond pin. In love with Mr. Perkins, the head librarian. As far as everyone knew, he didn't know she existed.

As the library clock struck five, Jenny grabbed her jacket, ready to make the run to the far parking lot relegated to students. Bud would be there with their old, leased Corvette.

"See you in the morning, Miss Lindstrom. I've got calls in to four of the speakers. Maybe we can nail them tomorrow."

"Thanks, Jenny. Have a good evening."

"Will do."

As Jenny strolled the campus, she felt surrounded by carefree coeds, minds on books and boys, the latest hot spot in college town, and Saturday night frat parties. She felt protected, almost distant, and in some frightening way, a little bit envious. Bud was there on time.

"Hey, Babe."

"Hi, Bud."

"How was work?"

"Good. Same old stuff. Phone calls, paper work, inter-semester week planning. How did practice go?"

"Good. The guys are getting better all the time.

"Say, Jen. Could you drive yourself home? I've got exams tomorrow. Got to hit the frat files. Jason says he'll drop me off on his way to his own apartment."

"Sure, Bud. I'll keep dinner warm."

"Don't bother. I'll grab something at the house. Don't wear out the old television."

As Bud pulled her tight for a long, slow kiss, he left her wanting more. As she stepped on the accelerator, the old Corvette skidded on a pile of autumn leaves, newly lost from the large, grand, overhanging trees of the parking lot.

Chapter Seventeen

S parky was splendid in a swirly denim skirt, ruffled top, and heavy, clunky sandals. Her long, limp, pale brown hair, usually hanging loose, was plaited into a braid that hung neatly down her back. Her glasses, usually plain or steel-rimmed, were sporting bright, red frames.

"Gee, Sparks, you look positively artsy."

"That's the idea, Jen."

"I'm so glad you could come. I can use the company. It's been a busy season for Bud."

"Glad to be here. Great after-midterm break."

"What a great car, roomie. Great guy magnet. That oughta get you some hot, Saturday night dates."

"Aw, Jen. It's my transportation. I go home now just about every other weekend. My dad thinks he can get me a summer internship with one of the larger engineering firms in The City."

"Great, Sparks. But, what ever happened to those dreams of settling down here, growing your own food, and rolling up your jeans to wade along the beach like we used to do?'

"Gone with the age of practicality. I hear they need engineers, and the place to be right now is New York."

"Okay. Let's get cracking. Dinner's in the oven. We need to make the salad and get to the art show by eight."

Making dinner with Sparky was not like making dinner with Mother. They chatted and chatted while the chicken sputtered in the oven and Jenny stirred the champagne sauce. Sparky tore the lettuce, chopped the tomatoes, tossed in the olives, and crumbled feta cheese over the top.

"Where are your dishes? I'll set the table."

"Right over your head in the left-hand cupboard."

"Great. I choose the chipped, red-flowered ones."

"Courtesy of a nearby flea market. Lots of bargains."

"Someday you'll be a proper matron and have a set of Spode china."

"Right now it looks like it's a long way off. Bud's dad promised him a partnership only if he stays on the team and keeps passing grades. I've written a lot of papers."

"What about your art work?"

"I'm working on a canvas in a once-a-week class. It's my only free time."

"Well, good. Maybe we can find a prospective buyer for it tonight. We'd better get chowing down.

"Jen, this is great. Where did you get the recipe?"

"From Aunt Gert's files. She slipped it to me last visit."

"I run into her on campus every now and then. I'll look in on her for you."

"I'm not sure who looks in on who. She's pretty resilient. But, I'd sure appreciate it."

"My pleasure. The girls love her. Kate Donavan who had her for three classes can't stop talking about her."

"Well, talk about her influence, we're about to taste her favorite dessert, the one she's been making since I was carted there in an oversized carriage. Voila, the chafing dish and the dramatic set up of cherries jubilee."

"Brilliant, Jenny! I'll start it on fire, since I'm the engineer. If we succeed in not burning the house down, we get an early start for the art show."

Sparky's robin's egg blue convertible was a fitting chariot to whisk to the art show in. Breeze whipping through their hair with the radio on full blast. Memories of their idle times at Keuka.

"Hey, Jen. I see one lone parking spot. What kind of a shindig is this?"

"I don't know, Sparky. Miss Lindstrom didn't say."

"Why don't you take a peek at the invitation and let us in on it."

"Everson Museum of Art invites you to attend 'Artists of New York State Retrospective: From Grandma Moses to Andy Warhol.' Curated by the Brooklyn Museum of Art. Andy Warhol, guest artist. Reception, 7:30-9:00 pm."

"Wow, Jen, Andy Warhol. He's the hottest on the New York art scene. Maybe some of it will rub off."

As they followed the crowd, Jenny saw a building of three red brick blocks set out on the Syracuse plaza like an enormous sculpture. Art was everywhere. An arced sculpture set out on the lawn to offset the blockiness of the building. Large, white canvases with streaks of color at the entrance. And, delicate, porcelain vases on stands with vivid hues of blues and reds, birds and flowers, a testament to survival through the centuries.

"Hey, Jen, wake up. We're about to be stampeded. Maybe we'd better circumvent Andy Warhol and head for the back and the exhibit. I value these sandals."

Jenny had never seen so many people with objects in their hands. Students on benches penciling strokes into sketch pads of all sizes. Women with heavy mascara peering intently at the paintings through their gold-rimmed lorgnettes. Men, turtlenecks rumpled, leaning toward the artwork, aided by the thick-lensed spectacles carelessly dropping upon their noses. And people everywhere with notebooks in their hands, listening and writing.

"Sparky, have you ever seen these paintings?"

"Not these, Jen. But, some by these same artists.

"But, I've never seen any Grandma Moses. It says here her paintings hung in the homes of movie stars and she was invited to the White House by President Harry Truman."

"I didn't know art could get you there."

"Art can get you everywhere. Warhol's paintings hang on the walls of every Manhattan penthouse and Hamptons mansion whose owners can afford them."

"Gee, Sparky, I wonder if I'll ever get there."

"You'll get there, Jen. You've got grit."

"Hey, chick. Are you an artist or a buyer?"

"An artist. I'm sorry, do I know you?"

"Of course, you don't know me. I don't live here. But, I'm here to pick out the artists and the buyers. I helped curate this exhibit, and I have a gallery in Soho. Chip Everly."

"Jenny Thompson. Pleased to meet you, Chip. Welcome to the backwoods of New York's southern tier."

"Thanks. I like your traffic patterns."

"This is Amanda Parker, better known as Sparky. She's a fellow New Yorker."

"High five, Sparky. I bet you like the traffic patterns, too."

"Better than the Lincoln Tunnel at five."

"Jen, do you have anything to show me?"

"I've only got one canvas at the moment, and the paint is still wet. I'm newly married. I don't have the time."

"Trust me, Jen. Make the time. Otherwise it'll never come.

"If you chicks spot any new talent, or Jen, if you get there yourself, give me a buzz. Here's my card. Great to meet you."

"Gee, Jen, you made a contact."

"He'll probably be retired by the time I can get something to him."

"Well, stop writing papers for Bud and maybe the time'll come sooner.

"Say, Jen, I've gotta get back. How about meeting Andy Warhol and making an exit?"

As Jenny pumped Warhol's hand, she looked directly into his eyes. Warhol's imposing figure, tall as it was, was intense. Shy, quiet, direct. A thatch of blond-white hair. According to his posted bio, he had been born in Pittsburgh, the son of working class immigrant parents. A transplant to New York in '49, he had pushed himself to the top of the heap by sheer hard work and guts.

Jenny found herself thinking of Jake. The summer and her marriage had separated them. She wondered how kind the Big Apple would be to Jake.

Chapter Eighteen

Football game Sundays brought panic to Bud the moment he woke up. Jenny tried to soothe him.

"Hey, Bud. You've practiced and practiced. You said the guys are doing great."

"Yeah. Well, that doesn't tell you how well the opposing team's doing. We're up against Temple. Those guys don't have to get through school. All they have to do is play football."

"You'll slaughter them. They're playing here. They won't know where they are."

"I hope Mooney gets his game together. He lost his girl over the weekend. They split."

"That's too bad."

"Not really, but he doesn't know it. She was a loser. Always nagging him. He was never around."

"Well, maybe we can have him over for dinner. Cheer him up."

"Good. Settled."

"How about a back rub?"

"Never turned one down yet."

As Jenny gently kneaded the muscles of Bud's arms and shoulders and back, she reveled in the delights of a newlywed. A private world, a private man, the scent of autumn wafting through the screens of a second floor, makeshift apartment.

"Oh, that's good, Jen. Good.

"Hey, how about giving us the real thing."

"Ready when you are, captain."

Jenny looked at Bud with admiration. A shock of blond, sleep-worn, hair hanging over a face of intensely, chiseled features. Muscles honed to perfection. As they made love, the sounds of the neighborhood children playing freeze tag on the sidewalks below drifted in on the autumn air.

"Jeez, Jen, we gotta get going. Coach says we gotta be there before noon."

"I'll get on it right away. How do you want your eggs?"

"I don't care. As long as we get going."

"Say, Jen, I've got something to tell you."

"Great. Save it for over the eggs."

As they sat, the second-hand chrome and formica table between them, Jenny looked out through the open window which hung above the postage stamp-sized backyard. A farmer lazily tooling along on his old John Deere was clearing a long, narrow field below them. Jenny admired the contrast. The open field surrounded by small, frame hastily built 1960s houses. A rebel farmer fighting the urban sprawl.

"Hey, Jen. Wake up. I've got a surprise for you."

"What, Bud?"

"My folks bought us a house."

"But, I thought we were going to be here for two years, What about my art classes?"

"Well, we can move back, and you can paint all you want. That way you can get the house ready for when I graduate."

"But, Bud, I like my job here."

"You can get one in Penn Yan. That way I'll be all set to move in with my dad at the agency."

"What kind of a house, Bud?"

"A great, old farmhouse on the edge of town. It's got five acres."

"But, I was kinda hoping for one of those bungalows Carl and Lyman Andrews are putting up over by the old Seneca Dairy."

"You'll love it. Give you a chance to put all those art classes to use fixing up the place."

"What does it look like?"

"White frame. Needs paint. You can paint it any color you want. Structure's good. Plumbing needs replacing. Owner lost his job and had to sell. The folks got it for a song."

"When do we have to go?"

"As soon as we can. This lease is up in January."

"Well, I'll have to tell Miss Lindstrom so she can start looking for somebody else."

"Don't worry, Jen. She'll get along. She's been there for thirty years. She's a tough, old gal."

"Just the same, I'll miss her."

"Okay, let's get going. We gotta cream those guys from Temple to even have a crack at the finals this year."

"You'll make it, Bud. The guys look good on the field this year. Everyone's pulling together."

"I hope that Mooney gets a grip. He's our only holdout."

"Good luck. I'll be in the stands."

"See ya, Babe." As always, Bud's long, slow kiss kept her wanting for more. She buried her desire under the heap of household tasks she knew were waiting. A slam of the door and he was gone.

As she tidied up, she thought about what she would wear. A player's wife was always on display. A new pair of Calvin Klein jeans ought to do it, set off by brown leather ankle boots and a wild scarf through the belt loops. A white turtle neck and a nubby pink crew neck should keep her from the autumn chill. She would sit with Coach Jensen's wife and the other players' girlfriends in the stands.

The noise of the farmer's tractor still drifted through the screen. Somehow, she desperately wanted to photograph the scene. She knew they had received a simple, SLR as a gift. But, where might it be? She dropped the dishes and ran to the very, small bedroom. It lay in the storage chest, nestled between an extra blanket and a quilt.

As she grabbed it and ran down the stairs, the sun rose in the sky toward high noon. She knew this photograph would be good.

Chapter Nineteen

Hanging curtains in the old, frame house they had moved into in January had had its problems. Warped window sills and rotted wood. Frames that never measured the same on either side. But, Jenny was determined to make it work.

As she stood on the second rung of the rickety ladder, the hammer above her on the top rung, a beautiful, new antique brass curtain rod in her hand, she surveyed the challenge. The heavy side drapes she had purchased would keep out the winter cold, and their bright reds and royal blues would add color to the presently drab living room. Simple sheers would let the sunlight in.

Federal blue on the walls would give it a more pristine look, and the replica of the Egyptian vase she had purchased at the Everson, with the deep, blues and greens of its peacocks and bright reds of its Egyptian blossoms would tie it all together. Slipcovers would make the second-hand attic furniture the Andersons had dumped on them all but disappear.

As she stood, the phone jangled from the kitchen she had painted a cheery, bright yellow. She ran to answer it.

"Hey, Sparks. What gives?"

"How about a walk on the proverbial beach this afternoon. A break for you and me. The trees are starting to bud and deliver their native greenery, and the smell of spring is in the air."

"Sounds good. I'll pack us a lunch."

"Jenny the homebody. Nah. This time I'm buying. Seneca Dairy is opening for the season."

"Okay, provided some of their ice cream goes along with it."

"Choose your flavor. I never knew anybody addicted to ice cream before."

"Only to theirs. I was practically raised on it."

"Well, then, be prepared to order a double scoop. You're looking a little thin lately."

The shore along the lakefront of the college looked the same. Jenny realized she hadn't walked its shores since sophomore year. She picked up a few shells and shards of colored glass as they strolled.

"Jen, what would you think if I bought a house here?"

"Well, Sparks, you did tell me you were angling for a job in New York City."

"Yes, but I thought about what you said. How my dreams for the future were here when I first met you. Subsistence farming and going barefoot in the dirt."

"Well, practicality always interferes with dreams. If I had

115

my way, Bud and I would live in the Village in New York and I would be working on making it in the art scene."

"I think I can make it here, Jen. There are some good engineering firms in Rochester and Syracuse. I can work there by day and be an inventor by night. I still have some good connections in The City."

"Sounds good, Sparks. If you need a place to stay, we have plenty of room."

"Thanks, Jen. But, my folks are giving me big bucks for my graduation. I think I'll use it for a down payment on a house."

"Swell. I can help you look. We've got a year."

"So, how's the devoted housewife?"

"Pretty good. Making a dent in that old farmhouse. I should have most of the rooms done and ready for entertaining by the time Bud finishes this semester."

"And, what are you doing for yourself, Jen? Are you painting anything but the walls?"

"I've got a studio ready to go in the attic. Aaron Hartwell is going to put a skylight in for me when he finishes helping his father in the furniture shop."

"Good. Maybe now you'll get busy and give Andy Warhol a little competition."

Jenny looked at her former roomie. Her limp brown hair still hung in a braid along her back, her perky polka-dotted red-framed glasses had been replaced by contacts.

"And, how about you Sparks? Have you corralled any men lately? Has anybody been lucky enough to swing a date with you?"

"Well, I have been dating a guy. Westin Embury, III. From Short Hills.

"He's a serious student. One of the few around here. We study together, and once in a while we take in a flick in town or, if we feel adventurous, drive to Syracuse in his new Ferrari."

"I'd like to meet him. He sounds like he has style."

"We'll drop over sometime. Maybe we'll even take you out with us on one of those nights when you're a football widow."

"Great. I'll be waiting.

"Okay, let's hit the Seneca Dairy. My curtains are waiting. I promised Bud I would have the living room done in two weeks. He's invited the whole football team over for an open house."

"Jenny the devoted workhorse. I'll race you to the parking lot. Last one there pays for the ice cream."

As Jenny fell behind Sparky, she checked out her former roommate. Jeans outlining a pair of very athletic legs. Sparky was an avid tennis player, swimmer, and beach comber.

Jenny realized she had let herself go in an effort to keep up with Bud and his needs and her job. She promised herself a half hour a day in front of the television with a Jack LaLanne workout. Summer was coming, and she would soon have to pull her bikini from its storage place in the basement. She was certain Bud's family had been busy booking pool parties at the country club for them to attend since before the crocuses had poked their tiny white and purple heads through the fertile soil to signal the start of spring.

Chapter Twenty

J enny looked down at her spreading figure. At four months pregnant, she was beginning to show.

Bud had graduated from Syracuse, barely squeaking by. The Andersons celebrated the occasion with lavish parties nevertheless, including a late-night stag affair for his former teammates to which she had not been invited.

Mary Lou Anderson had been furious at Jenny's pregnancy, never bothering to stifle her discontent. Although she never attacked her directly, she complained incessantly to Bud, pointing out that she had expected Jenny to work a few years to help out until Bud could get on his feet with a new dealership of his own or a major share of Leland's agency so he could retire that much sooner. Although Bud had agreed to starting a family, even telling Jenny she could have as many children as she wanted, he took to spending more evenings at the agency to hide out from the obvious mounting tension.

Jenny's complaints to Mother had fallen on deaf ears. "Let's hope it's a boy so he can be groomed to take over the agency when he's of age," was all she could say.

Only Aunt Gert had been sympathetic, helping Jenny to plan the nursery and getting her friend Alma Miller who had a yarn shop in town to knit a few caps and booties and sweaters to set the baby up for the coming cold winter.

As Jenny surveyed the nursery which she planned to do in yellow, with a starry, dark "sky" on the ceiling and several twinkling stars, she thought of the pictures she could paint to compliment the yellow of the walls. Peter Rabbit, a jack-in-the-box, the three little pigs, and a cow jumping over the moon. As she thought of the subjects that would entertain a wee person and perhaps help him or her to dream, she thought of Jake. How they had once read nursery rhymes to the littlest of his family, who had been used only to Bible stories, and how their eyes were as wide as saucers.

She had heard Jake was in town for a few weeks to help his father with the tending of the crops and preparing the barn for the autumn harvest. She must see him before he left. His visits had become less and less frequent and she heard he would be starting law school in the fall.

She must see him at dusk just like they used to meet. Mother was gone for the day with her card club and a re-do of her permanent. Father was at the tire store while Jackson was out of town.

Jenny hopped in the car, out of the driveway and along the unpaved, dusty road. The setting sun was a beautiful finish to a very beautiful day. Blue skies, and the brilliant sun of August.

As the sun set, Jenny admired the shades of red in the fast darkening sky. Surely, the sun set with such a feast of color only over Jerusalem.

120

She would rouse Jake with the sound of the whippoorwill, the signal of their childhood years, to preserve the social comfort of their respective families. As she drove up the driveway of the Thompson homestead, and left her car for the direction of the barn, she could hear the sounds of the Martins working steadily in the fields, their happy chatter interrupted only occasionally with the slow, methodical voice of Mr. Martin firmly issuing directions, carried through the still, windless day.

"Whip-poor-will," called, Jenny, the childhood signal bringing the sound of heavy boots crackling on the gravel of the lane which connected the Thompson and Martin farms.

"Jen." Jake stood in front of her, the awkward farm boy now morphed into sophisticated city dweller, despite the conventional overalls. "Do you mind if I hug you?"

"Oh, Jake." She wrapped her arms around him, taking comfort in the warmth of his embrace.

As he stood back, he surveyed her formerly lean figure.

"I see there is another Anderson on the way."

"Yes. Due in January."

"Congratulations, Jen."

"Thanks, Jake. And, what about you?"

"I start law school in the fall. I got a full scholarship to Columbia."

"Congratulations, Jake. You'll make a fine lawyer."

"Thanks, Jen. And, what will you name that new arrival?"

"Amanda, if it's a girl. Mandy for short. Leland Anderson III if it's a boy."

"And, what will you call a boy for short?"

"I thought Josh. Remember when we thought that if your Ma had another boy she should name him Joshua?"

"I do. What do the Andersons think of that?"

"Bud says he doesn't care what we call him as long as his formal name carries on the family line."

"And, how goes the marriage?"

"Fine. Bud is pretty busy at his dad's agency so it gives me a lot of time to plan."

"I wouldn't leave such a beautiful new bride alone so much if I were him."

"My former roommate from Keuka keeps me company in the off hours. She bought a house down the road."

"Sounds like a good friend."

"And, how about you, Jake? Do you have a girl?"

"Haven't had time. Too much study and hard work.

"Have to run, Jen. I have packing to do. I'll be taking off next week for good. Good luck on the baby. If you ever need me, Sarah and Anne will have my number and my address."

Jake looked down at Jenny, remnants of the farm boy still visible beneath the smooth exterior. He kissed her on the cheek and then he was gone.

Chapter Twenty-One

Leland Anderson III was born at 3 a.m. on a very stormy January morning. Jenny's water had broken and contractions were coming nearly a minute apart when she and Bud reached Sailors and Soldiers Memorial on roads barely visible 6 p.m. the evening before.

As her contractions eased, and the medicine they gave her took hold, Bud pulled out a deck of cards.

"C'mon, Jen, this'll take your mind off it."

"What do you want to play?"

"How about gin rummy? You're always good at that."

"Okay, Bud, loser does dishes for a month."

"I was going to talk to you about that, Jen. I have a surprise for you."

"What kind of a surprise?"

"Well, I wanted to wait till you got home to tell you.

"I'm hiring someone to do some light housework and take care of the kid."

"But, Bud, I want to stay home with the baby."

"I'll get some little Mennonite girl. They work for very little."

"But, I don't want someone else taking care of my baby."

"You'll get used to it. And, that way, you can come into the agency and save us a full-time salary."

Jenny put out a three of diamonds and said nothing. But, she was determined to stay home with the baby for at least three months, the length of time she had scheduled to nurse the baby herself.

Suddenly, as she drew a card that would make a meld for herself, a long and especially painful contraction hit. "Bud, get the nurse."

"Aw, take it easy, Jen, they know what they're doing."

"If you don't, I'll scream so loud they'll be sorry they admitted me."

"Okay, okay. I'll call her."

As Jenny was wheeled down the hall to the delivery room, her screams scared even herself. "Hang on, Jen, we're almost there. We'll give you a little nitrous to relax you."

Strapped onto the table, her contractions came even faster. Margie, the delivery room nurse, held her hand. "Push, Jenny, push." Dr. Reynolds, gentle and sweet in his office during examinations, had turned martinet.

Jenny had never felt such pain before. "C'mon, Jen, the head's out. A few more pushes and we'll find out what the baby is."

In what seemed forever and the space of no time, a loud squall filled the room and she saw Dr. Reynolds holding the baby's feet. "Jenny, you've had a boy. Congratulations." Their audible sighs of relief barely cut through Jenny's euphoria.

"Would you like to hold the baby?"

"Oh, of course, can I now?"

"Well, we'd like to get him cleaned up, but we'll let you hold him for a minute."

As Jenny cuddled her newborn, "Josh" as she proposed to call him, she thought of the nursery she had painted and the hours she planned on laughing and playing and showing him the world. She stared at his tiny fingers and toes, inspired by a feeling of awe.

"Okay, Jen, we're going to clean him up. The Andersons are waiting along with Bud, and I'm sure they want to get a look at their new heir. Your parents are waiting in your room. Nancy will help you into the things you brought from home."

"Thanks, Dr. Reynolds."

"You did a great job, Jenny. That baby looks like he could mow the world down already. I'm going home to get some sleep and tell Millie you had a boy. I'll see you in my office in six weeks."

As Jenny put on the nightgown and bed jacket she had brought from home, she thought of the future. Josh would become a great scientist and she would be the toast of the village. His sister, more reserved, would accompany her on shopping trips to Syracuse and New York.

"Okay, Jenny, snap out of it. I'm going to brush your hair. You're going to knock 'em dead when we send you back to your room. Here's Ginny to take you back."

Ginny's transport skills seemed at a low ebb, and Jenny felt the pain as they whizzed through the old halls of the small-town hospital. "What was it like when you had your first baby?"

"The same as you, Jenny. But, now, they're both in school. I have more time, but they're more work. So, it all evens out in the end."

Mother was waiting along with Aunt Gert. Father was pacing the halls.

"You did it, Jenny. You gave the Andersons a boy."

"The baby is his own self, Mother. He doesn't belong to anyone."

"Nevertheless, the Andersons are ecstatic. You should be very proud, Jenny."

"Congratulations, Jenny. He's beautiful. We just got a peek." Aunt Gert bent down to hug her niece.

"Thanks, Aunt Gert."

"You look tired, Jenny. Maybe we'd better go."

"No, Father, stay. I'm glad to see you."

"The baby looks just like a Thompson. Your father was a handsome man when he was younger, Jenny."

"He still is, Mother. Was he awake when you saw him?"

"Yes. He was. He looks like a strong young man already. You'll have to feed him soon, Jenny."

"They'll bring him in when they're ready. He's going to stay here with me."

"You need your sleep, Jenny. He should stay in the nursery."

"It's just for a day, Mother. We'll be fine."

"We'd better go, Jenny. We'll see you tomorrow at home."

"Thanks, Father. I'll get Josh all fixed up for you."

"I thought his name is Leland."

"That's his formal name. I'm going to call him "Josh".

"After some Mennonite, or some cabinet maker's son?"

"After himself, Mother."

"I'll have a book already for him tomorrow. He can look at the colored pictures."

"He needs a more masculine toy, Gert. After all, he's an heir to a long, proud lineage."

"Let's go, ladies. We'll let our new mother get some rest."

As they left, Bud raced by, barely giving them a hello.

"You did it, Jen."

"We did it, Bud. He's both of ours."

"Well, yeah. That's what I meant. So, what are they giving you for breakfast?"

"I don't know yet. They haven't brought it."

"I think I'll go down to Capn's and grab some breakfast. The guys are waiting for the news and I have a whole box of cigars to hand out. Whit called from Hawaii with congratulations. He said to get him started early in the agency, and he's going to give him polo lessons."

"That's great, Bud, but he'll have to grow a little bigger first."

"Whatever you say, Jen. Listen, I have to go. I'll drop in tonight. Anything you need?"

"Just remember to lay out the linens for the nursery and for our room. Sally Jenkins is going to help out for the first few days."

"Will do. See you later, Babe."

As Bud bent down for a quickie kiss, grabbing his cigar box as he sped out the door, Jenny drifted off to sleep. She would need her strength for Josh's first feeding.

Chapter Twenty-Two

Josh's gurgling and baby noises brought Jenny from the kitchen to the nursery. Now three months, Josh delighted in the mobile hanging from the ceiling Jenny had made him. A red-nosed clown, an elephant with a hat, a walrus with a big, pink bow, a miniature boy with a blue plaid suit, and a leprechaun. All were dancing round to the tune of the breeze blowing in through the open window, and the sparkles on the leprechaun's shamrock were glowing in the rays of the noonday sun.

Jenny felt so free as she rose from the easel she had set up on the kitchen table. Her wildflowers, the image of the newly sprung blossoms in the fields beyond the farmhouse, lent a lovely contrast to the bright yellow of the kitchen. She laughed as she bent over Josh, his gurgling continuing as he studied his fingers, moving in front of his face.

"Time to eat, little man?"

As if on cue, he started to whimper. "Caught you just in the nick of time?

"How about if we sit on the rocker and listen to the birds. When we're finished, we'll check out the trees and see all the new green leaves of spring. Then, maybe we'll go outdoors if it's warm enough and fill the bird feeder. You can help me chase all the barn cats away."

Josh's answer was a hungry and satisfied sucking at her breast, but that was enough of an answer for Jenny. She sat quiet until he was full, then burped him in front of the open window, pointing out the willows and the maples.

As they stood, the back door slammed.

"Hey, Jen, are you here?"

"Of course, I'm here."

"I got somebody here to meet Josh. Sarah Martin. She's Jesse Watson's new bride. He makes our office cabinets."

Jenny swallowed her protests as she greeted Sarah. "Sarah. You're all grown up and beautiful. Marriage must agree with you."

"Thanks, Jenny."

"Okay, you ladies chat later. I gotta run. Jenny, see if you can drive Sarah back to her house. I've got a client waiting."

As the back door slammed once again, Jenny looked over at Sarah Martin. Slim and young, with a resolve found only in a woman at peace with herself.

"May I hold him, Jenny? He's beautiful."

"Of course, Sarah. But, I don't know if Bud mentioned I haven't agreed to this."

"He didn't say, Jenny. Just that you were looking for help."

Jenny sighed and handed Josh to Sarah. Josh, already enchanted, his eyes drawn to the plain black dress and plain white cap, began playing with Sarah's hair.

"He's beautiful, Jenny. I hope Jesse and I have a big family."

"You deserve to, Sarah. You put in a lot of time taking care of the little ones."

"Can I help you bathe him, Jenny?"

"Of course. You get the rubber duck in his toy box, and I'll fill the bassinet."

As Jenny filled the sturdy bassinet, a gift from the Andersons, Sarah entertained Josh with giggling noises and a chance to pull on her hair when she'd let him. Josh was smitten, and rewarded her with what passed at that age as a smile.

"Sarah, why don't you lay him in the water and hold his head up. That way you'll get the hang of it."

"Sure, Jenny. I always bathed Hannah and Matthew in the sink, but I'm sure it's not much different."

Josh followed his yellow duck with his eyes while Jenny washed and rinsed him. Sarah picked him up and wrapped him in his waiting yellow towel.

"He's rubbing his eyes. He's ready for his nap. What do you say we both put him to bed and we can catch up on old times as he sleeps?"

"Great, Jenny. You don't have to take me home. I'll walk. I like to keep the Mennonite laws when I can. It's been hard enough on Ma and Pa to see Jesse and me go modern."

As Jenny poured tea for Sarah, she set out a plate of half-moons, the cookies the Mennonites were famous for at the market.

"How are your parents doing?"

"They're doing fine. Jesse and I go over and help them on the weekends, and Hannah and Matt are big enough to follow after Pa in the fields."

"I'm glad." Jenny hesitated. "How is Jake doing, Sarah?"

"He's doing fine. He's busy. Keeping his grades up for the scholarship and working for his professor the rest of the time. But, I know he thinks of us. Once you've worked the land here, Jenny, you don't forget."

Sarah's words brought the memory of her own times on the back of Father's tractor and the image of a farm boy done with his day's work. But, she quickly changed the subject.

"How about coming in to help Tuesdays, Thursdays, and Fridays. Would that suit you?"

"That would suit me just fine, Jenny. That would give Jesse and me a start. He's doing real well with his cabinet making on his own, but we could use the help."

"Okay, Sarah, I'll see you next week. I have a few errands to run, so you and Josh can get better acquainted."

"That would be fun. I better go now. It's almost supper time, and Mennonite men don't cook."

As Sarah, started down the open road to the village, closing the door gently behind her, Jenny felt a new life begin.

Chapter Twenty-Three

Jenny chewed on a pencil as she lifted her head to look out the large front window of the Anderson agency. Spring was in the air and the soft breeze floating through the open door was misty from an earlier rainfall. Her old, wood desk, shoved out of the way of the showroom, was piled high with paper work.

Sammy Walker strolled through the showroom, careful not to acknowledge her presence as the boss' wife, on the way to seek the advice of Alfred Stoller, pompadoured raconteur and ace number two salesman, almost as good as Bud. His new third wife enjoyed a number of trips to Atlantic City and New York, thanks to his expertise.

"Hey, Jen, look at Sammy. I guess he's gonna stay with us." Alice Masters chuckled as she placed yet another sales transaction on Jenny's desk for typing, filing, and mailing.

"I guess. He's sure good for the agency. He's won top prize for the best repairs in the southern tier ever since he's been here."

"Bud never treats him well, Jenny. I'm surprised he's been here this long."

"He's closest to his family here. He fixes cars after hours and makes a little money on the side. That way he can take care of Etta and her brood. Her husband lost a leg in a threshing accident last year."

"Just the same, he almost lost him to Mack Jones in Elmira. Bud should be more careful."

"Try and tell him that. He keeps Sammy just above pay scale so he doesn't lose him."

As Jenny turned her attention to the mounting pile of paperwork, Sammy stopped by.

"How's it going, Jenny?"

"Good, Sammy. And, you?"

"Can't complain. Put together an old Chevy for the folks and an old Ford pickup for Etta and Bert. He gets his new leg next week at Clifton Springs. This way I fixed it so he can drive it, too."

"Sounds great, Sammy. They're lucky to have you. Going to the American Legion dance next week? They're going to have a fiddler, a caller, and a barbecue."

"Aw, I don't have anyone to take, Jenny."

"Why don't you take Janey and Fran? They're old enough to know the reels and they'll love the fiddling."

"I guess. Ma and Pa would like that."

"Okay. See you there. Now, we'd both better get back to work before we get fired."

"Thanks, Jenny. I don't know what I would do without you to talk to. Those guys in the back get pretty rough sometimes."

"Hang in there, Sammy. Someday you'll make assistant manager."

"Aw, I'm happy bein' just a regular old grease monkey."

As Sammy headed for the back bays, Sarah came in the front door, carrying Josh in her arms. "Hey, Jenny. We came to town for ice cream."

"Sounds good. Why don't I hold Josh while you walk over to the dairy?"

"Thanks, Jenny. I brought Anne. She's out by the stroller. You want us to get you a cone?"

"No, thanks, Sarah. Gotta fit into my bikini in six weeks."

As Jenny cradled Josh, all the women in the office migrated as one to her desk, cooing and chucking him under the chin, losing all command of the English language. Alice Masters waved an old beaten-up Teddy Bear she had won at a Kiwanis bingo years ago she kept as a work mascot.

"Hey, Jen, can't you get him outta here? He's disrupting business."

"Gee, Bud, I'm just keeping him till the girls get back with their ice cream. I thought I would show him around. After all, he's going to take over the business someday."

"Okay, as long as everybody gets back to work. Dad is furious."

The women returned to their desks, but Josh kept cooing and gurgling, keeping everyone silently amused as they bent over their paperwork. Jenny kept him distracted with a set of plastic keys and the old Kiwanis teddy bear.

"Hey, Jen, are those Jake's little sisters?"

"Yes, Sammy."

"They've grown. The last time I saw them up close they were littler tads in their Pa's fields."

"Sarah's married. She's married to Jesse Watson. You know him?"

"I've seen him. Those Mennonites bein' home-schooled, I never saw him except at Mr. Adam's dry goods once in a while.

"Is Anne married?"

"No, Sammy. She's barely seventeen. But, I didn't know you were interested in girls. All I see you do is work."

"I'm not, Jenny. But, Anne is different. Her face has a shine to it. She's pretty."

"Well, we'd better get back to work before we both get fired. Josh has already caused enough of an uproar."

"I don't know why. He's the best thing we got to look at around here."

"Thanks, Sammy. I miss him during the day. But, I know he gets good care. He loves Sarah."

As Jenny waited for the girls to return, she bounced Josh on her lap while she put her papers in neat piles upon her desk, jiggling her keys to keep him amused at the same time. As Sarah and Anne pushed open the great glass doors that announced the Anderson Agency, the gale of spring air they brought with them sent her neatly stacked papers across the yellow squares of the cheaply tiled floor. Josh burst out into gales of laughter.

As Sarah took Josh in her arms, the whiff of spring air wafted along Jenny's nostrils, bringing memories of riding the tractor with Father at planting time, the sun so strong on their backs, and the hours after spent up in the hayloft, the sun giving way to the quiet of the evening, the sounds of the whippoorwill, and the silver shine of the moon on the newly tilled fields.

Chapter Twenty-Four

T he Penn Yan Country Club was decorated with the
flowers of summer, the soft pinks and the purples giving
way to the simplicity of their surroundings. Mary Lou
Anderson was everywhere, rearranging the flowers, directing
the staff to replenish the hors d'oeuvres, and shaking the
hands of just about everybody.

Throwing lavish parties at the country club to increase
contacts for the agency was nothing new to the grande dame
of the Anderson dealership. She was holding court in a
beautifully tailored off-the-shoulder cerise silk gown which
she had flown to New York to get designed and fitted all
before the previous Thanksgiving holidays.

The governor of the state was due to arrive at any moment
and Mary Lou was making sure that every petal of every
flower and every cracker that held an hors d'oeuvre was
worthy of his presence. The Andersons had been heavy
contributors to his recently successful campaign.

Jenny took refuge in the pool.

"Hey, Jen, why the long face?"

"Hey, Whit."

"Where's the big guy?"

"I don't know. I haven't seen him since we arrived an hour
early."

"Oh, he's probably helping his dad make sure everything's in place for the big arrival. And, how's the little big guy?"

"Oh, he's fine, Whit. Growing like a weed. I can't keep up with him."

"I gotta get over and see him. Someone's gotta teach him how to sneak out on his parents. But, honestly, Jen, I've been so busy setting up our new office in Hawaii that I don't even remember my own name. If I didn't shave in the morning, I wouldn't know who I am."

"That's great, Whit. You're soon going to be the largest liquor distributor on the globe."

"Not yet. I haven't conquered Europe or Asia. But, distributing the stuff isn't nearly as much fun as drinking it. What do you say we ditch this place for the cocktail lounge?"

"Great idea. I'll see you in a few."

As she switched her lime green bikini for an aqua ankle length silk and chiffon she had eyed at a Syracuse mall, she thought of how Whit had still kept his former athletic figure. Maybe Sparks would be interested.

They strolled the hall, the most austere Jenny had ever seen, perked up only by one enormous floral ceramic vase filled with a few large, dusty, silk tiger lilies.

"Have you got a girl, Whit?"

"Too busy, Jen. Say, how well do you know Katt Johnson?"

"Not well. Roomed with her a few times at Syracuse."

"I hear she's in town to get over a divorce with a visit to her cousin. Do you think you could arrange an introduction?"

"Do my best. Now, we better get set to meet the important figures of our state. It looks like Mary Lou has them lined up already."

Governor Cuomo shook her hand with the firm, hard grip of a seasoned politician. As she left the receiving line, Bud's voice came loud and clear across the atrium, a tipsy and slightly raucous Katt Johnson on his arm.

"Hey, Whit, when did you blow into town?"

"Yesterday, old man, but no time to call. I had to unearth this tux so I could attend your shindig today."

"Well, Whit, I guess you won't have to wait long for an intro to Katt Johnson."

"Hey, Whit, glad to see ya, buddy. This here is Katt Johnson from Long Island. You might remember her from prom night at the Castle way back when."

"Glad to re-meet you, Katt. What brings you to our small town from all the action on the Island?"

"A messy divorce and a yen to live it up with the country folk. How goes it with you?"

"Not bad. Global travel seems to agree with me.

"Say, Katt, would you like to dance?"

As she nodded her head to the detriment of her balance, the band struck up a hot mambo.

"Say, Bud, do you think we could do that?"

"Aw, Jen, you know how I hate that stuff. Why don't you get a drink and mingle. I gotta get going. Dad will have a fit if I don't pick up some new sales."

Bud walked off, taking Mandy the new temp along with him to keep track of new sales leads. Jenny headed for the lobby phone.

"Hi, Sarah, how's Josh?"

"He's fair, Jenny. He's crying and I'm quieting him down. He keeps rubbing his ear."

"He just had his shots. Is his medicine nearby?"

"Yes, but he's not due for a dose for another two hours."

"I'll be over to check if you need me."

"Thanks, Jenny."

As Jenny returned to the festivities, she spied Whit slugging a Jack Daniels with no mixer but a lemon.

"Where's Katt?"

"Powdering her nose. She's taking a long time."

"Cheer up, Whit. We'll get her over for a barbecue. With your charm and my chili sauce she'll be your conquest in no time."

"She seems to have her eye on a lot of other guys."

"Just post-divorce syndrome. Have you seen Bud?'

"Not for a while."

"Well, if he appears, would you tell him I went home to check on Josh?"

"Gee, Jen, shame to spoil the festivities. Can I help?"

"Thanks, Whit, but duty calls. See you later around the dinner hour."

As Jenny walked across the parking lot, she barely noticed the setting sun. The newly tarred surface was hot and sticky. All her thoughts were on Josh. Lucky for her confidence in Dr. Reynolds. He had pulled her along with Mother and Father through every childhood disease. He was starting on his third generation.

Chapter Twenty-Five

The patio that Bud built on the back of the old farmhouse was laid with the beautiful grey stone Jenny had found at the nearby quarry. A set of white wicker furniture fit perfectly.

Bud was busy serving drinks and getting the old, brick barbecue started. Jenny marinated the steaks while Josh gurgled and giggled in his playpen, surrounded by plastic trucks and trains, a stuffed frog that croaked, and numerous stuffed animals which either squeaked, talked or rattled.

Jenny looked out over the vista beyond their yard as she added the red wine, the olive oil and the onions to the soy of the marinade. The pinks, the purples, the oranges and the yellows of the wild flowers stood out among the field grasses as they stretched their way to the blue of the horizon. What a painting that would make.

"Hey, kid, a penny for your thoughts."

"Hey, Whit. Just thinking what a great painting that would make out there."

" Have you painted lately?"

"No. Being a wife and a mother and a full-time office worker has done me in."

"You should be painting, Jenny. You were the best in the school."

"Well, I don't know about that. But, I liked it."

"Maybe I can get Dad to commission a painting for our new headquarters. Then, you'd have to do it."

"Thanks, Whit. That would be nice. But, I don't know that I'd have the time."

"You have to make the time, Jenny. We wouldn't want great art to go dormant."

"Say, Jen, do you have dessert?" A drunken Katt poked her head through the open doorway.

"I have a raspberry pie I just baked."

"How about some vanilla ice cream to go with that? Bud and I can hop down to Byrne Dairy and get some." Without waiting for an answer, she disappeared back into the grass of the fair sized yard.

"Hey, Whit, man. Keep an eye on the barbecue." Bud's voice came through the well-patched screen door as he jumped over the door into the driver's seat of the borrowed red Corvette convertible. "We'll be back in time to throw those steaks on."

As the car squealed off, Katt in the passenger seat, Whit stared after it.

"Hey, Whit, how about giving Josh a break and getting him out of that play pen?"

"Okay, little man, here comes Uncle Whit. Now, we're going to have some serious play."

As he dangled the chain of plastic keys over the netting of the play pen, Josh began to whimper.

"What's the matter little man. Don't like keys? You'd better get used to them. They get you into the executive washroom."

Jenny laughed. "He's just hungry, Whit. His bottle is on the back burner. Would you mind feeding him while I finish this salad?"

"I'd like to, but I don't know how."

"It's easy. You just sit over there, fit him into the crook of your arm, and give him the bottle."

"Okay, let's go at it, tyke."

Jenny tested the bottle of formula on her forearm, handing the bottle to Whit. As he sat, the pleasant noise of Josh's sucking filled the room.

"Why, Whit, you look positively domestic. You look like you were born for it."

"Maybe, but I haven't had a chance to have a proper date, much less settle down. Katt is a strange girl. Sometimes hot, sometimes cold."

"Just nerves and post-divorce syndrome. She'll come around."

"I don't know. The guy she dumped sounds like a fairly nice guy. Nice family, plenty of money. Just not ambitious enough for Katt. She divorced him before their first anniversary."

"Well, just show her the town and keep your wits about you. I think she likes it here."

"I'll try. But, I'm not ready to be hurt yet."

"Say, they're gone a long time. I'll take Josh and put him in for the night. You take the steaks out to the grill."

As Jenny lay Josh down into his hand-made oaken crib, his wooly lamb and his ragged green frog beside him, the Corvette returned, tires squealing, and raucous laughter spilling over the blare of the high-volume radio. Jenny gently closed the window and tiptoed out.

"Hey, Jen, where are the steaks?"

"Out with Whit at the grill."

"What say we get those babies on? You get the stuff out, and Whit, old buddy, and I will grill them to perfection." Loud, raucous laughter from Katt.

"You were gone a long time. Was Byrne's out of vanilla?"

"Uh, yeah, we had to go to Seneca. It was mobbed."

Jenny pulled the salad from the fridge and Aunt Gert's lyonnaise potatoes from the oven. Katt dropped into the easy chair for a snooze.

As Jenny set the glass-topped table on the deck, the evening breeze swirled about her, making even more memorable the vision she had as the sun was setting over the horizon of a perfect painting in oils.

Chapter Twenty-Six

The fight that Jenny and Bud had after the dinner party was lengthier than any they had ever had. Jenny, generally placid, had pretty much always held her tongue.

"What do you and your new assistant do after hours when everyone else has left? You sometimes don't get home until eleven."

"Aw, c'mon, Jen, there's a lot of paperwork to catch up on. And, sometimes I just need to unwind."

"Does little Miss Mandy need to unwind as well? I hear from Jackie at Pat's that you're both down at his bar at about ten."

"Oh, for gosh sakes, Jen, she's just a kid. And, she works hard all day. I wouldn't have had to hire another assistant if it wasn't for you insisting you had to stay home with Josh. Dad was furious."

"Did you forget you have a family?"

"How could I forget? You're on me all the time about it."

Jenny held her tongue after that. No use arguing with Bud. She couldn't go to Mother because Mother would find fault with Jenny and take Bud's side. Instead, she and Josh became regulars at Sparky's back-to-the-land farm, sometimes with her alongside Sparky hoeing the soil to encourage the growth of the crops as Josh giggled and laughed outright in his playpen nearby, sometimes jangling his circle of plastic keys, sometimes pulling his shaggy bear's string to make it talk, or pulling down on his mobile of musical instruments to listen to a favorite tune.

They also visited Aunt Gert and Sarah and Jesse. Aunt Gert would cook dinner for them while Chaucer would lick Josh and try to get him to play. But, Josh couldn't run yet, and Chaucer would give up with a sigh and settle down next to him, falling asleep with the exertion of it all. At Sarah's, Jesse would sometimes let him watch while he fashioned a high-boy dresser or grandfather clock.

At Aunt Gert's, conversation often turned to the greenhouse and what plants they had to pinch back to help them grow. Jenny painted the new orchids on small canvases to distinguish the new species from the old.

"Thanks, Jen, we can use these for our advertising. We can also give them out to our florists as handouts for their customers.

"How's Bud these days? I don't see much of him."

"Neither do I Aunt Gert, He's not home often, and when he is, he's dead tired. Too tired to play with Josh or spend time with me."

"Have you talked to him about it?"

"I've tried. But, it always turns into a fight. He says I'm no help to him anymore. I don't go to prospective client parties and I don't look as glamorous as I used to. He says I spend too much time with Josh."

"Have you talked to Wycliff Lyndley about it?"

"I haven't seen Pastor Lyndley since the wedding. Bud won't go to church with me and I can't get anyone to watch Josh. Mother thinks I will end up in eternal damnation."

"Well, make an appointment to see him. He's very anxious to be of service. He has a Ph.D. in counseling and a very sympathetic ear. And, he's young, too."

"I will, Aunt Gert. Thanks for the help."

"Oh, forget it, Jen. You are my favorite niece, not just because you're my only one. Now, let's stop clipping the orchids and give Josh some quality time."

Sparky took a different tack.

"Why don't you hire a nanny for Josh, take up painting and get famous, and give Bud the heave-ho?"

"Thanks, Sparks, for the sympathy. But, I suppose I could work harder at this marriage. I've gotten pretty tied up with Josh."

"Well, for gosh sakes, he is an infant. And, you're his mother. It's supposed to work that way."

"Well, maybe I've let myself go. Mother says I should improve my wardrobe. She says it makes Bud look bad if I don't keep up."

"Well, I don't know that she was a glamour queen when you were growing up, but I wasn't here."

"She says it was different for her. She was only the wife of a farmer. But, she always made sure she looked good, getting her hair done at Mayva's every Saturday and getting the latest at Hal Barker's apothecary and dry goods when the shipments came in."

"Well, I think you look pretty good to me, Jen. You're gorgeous. Just maybe a bit underappreciated.

"What say we put some effort into getting that field plowed. Josh looks content with two dogs and three cats looking after him. This should tone your muscles without a morning workout with Jack LaLanne."

As Jenny helped plow, beads of sweat rolling down her forehead, her jeans and her tee stained with streaks of earth, she thought of the many sunny afternoons she had tagged after Father as he perched her alongside him to till the earth and make it fertile. As she helped Sparky, she felt the wind suddenly on her shoulders, bringing a cool breeze to her sun-soaked long, sandy-brown pony-tailed hair.

Chapter Twenty-Seven

Jenny rang the bell of the parsonage as she stood not far from the bright red enameled front door of the white frame church. Pastor Wycliff Lyndley answered the door, his dress a pair of jeans and a soiled white tee shirt.

"Come in, Jenny. Sorry for the attire. I was just attending to a burst pipe in the basement. Saves the congregation a few dollars."

"Thank you, Pastor Lyndley. It's nice that you are so handy."

"Well, it's definitely a learned skill since I've been living here. Please call me Cliff. That way we don't have to be so formal.

"I've seen your mother on Sundays, Jenny. She is very proud of you. She feels you made an excellent marriage."

"Well, that is some of the reason I'm here. I appreciate your seeing me."

"Would you like some tea or coffee?"

"Oh, thanks. Could I help you make it?"

"No need, Jenny. I have become a very handy bachelor and a fair cook. What say we get right down to business. I'm sure your time is valuable, since I understand you're also a mother."

"Oh, yes. Josh is eighteen months now."

"How nice. I would love to see some photographs later if you have some."

"I do. What a pretty table you have laid out."

"Well, my mother, who lives a distance and can't visit often because of ill health, insists on a red-checkered table cloth. The oatmeal raisin cookies are here not only because they're my favorite, but because she thinks I will starve without her care packages."

"Well, perhaps she's right. How nice to have a mother who looks after you so well."

"Please sit. Shall we get down to business? Can you tell me why you've come to see me on such a nice, bright, sunny afternoon?"

"I've come to see you about my marriage. It's a bit strained lately."

"How long has this been going on?"

"Oh, mostly since I quit working full-time at the agency. Bud was mad that I decided to stay home with Josh."

"How does he feel about having a family?"

"He seems pleased to have one. He just doesn't think it should take any work."

"Well, he's never had one. And, he is heir to a business that he knows takes work.

"Do you and Bud ever have 'alone' time?"

"I try to get Bud to take some. But, he's very resistant. He is very dedicated to the agency.

"I have planned nights out, sometimes alone, sometimes with friends of Bud's. But, he never seems satisfied with me. He either feels I don't talk enough, or I talk too much and don't fuss enough over his friends."

"What do you want to keep going in this marriage?"

"I see a home for Josh. And, a home for me, of course. I try to make a good home for Bud so he can relax when he gets there."

"What attracted you to Bud in the first place?"

"Well, I was very flattered that he preferred me over the other girls. He was very popular, you know. He was so very handsome, and he was the high school football star."

"Did you like being with him?"

"Well, Bud was always a lot of fun."

"How well did you know other boys? You were an only child, without a brother to learn how boys might think. Did you have a friend who you could get to know well who might have given you those clues?"

"I had Jake. But, he was a Mennonite. Mother didn't approve of Mennonites.

"When the Martins moved in next door, Jake and I became instant friends."

"What did you and Jake do when you were together?"

"Mostly, in the beginning, we used to play with his sisters and brothers. Then, when they got busier, we used to meet in my family's hayloft after the chores were over."

"What did you talk about?"

"Everything. My social life. Our families. Our hopes and dreams."

"Did you ever try to talk to Bud like that?"

"Sometimes. But, Bud doesn't seem interested."

"Well, maybe we can find out where some of the problems lie. I think we should end our session now. If Bud won't come with you to see me, maybe we can talk on a regular basis or when the need arises. You be the judge, Jenny. But, know that I will always be here for you. You can call me at any time. You have my number."

"Thanks, Cliff. I so appreciate it. I do feel like I have a friend in you."

"See you next time, whenever you decide. In the meantime, treat yourself well. You deserve it. You are a lovely, talented woman, Jenny. I hope we can get you to see that."

As Jenny headed home, she made a mental note to ask Sarah for a Saturday to stay with Josh. She would travel to Syracuse, maybe take Sparky with her, and add to her wardrobe the most sophisticated outfits she could find. Some new lingerie as well.

Maybe she had let herself go as Mother suggested. Maybe Bud's absences were her fault as he insisted. When did marriage stop being a symbol of hope and become a prison of doubts?

Jenny stepped on the gas. All about her, the mist of a recent rainfall was glistening on the lawns of the small, shabby houses she was passing, turning the grasses a beautiful emerald green which sparkled like Irish crystal. Jenny barely took notice.

Chapter Twenty-Eight

"Why do we have to go so far for dinner? Can't you make something, or can't we go into town to Capn's?"

"Cliff thought it would be nice if we took some time together to have a sort of "date". He said couples should pay attention to their romantic side."

"What do you listen to him for, Jen? He isn't even married."

"He has a degree in counseling. Besides, we haven't been out in ages. I thought we might take in a show or movie as well."

"I'm not going to see those sissy dancers playing at the Opera House. Maybe a movie, if it's got a lot of action. Not one of those art things you like."

"We can check out the Cinema when we're there. We better get going. Josh needs his bath, and then I'll be ready."

"Okay, I'll go down and get the car gassed up."

The ride to Belham's Castle, where Jenny had made reservations days earlier, was silent. The trees and the fields looked positively artful beneath the setting sun.

As they walked up to the imposing red door of the former mansion, Jenny noticed the sparkle and the shadows of the old, stone exterior. "We haven't been here since the prom. Do you remember, Bud?"

"Of course I remember. Whit had his Jag then. And, that's the night we all met Katt."

"Right. It was the first time I had been here. The dinner was so lovely."

"Let's get a move on. Maybe I'll have time to get back to the office."

Jenny swallowed her hurt. "Tonight is our night, Bud. No Josh, no office, just us."

"Well, okay, let's see what they have to eat."

As the hostess seated them at a table Jenny had requested with the reservations she had made three days earlier, along the bank of windows at the old front porch, Bud began to relax.

"Hey, Babe, what are you going to get?"

"I don't know, Bud, I haven't seen the menu yet."

"Well, I could go for a nice, big old steak. We haven't had one since Mayer's Meats moved out and we have to go to the Market Basket or the Mart."

"I hear that Jeb Martin's going to get some better meat at the Mart. Maybe things will get better."

"I hope so. A man's gotta eat.

"Say, Jen, here's a steak dinner for two. Filets and New York strip. Wanna get it?'

"Sure, Bud. Sounds good."

"And how about a bottle of wine to go with it? Would you like some Cabernet? Whit's favorite wine."

"Sounds positively gourmet."

As the waiter returned to take the order, Jenny found herself staring out over the lawn, its deep green manicured grass dotted by heavy, old freshly-painted white chairs and grand old elms and oak trees. The blue water of the lake still sparkled in the softly setting sun.

"Hey, Jen, what are you thinking?"

"I'm thinking that would make a beautiful painting."

"Would, Babe, but those days are over for you. You're a wife and mother now."

"I was thinking that as Josh gets older, maybe I can take some art lessons."

"Well, I wish you'd think about coming back to the dealership. Dad is furious because we had to hire someone to take your place."

"I want to be home for Josh, Bud. Maybe when he goes to school."

"It's our bread and butter, Babe."

"I know."

"I thought I was getting a gal who could get out there and schmooze. For gosh sakes, Jen, Mandy's better than that. And, she's just a kid."

"Of course. She doesn't have a baby to take care of. She's got plenty of time on her hands."

"Yeah. And, she knows how to dress."

"Of course, she can spend her whole salary on her wardrobe."

"Well, the guys like looking at her. And, sales have risen."

Jenny tried hard to quell the hurt that was running through her. She wanted desperately to have a nice evening.

"I'll try harder, Bud. I've arranged to go shopping with Sparky in Syracuse on Saturday."

"Why her? She wouldn't know a chic outfit from a pair of overalls. You should take Katt. Now, there's a girl with a sense of style."

"This wine is good, Bud. Where's it from?"

"France, of course. Can't you tell? It's the real stuff."

"You've always been so good at picking wines."

"I learned early from Whit. He's got connections all over the world."

"How's he doing with Katt?"

"I don't think he should be going after her. She's too restless. She just wants to have fun. He should be looking for someone to settle him down."

"Well, he's pretty stuck on her."

"We'll see. He's also got a big job setting up that new office in Hawaii."

As they spoke, the waiter came with a tray of carefully balanced dishes. A hot metal plate with a sizzling steak which he prepared to slice on a separate silver cart, and perfectly whipped potatoes which he piped around their individual servings.

As they ate, Bud pushed Jenny to eat so they could order dessert.

"I think I'll go back to the office, Babe. I've got a big contract for several cars in Westchester County."

Jenny gave up on trying to make this a special night. As she looked at Bud, talking about everything and yet nothing, she wondered where the football hero had gone. The team player. In his place was a man who was already looking haggard, somewhat thick around the middle from too many boozy nights entertaining prospective clients.

She promised herself she would get out there and do what Bud asked. She would buy herself some frilly outfits and some new makeup and entertain prospective clients as well. After all, it was her bread and butter, like Bud had said, and it was Josh's also.

As Bud paid the check, Jenny looked around at the old, wide circular staircase and the antiques that were scattered all about the former mansion. As they left, the romantic aura of a former era and a dinner by the beautiful, manicured grounds overlooking the pristine waters of a beautiful, blue lake all but disappeared. The glow remained only by looking at the sky, now clear and dark and full of the bright shine of the moon and the stars all twinkling about it.

Chapter Twenty-Nine

J enny looked round the great hall now used only for banquets and large parties. The outside clapboard of the Penn Yan country club had a new coat of paint thanks to Leland and Mary Lou Anderson. The great hall was newly painted as well. Mauve, as Mary Lou had specifically instructed. There was a small plaque in the corner commemorating their generosity.

A large orchestra, imported from New York, was playing a batch of oldies, allowing couples from any era to dance without the difficulty of formal dance lessons. Mary Lou and Leland were working the crowd, all chosen from a faithful client list, or from a list of prospective wealthy clients.

Whit's father had supplied the liquor. Both Whit and his father were in attendance in identical tuxes. Sparky and Cliff Lyndley were there as well, guests of Jenny herself. The choices had caused some difficulty, bringing Mary Lou to comment to Bud that there was no way a parson was going to spoil her party, intimidating many of the rich and wealthy. And, Sparky was too much of a liability since she had taken up farming and practically departed from the good breeding she had been raised with.

However, in the end Jenny won out. It would not look

good if the lovely, young wife of the heir apparent to their agency pulled a no show.

As she mused, Cliff appeared at her side, drink in hand. "Nice party, Jen. Thanks for asking me. I like to sometimes mingle with my parishioners in a more relaxed setting."

"They'll be plenty relaxed soon, Cliff. The liquor is flowing."

"Maybe I can enlist a few new parishioners. I see a few who have strayed already."

"I'd like you to meet one who hasn't signed up yet. A friend of mine, hiding herself in that corner over there."

"Glad to, Jen."

As they walked to Sparky's tentative hideout, Mary Lou glanced in their direction, her slight sneer very apparent. As they reached Sparky, the former Long Island debutante pulled herself up out of the chair she had slunk into.

"Hey, Sparks, what are you doing holding that plant up?"

"Just leaving room for you to be belle of the ball, Jen."

"Sparky, I'd like you to meet Cliff Lyndley, pastor of our church. Cliff, Amanda Parker, former deb from Long Island and present dirt farmer. Not much of a church goer."

"Nice to meet you, Amanda. Is it possible to get you out of this corner?"

"Of course, but only if you call me Sparky."

"Will do. Sparky, how about a spin around the grounds? I've never been here."

"Good idea, Cliff. I've never been here, either. We'll explore together."

Cliff's sensitivity touched Jenny. Mary Lou's sneer had not gone unnoticed.

"Hey, Jen, have you seen Katt?" Whit had sidled up, tipsy as usual with drink in hand.

"Not yet, Whit. But, it looks like you've seen the bar."

"Why not? Dad and I put a lot of effort into making the liquor flow. Why not enjoy it? Say, have you tried one of these mushroom caps with lobster? Scrumptious."

"Thanks, Whit. I'll take you up on it later. How's Hawaii?"

"Hawaii's great. Wahines are good. The office will be ready in a few months."

"Are we going to lose you to Hawaii and one of those grass skirts who can hula?"

"Not a chance. We're staffing it completely local."

"So, you'll be able to oversee it and get a tax break at the same time for spending your off hours in the sunshine."

"I told you Dad was a business genius. And, what about you? You look like a knockout. You're putting Bud's new, young assistant to shame."

"Little Syracuse shop who's owner goes to New York."

"And, who's that weird femme who was sitting in the corner?"

"Amanda Parker, former roommate, former deb, and present dirt farmer."

"Oh, the one who goes around in overalls and a pigtail? What did she do, suddenly discover clothes?"

"Sparky's okay. She just prefers Penn Yan to Long Island."

"Well, I'm going to find another Long Island exile. She went to powder her nose a while ago and I haven't seen her since."

"Good luck, Whit. Maybe she'll surprise you."

As Jenny surveyed the crowd, Mary Lou Anderson headed in her direction.

"Jennifer, where is Bud?"

"I don't know, Mary Lou."

"Well, it's a wife's job to keep track of her husband."

"He was here about a half hour ago."

"Well, that's not good enough. He should be right here now mingling."

"I'll see what I can do."

"Honestly, Jennifer, you're a slipshod wife, a poor mother, and you have no sense of fashion. You spoil that child. I need to take him for a day or two to shape him up."

"I'll look for Bud, Mary Lou."

Jenny headed for the women's locker room to freshen up and take the edge off Mary Lou's assault before she began her hunt. As she passed the employees lounge, she heard loud noises inside, moans and groans added to a few loud shrieks. She stood still, wondering what to do. One of the staff, a long-time regular, came up behind her.

"What's goin' on, Miz Jenny?"

"I don't know, William. Perhaps we better find out. Do you have a key?"

"I do. If you step out of the way, I'll open the door. You can call for help if we need it."

William pushed open the door. There on the lone cot along the far wall lay the tangled heap of two naked bodies in the heat of passion. All noise had stopped. Bud's face, turned toward the door, was scarlet, his mouth dropped down like a door ajar, the stare on his face frozen as he recognized Jenny beyond William's shoulder. Katt searched for a towel to cover her lean body.

William quickly closed the door.

"You better not look, Miz Jenny."

"I already saw, William."

"We better get you some help. You don't look so good."

"I'll be fine, William. I just need some air."

As Jenny tried to keep her composure, she fell over the nearby plant on the way to the heavy exit door. William grabbed her arm, leading her through the heavy metal door to the outside, a path to the newly planted garden. There on a bench in a grove of sycamores sat Cliff and Sparky, engrossed in the intensity of their newly discovered conversation.

"Jen, what happened?"

Cliff caught Jenny as she started to fall. Sparky reached out to grab her hands.

"Let's get you home. Better still, let's get you to my house."

As they drove in the direction of Sparky's dilapidated farm, Cliff at the wheel with Sparky comforting Jenny in the back, Jenny filled them in on the details. The trees whizzed by, a blur of green in the thoughts that once held the hopes and dreams of a marriage.

Chapter Thirty

Jenny looked round at the shabby but comfortable bedroom Sparky had generously offered. Josh's small bed sat across from the high colonial double bed that filled the room, a hand-me-down from Sparky's great aunt, an heirloom as she called it.

Jenny had moved out from the home she had shared with Bud, leaving behind her artistic touch and the loving décor she had so graciously bestowed upon it. Mother showed up every day at Sparky's, hoping to talk "some sense" into Jenny's muddled head.

"You haven't given Bud a chance, Jennifer. Boys will be boys. Especially those with an upbringing like Bud's. He just needs to work things out."

"I've tried, Mother. Bud refuses to get help."

"Well, maybe he doesn't need help. I wouldn't give you a nickel for those psychologists. Maybe he just needs to sow his wild oats for a while."

"You wouldn't like it if Father strayed."

"Well, your father is not like Bud. He came from a poor family. Rich people feel they have more privileges."

"I don't think that, Mother."

"You're so stubborn, Jennifer. It's not a good characteristic."

"Josh and I will get along, Mother."

"You're such a romantic. Just like your father. That's why we never had anything."

Aunt Gert tried to give support to her niece without ruffling her sister. Father remained neutral. Aunt Gert appeared whenever she could, loaded up with various toys for Josh and a few ribbons and hair ties for Jenny. She took them to her place whenever she could, Chaucer bringing chuckles to Josh despite his difficulty in getting around these days.

Bud had been less than apologetic.

"Geez, Jen, it wasn't anything. Katt was drunk and I was drunk. It was nothing."

"I don't think it was 'nothing'."

"You're so uptight, Jen. You should get out more often and stop doting on that kid."

"That 'kid' is our son, Bud. He needs and deserves good care. And, how can I dote on you when you're not ever here?"

"Aw, c'mon, you know I'm under a lot of pressure. Dad has stepped up my duties at the agency."

"Does that include late nights with Mandy?"

"Oh, for gosh sakes, Jen, you're so possessive. Your jealousy is causing us problems."

As Jenny mused on her fate and what she could do to improve it, Josh's screams brought her back to reality. His teddy bear had gotten stuck behind a dresser down the hall and his arms were too small to retrieve it.

"Hold on, little man, help is coming."

As Jenny got the toy back into his arms, and his tears turned to laughter, she looked at the child caught up in his own little world. Right now, Josh was happy just being fed and changed. His entertainment was simple and his attention span was short. But, what of the future? Could she be both mother and father? Could she provide for his needs relying on herself?

The door slammed, cutting into her self-imposed reverie. Sparky was back, bearing gifts from New York.

"Hey, Jen, what goes? Why the long face? I've brought you mega oil paints, straight from the Winston Newton store. A few canvases to daub as well."

"Oh, Sparky, thanks! It's been so long since I dabbled in the richness of oils."

"No sense letting Mother Nature and this old dilapidated farm go to waste. At least you don't have to pay it to sit still.

"And, for Josh, a few items as well. A ball that plays "Over the Rainbow," a stuffed Scotty dog, and a myriad of colored nesting boxes that would keep any self-respecting nearly two-year-old busy for hours."

"Thanks, Sparks. You're too good to us. And, what's new in the world of engineering?"

"Well, we've got a new product ready to unveil, but we're

going to wait until next spring so the excitement can mount and the patent will be cleared by the lawyers."

"Well, the farm held up while you were gone. But, the tractor broke down. Sammy will be here next week to take a look."

"He's a good guy, Sammy. I don't know how the Andersons keep him. He's underpaid and overworked."

"He's happy here. His family depends on him and he's saving up for a house of his own."

"Okay, time to eat. I'm starved. Long wait at the airport. Let's let Seneca Dairy do the cooking."

"Sounds good. How about we pick up some for Aunt Gert and some for Cliff Lyndley and stop by for a couple of visits. Josh and I could use some socializing."

"Okay. Let me get out of these Big Apple duds and into something that makes sense. Then, we can do the town."

As Sparky changed, Jenny fingered the oils Sparky had brought her. The shades of oranges and reds and the ochres brought visions of the fields and the hills in the fall. She would transfer those thoughts to canvas as soon as Josh was safely in bed.

But, for now, Jenny thought of the future. She must provide for Josh and for herself. As she pondered the best way to do this, she pulled from her belongings set beside the dresser the slim volume of Blake excerpts Jake had given her at graduation. It had been long since she had thought of Jake, or had taken the time to read poetry at all.

She scanned the lines of "Jerusalem." "And did the Countenance Divine, Shine forth upon our clouded hills?...I will not cease from mental fight, Nor shall my sword sleep in my hand, Till we have built Jerusalem, In England's green and pleasant land."

Jenny's and Josh's Jerusalem was here in the hills and valleys that surrounded them and in the fields where Mennonites and poor farmers pulled bounty from its earth. Jerusalem would always be home. But, as she packed away the volume of poems, Jenny realized that, for now, Jerusalem would have to be, as it had been for the poet, a sustaining and beautiful vision.

Chapter Thirty-One

J enny packed her things with care. She would have to make them last. She had brought the clothes she had accumulated during her marriage and the furniture she would be taking she had moved to Sparky's basement.

The divorce was final, and the judge as lenient as he could be. She had asked for the venue to be changed from Penn Yan, and the court had complied. The case was tried in Syracuse, but the long arm of the Andersons' influence reached there as well. The maintenance was poor, and the child support even less. She would have to work to support both her and Josh.

She had gained full custody, however. The Andersons were not interested in another mouth to feed or a child to supervise, so the terms were amiable.

As Jenny packed, she thought of what lay ahead. She would have to brush up on her shorthand skills, and Miss Ransom, who she had approached after the divorce, agreed to use her influence and connections to help get Jenny a job in New York City. New York would be a place where she and Josh could get lost in the hubbub of daily life and be more anonymous than they could be in Penn Yan. Away from the controlling Andersons and the egocentric antics of Bud.

"Hey, Jen, I am contributing to that suitcase. Ron Martin is giving up his dry goods store to go back into the practice of law. I have bought up all his sweaters to keep you warm in New York."

"Oh Sparks, I owe you so much. You have been too good to us."

"Not too good, Jenny. You just have to remember to be good to yourself."

"Mom and Dad called. They found you an apartment in Brooklyn. It's a walk-up. But, it has heat."

"Thanks, Sparky. I so appreciate their help."

"No problem. They're looking for something to do since I'm not there to give them trouble."

"How much time do I have before the big shindig you decided to throw?"

"All the time you need. Our guests won't be here till seven."

"I wish you wouldn't fuss, Sparks."

"No fuss. They wanted to come. And, they're bringing the goodies."

"What about Mother and Father?"

"They turned us down. But, give them time, Jen. Your mother hasn't gotten used to the divorce yet. And, they'll be here in the morning to see you off."

As Jenny thought about how she could placate Mother, the small, plaintive wails of Josh's ended nap reached the room.

"I'll get him, Jen. He needs to talk things over with old Auntie Sparks."

"Thanks, Sparky. I'll pack his toys last. He'll need a few for the drive."

"He'll be fine, Jen. Let's look at it as an adventure. His first trip."

As Jenny heard the sounds of Sparky's attempt at relating to an eighteen-month-old, she thought about his future. Would she be able to summon the strength and the skills to provide for a toddler and herself in a city the size of New York?

She lay the sweaters Sparky had given her carefully in her suitcase. The warmth of the afternoon sun creeping through the old, farmhouse windows warmed her back, much as it had when she had ridden as a toddler on the seat of Father's tractor. She would work to give Josh the strength he would need to find his place in the world, but first she must brush up on her shorthand skills so she could support them.

Chapter Thirty-Two

A unt Gert had outdone herself. The best champagne, pastry cheese puffs just out of the oven, salmon mousse, and the finest brie cheese she could find.

"This is not a going away party," she emphasized. "You will always have a place here. This is just to wish you and Josh the best of luck in your quest to mow the world down."

"Sweet sentiment, Aunt Gert, but I am only hoping for survival on our own."

"You'll find it , Jenny. You have a lot of gifts and a lot of skills."

"How about setting out the tableware," shouted Sparky, her voice rising from the kitchen over a very loud clatter of pots and pans. "I'm warming up Aunt Gert's pot roast."

"Cliff's not here, yet."

"He'll be here in a flash. Held up by a pushy parishioner.

"How about putting on some music? I've got tapes of Fleetwood Mac, James Taylor, and, of course, The Grateful Dead."

"Will do. How will that go over with Cliff? Shouldn't we have something tamer?"

"He's cool. I found we share a love of music. I also found despite his rather square demeanor he has a slightly wild side waiting to come out."

"How about you, Aunt Gert? Wouldn't you like something more period?"

"Not me, Jenny. I try to keep up with the students. To do that, you have to know their music."

Jenny chose the James Taylor LP. More upbeat, she thought. His people had lives and dreams. The cowpoke in "Sweet Baby James." They had loyalty. "You've Got a Friend." She was lucky. To be surrounded by friends who gave her the hope she needed to face an uncertain future.

"Hi, folks. Sorry I'm late." The door slammed as Cliff came through it with a bunch of flowers in one hand and a bottle of wine in the other. "Some of the parishioners believe they have a divine mandate to cause as much trouble as they can."

"Don't pay them much mind, Cliff" said Aunt Gert. "I've heard nothing but good things about the church since you have worked so hard to bring it into this century."

"Some people don't think so. They think young people should be seen but not heard. They think the Sunday morning youth services with guitars are nothing short of heathen."

"Hi Cliff. What beautiful flowers. And, a bottle of Dr. Frank Pinot. How perfect for a first-class pot roast dinner." Sparky had reappeared from the kitchen, her old, red and white checkered apron still generously spattered with Aunt Gert's pot roast gravy.

"I see Sarah and Jesse's buggy in the driveway. Let's set that table."

As they sat around Sparky's idea of a dining room table, a large door she had salvaged from the old barn, Jenny looked round at her friends and at the aunt she was closest to in her childhood. She would miss them and the warmth of the small town she had grown up in. She secretly resented the Andersons and the strength of their far-reaching influence. But, she promised she would look at this as a new and exciting adventure.

Sarah announced the news of her pregnancy. She and Jesse would be parents in June. Everyone offered their congratulations and they all proposed a toast.

"Will you see Jake when you get to New York?"

"I don't think so, Sarah. I don't think he needs a runaway divorcee on his hands."

"He graduates from law school this June. He has been promised a very good job with a big law firm there."

"How nice. He has certainly achieved success."

"It depends on how you look at it. We miss him and he's not here to take care of Pa as the eldest son should."

"Well, perhaps now that he has finished law school, he'll have more time to look in on you and your family."

The conversation turned to what Jenny would do in New York, Sparky's spring planting and Aunt Gert's delicious pot roast. Sarah presented Jenny with a beautiful star point quilt she and her sisters had made and a little knit cap for Josh. Cliff gave her his favorite quotes in a beautiful leather bound book. Aunt Gert gave her an envelope of introductions to Miss Ransom's business acquaintances and a promise to visit whenever she could.

As they cleared the table and set it for dessert, a scrumptious cherry pie Sarah had baked, Jenny realized how much she would miss the warmth of their friendship. But, Josh was depending on her now to lay the groundwork for their future. She laid their gifts carefully in her suitcase after they left.

Chapter Thirty-Three

Jenny hammered nails into the wall of the newly painted but dilapidated apartment. Mrs. Caputo, the landlady, had given her permission to hang any artwork she wanted without penalty. Jenny was determined to turn the corner of the rather drab studio apartment into a proper nursery for Josh. In that spirit, she hammered a nail squarely into the ochre-hued wall, hanging a brightly colored picture of a cat and mouse fishing together along a very blue stream. The stream reminded her of home.

Not that there wasn't an outside in New York or Brooklyn. There was, but Jenny didn't seem to notice, The buildings were overwhelming, and getting a toddler up seven flights of stairs seemed to put a dent into the natural curiosity of her surroundings.

New York City was an enigma, defying every law of nature. Buildings everywhere. Some ancient, with every bit of ancient architecture intact, though old and crumbling. Some ultra modern, some in the process of being built, or certainly remodeled. Scaffolding was everywhere.

Streets were lined with the backs of these buildings, or the fronts, depending on which route a walker chose. The main idea was to get from one place to another, ignoring the buildings, which were too tall to see in their entirety, unless one stood back and gawked, risking the ire of the passersby who were all trying to get someplace. New Yorkers were intent on getting someplace.

Brooklyn, of course, was filled with rows and rows of drab buildings. No nature, or at least it seemed that way to Jenny. She barely heard the pigeons that cooed and made a mess of the buildings, or saw the sparrows that lined the telephone wires in their need to find a place a roost.

Jenny had been in Brooklyn almost a week and had met no one except for Mrs. Caputo. Sparky's parents were away for a month but were expected back next week. As Jenny hammered, a knock at the door interrupted her avid concentration. She opened it to find a fidgety young woman in jeans and a tattered tee-shirt.

"Hi, my name is Dee Donetti. I live down the hall. Mrs. Caputo told me you just moved in."

"Thanks for stopping by, Dee. My name is Jenny. Would you like to come in?"

"Sure."

"Would you like some tea, or coffee?"

"Coffee. Strong, with lots of cream and sugar."

"I'll just start a fresh pot."

"I see you have a little boy." Josh was sitting in the corner with his playthings, staring unabashedly at the "intruder."

"Yes, his name is Josh."

"Hi, Josh." Dee looked over at Josh, her face all aglow with an attempt at wiggling her nose. Josh laughed.

"He's cute. I have a five-year-old. Her name is Rosa."

"That's nice. And, where is she now?"

"She's in school. I got knocked up in high school. Nice guy, but bent on a different path. I've been trying to support Rosa and me and take a few classes at the same time."

"What do you do?"

"I wait tables over at McGinnity's two blocks from here."

"And, what do you take in school?"

"Secretarial. I hope someday I'll get a job on Madison Avenue in some big, modern office."

As Dee sipped her coffee and dug into the few cookies Jenny had left from the ones Sparky had packed for the drive to Brooklyn, Jenny assessed her neighbor. Street smarts, a few well-placed tattoos. Beautiful long, dark hair neatly wrapped in rollers. Long, very red nails and lots of makeup. The largest dark brown eyes Jenny had ever seen.

"Where are you from, Jenny? I'm from here."

"A small town called Jerusalem. Along the southern tier of the state."

"Sounds cool.

"Dee stands for Diane which I hate. What does Jenny stand for?"

"Jennifer. I was named after a great-grandmother."

"How nice. I didn't know my grandparents. My parents came over from Sicily."

"Well, I bet they have a lot of stories to tell."

"When they get a chance. We have a large family. I have two sisters and three brothers."

"I'm an only child."

"We can fix that. I'll take you to one of our family reunions. The noise will make you want to run for that small town of yours."

Jenny wasn't sure what she and Dee had in common. But, she was sure of one thing. Her new friend was amusing. And, despite her rough exterior, and a burden she was thrown at a very early age, remarkably sensitive, with a warm and loving heart.

Dee jumped up as she shoveled in the last of her cookie binging. "Gotta go. Rosa gets home now.

"Thanks for the coffee. Stop down anytime. Apartment 713."

"Will do. Thanks for the visit."

The door slammed as Dee ran out, at the same time trying to wave a quick good-bye to Josh who sat fascinated in the corner.

"Our first neighbor, Josh. I wonder what the others are like."

Jenny tried to calm her homesickness as she lifted Josh to take him into the bathroom with the cracked sink to wash his hands for his afternoon snack. As she coaxed the hot water from the tap, she made a mental note to begin looking for a shorthand job on Monday.

Chapter Thirty-Four

Pounding the proverbial pavements of New York was exhausting and confusing. Finding her way around took almost all of Jenny's resources, both financial and mental. Learning the subway and the bus system, the street cars and the taxis, took time. But, Jenny wasn't afraid to ask. She soon got used to the gruff exterior of almost every New Yorker, finding them friendlier than she so often had heard.

Josh was now with Mrs. Donetti, Dee's mother, almost every day of the work week while Jenny looked for a job. Mrs. Donetti had taken in pre-school children for the last twenty years. Her house was chaos, but she seemed to enjoy it. Children wandered everywhere, but parents were held to task for a proper lunch and a clean rest mat.

Often, Mrs. Donetti had to mother the parents as well as the children. If a parent forgot their duties of prepared lunches, snacks or perhaps repairing a favorite toy, they often got a lecture from Mrs. Donetti, but they often got a hug as well if they threatened to buckle under the stern exterior.

Jenny snapped out of her reverie as she jumped to avoid a cab moving slowly toward pedestrians who were hurriedly trying to run a red light. The cab driver yelled out of his open window. Jenny clutched her leather notebook and walked faster.

220 Madison Avenue. She was here. Her first interview. A friend of Miss Ransom's who ran the steno pool. She pushed the gold trimmed-revolving door to enter the lobby. The directory was straight ahead, perched to the right of the elevator bank, all encased in marble walls. Mallory, Hollander & Wexler. Import Export. Just what she wanted. Eighteenth floor. Jenny had never been on the eighteenth floor of anything. Most buildings in Penn Yan were not raised beyond a few stories.

She pushed the eighteen button at the elevator bank, invoking an immediate bong and the swift opening of an elevator in front of her face. Somewhat daunted, she entered it, stepping carefully onto its carpeted floor. Three people followed, pushing buttons as they entered. They stared at the ceiling or straight ahead as it rose, getting off at their appointed floor.

Jenny got off at eighteen, lit up on the monitor above the button panel. She followed the red carpet down the hall to 1855. On the heavily paneled walnut door hung a sign with the firm's name in gold, and the partners' names in small black letters underneath. Jenny pushed open the door.

The receptionist barely looked up, but looked directly at Jenny.

"Do you have an appointment?"

"Yes. With Mr. Masterson at 10:00."

"What is your name?"

"Jennifer Anderson."

"He'll be right with you. Please be seated. Would you like some coffee?"

"No, thank you. I already had some."

Jenny sat down on one of the upholstered maple chairs, eyeing the magazine pile laid out neatly in the center of the mahogany coffee table. Two other people were waiting, one drinking coffee, one intently reading a magazine, both with bulging briefcases at their side. Jenny chose "The New Yorker."

She had never seen a magazine without recipes or starlet gossip. Nevertheless, the cartoons began to fascinate her. Perhaps not for their concepts, for she barely understood any of them or got the drift of their humor. But for their drawings. She had never seen drawings where it was obvious the artists could let loose, bringing to life humor she didn't even understand. If only she could doodle like that, or sketch.

Suddenly, a middle-aged man, heavy set, appeared in the doorway that led to the private offices, calling her name. Jenny was startled, since she hadn't heard her name announced out loud from the receptionist's desk. But, she decided as she looked, that the complicated box of buttons on the receptionist's desk was responsible for summoning him. She rose immediately.

Mr. Masterson extended his hand. Jenny grasped his as he shook hers firmly and rapidly. "Please follow me. We will be

186

heading toward my office."

Jenny followed as fast as she could. As they reached his office, he motioned her inside. "Take either chair." Jenny chose the one closest to the door. Mr. Masterson followed, settling himself into the large, leather swivel chair behind his massive, mahogany desk.

"Do you have a copy of the letter of recommendation you sent us? I know you sent it on ahead, but if I want it, I'll have to hunt down Alma. That's Alma Bienvenuti, head of the steno pool. She's hard to find, sometimes."

Jenny pawed through the sheaf of papers she had neatly pressed into her notebook, pulling out the letter. Mr. Masterson scanned it, then looked up. "A pretty good recommendation. Do you think you can live up to it?"

"I think so, Mr. Masterson."

"I'll level with you, Jennifer. We're pretty shorthanded right now. And, this is a fast-paced pressured business. Lost two girls last week, one to maternity, one to going back home to Montana. If you think you can do the job, the job is yours."

"I'd like that, Mr. Masterson."

"You can call me Bill. Almost everyone here is on a first-name basis. We try to be as laid back as we can in the office. We are frantic with phone calls and mailings across the continents. It kind of gives us a leveler.

"Now, you can take your tests. Follow me and we'll go find Alma."

Jenny followed as fast as she could. She made a mental note to wear more comfortable shoes if she got the job.

"Ah, there you are Alma." Mr. Masterson was addressing a formidable but pleasant looking woman of an uncertain age, much makeup, a rather hard countenance, but with a large, welcoming smile on her clearly hassled face.

"Come in, Bill. Welcome to the world-weary cluster of support desks."

"C'mon now, Alma, it's not that bad. What do you have to worry about? All you do is sit here and type all day."

"Thanks for the vote of support. Now, what can I do for you."

"I have here a Ms. Jennifer Anderson. She's interested in joining your ranks but first we have to see what she can do. Do you have time to give her a test?"

Jenny peeked around Bill Masterson. A huge room filled with desks and typewriters appeared before him, filled with sun coming in from the very large windows which graced the outside wall.

"Come in, Jennifer. I think we can find someone to give you a test. Maybe in the meantime, Cathy can give you a tour of our offices." She motioned to a very young woman who sat two desks away and who was busily typing without looking up. "She's from Iowa, but she's practically like a native New Yorker already."

"Thanks, Alma. Nice to meet you, Jennifer. Good luck."

Bill Masterson turned to hurry down the hall as he spoke. Alma got up from her desk and ushered Jenny into the steno room.

Jenny looked round at the cluster of desks as Alma guided her to Cathy's. Alma introduced the two. "Maybe Jennifer would like a tour of our well-appointed offices. I'll finish your work for you, Cathy."

"Thanks, Alma. I could use the break."

As Cathy rose, Jenny noticed her height. Very tall, and very slender. Cathy walked with a slight limp.

"We'll tour the middle management first. The partners don't like a lot of intrusion."

As Jenny followed, she noticed a profusion of maps. Maps under glass, maps with pins, and old, artistic maps of an ancient nature.

"Have you gotten used to New York yet?"

"I haven't seen too much of it. I have mostly gotten settled in my apartment in Brooklyn."

"Nice choice. I live in New Jersey. An hour and a half commute."

"Do you like New York?"

"I haven't thought about it. I came here to learn this business."

"Where are you from?"

"A small town in Iowa."

"What made you come here?"

"Trade is my passion. I was an economics major at Iowa State. But, there are no jobs in global trade there. I was offered a bank job, but it was dead-end."

"Sounds exciting. How come you're a steno?"

"No jobs here for women except in the typing pool. Import export is still a man's world. I hope to go back to Iowa and start my own business. With the new upgraded shipping and the new improved transatlantic cable you don't need New York or the coastlines anymore."

The tour ended with a look at the partners' offices, at least the outsides. Mr. Mallory's was empty. Cathy explained he was away on a sales trip, so they could peek inside. A big fish hung on the only unencumbered amber wall. A souvenir from a fishing trip to Antigua, Cathy said. Jenny looked out the two huge windows at the street below. Tiny taxis, tiny buses, and dots that resembled people filled the streets and sidewalks.

Jenny passed the tests with flying colors. Her studying had paid off. Bill Masterson saw her briefly once again, this time to fill her in with a variety of company rules and benefits. Then, he passed her off to personnel. Endless forms and paperwork. When she was done, Alma took over.

"We'll see you here on Monday. By then we'll have a desk ready for you."

Alma surveyed Jenny. "Everything you have on is fine except for the shoes. You will want a more comfortable pair. Chasing after these execs take practice and persistence.

Tailored dress is preferred so you can stock your wardrobe accordingly.

"We look forward to seeing you on Monday. Watch out for the rush hour crowd you'll find down there when you leave. They are very unforgiving."

"Thanks, Alma. I will. And, please thank Cathy for the tour. I really enjoyed it."

"Will do."

As Jenny struggled to find the right bus that would take her to the train station, she could hardly wait to get back to her apartment so she could call Sparky and Aunt Gert with the news.

Chapter Thirty-Five

J enny arrived bright and early at Mallory, Hollander & Wexler Monday morning. She had gotten Josh off to Mrs. Donetti's where he was the resident toddler. Not old enough to play sophisticated games, but not too young to be considered an infant, he was sought after as an audience, where he would clap in delight at four-year-old Cora's antics, or sit admiringly in the corner for hours as three-year-old Brandon regaled him with his knowledge of every piece of every game in the cupboard.

Jenny hurried down to the steno room. There, under a window with a burst of sunlight making its way through the newly-cleaned panes of glass set into the modern building, was Jenny's desk. A "Welcome Jennifer" sign sat atop the laminate wooden finish.

"Jennifer, good morning. I'd like you to meet the managers. Follow me."

Jenny hurried to keep up with Alma. All the managers were cordial but curt. It was plain to see that serious business was the order of the day. Bill Masterson took the time to welcome her again, adding that any problems or questions he would be glad to handle if Alma was away. Jenny thanked him and followed Alma back to the steno room.

Alma pulled a sheaf of papers and some steno pads from

her desk. "These have been sitting here for a week. As Bill pointed out, we have been fairly short-handed for the last few weeks. I have three girls' pads in my desk waiting for transcription. Do you think you can do it?"

"I think so."

"Okay, most use the style you've been trained in. But, if anything comes up you can't understand, ask Cathy. She can translate anyone's notes, I'll bet even in Swahili. I have to be gone most of the day. Cross town meeting with Mr. Hollander. Have to catch a cab."

"Thanks, Alma."

As Jenny tried to decipher the shorthand symbols in front of her, she wondered if she had acted wisely in uprooting herself and Josh for New York. But, as she contemplated the decision, she decided she had no choice. Mary Lou Anderson had threatened to ruin her, insisting that the divorce was a vendetta on her part to destroy the Anderson image. She had threatened to block every employment opportunity Jenny might have and to fight for custody of Josh if Jenny opposed her.

Josh and Jenny were settling into the New York scene, albeit slowly. Josh was ecstatic with his new playmates at Mrs. Donetti's, and had made fast friends with Dee and her daughter Rosa. Jenny still had attacks of homesickness and tried to quell them with a call to Sparky or Aunt Gert, or singing a little ditty she had learned in grade school or reciting a stanza from Blake's "Jerusalem," or picturing the fields of the southern tier in all their autumn splendor, or the first daisies of summer, pure and white, rippling in the sway of a gentle breeze.

"Jennifer, do you need any help?"

Jenny looked up to find Cathy standing over her desk.

"Maybe. I'm finding it impossible to make anything out of this one pad."

"That's because it's Hedda's. She's from England. They use the Pitman method there."

"Well, I'm only familiar with Gregg."

"Most of us are. I'll take that one from you. I learned the others because I had nothing else to do when I first got here. I miss Iowa."

"Thanks, Cathy. I'll owe you one."

"No problem, Jen. How about lunch? Then we can rake everyone over the coals and I can really baptize you into the fold."

"Thanks again, Cathy. I'd really like that."

Lunch was fun as she and Cathy huddled in a vinyl-covered booth around the corner at Lindy's. The restaurant had lost its famous cheesecake and celebrity customers, and gained a lot of new locations, but Jenny felt at home here. The grease-spotted menu could almost double for the ones that Cap'n put out.

"Let me give you a rundown of the managers," Cathy said

between bites of a tuna on white. "They're the ones you'll deal with at first. The partners have their favorites who have been here for years.

"You've met Bill Masterson. He's nice, but they're not all like him. Tom Herrington is a bottom pincher. Eight kids and a lust for life. Malcomb Schuster seems portly and proper, but he can turn on a dime and blame the steno for all his mistakes. Bernie Torrington is the one you really have to watch. Eager to get ahead, he will use anyone who's handy, or naïve. He has been known to set up situations to get a person fired if they don't succumb to his will."

"Gee, Cathy, nothing like at Miss Lindstrom's. The only one we chatted with was the janitor at the end of the day."

"Well, this is New York. The sooner you get on to it, the sooner you can start to enjoy. Now, eat up. We'd better get back. Alma is a stickler for hours."

Jenny enjoyed the challenge of deciphering the other note pads upon their return. Despite the universality of the Gregg method, little squiggles and quirks of the pen could alter the look. She hardly had time to enjoy the afternoon sunbeams dancing across her desk.

Alma returned late in the day. She acknowledged no one as she pulled her typewriter from its spot underneath the top of her desk, typing furiously to transcribe her notes of the morning.

Jenny began thinking of where she would take Josh for

dinner. They deserved a night out. Maybe the diner around the corner from their apartment. They had both grown to like the place. A warm-hearted waitress and a tough but soft-hearted ex-marine who owned the place completed the picture. Ernie waited for their arrival and got pencil and paper for Josh to draw while he waited for his toasted cheese and the cook flipped her burger, which was so close to the ones at Capn's she could swear they learned from the same chef.

Jenny said her goodbyes to the other stenos as she left for the day.

Alma looked up briefly. "Hope you had a good day, Jennifer."

"It was fine, Alma. Thanks."

As she hurried for the cross-town bus that would take her to the train station, she congratulated herself on making it through the first hurdle of her move to New York. She must pick up a celebration toy for Josh in that cute little shop she had seen in Grand Central. What would he like? She thought of a push toy, then scratched it for a puzzle or an accordion.

Chapter Thirty-Six

Sparky's parents were as cordial as could be. They sent a car round on a Sunday when they returned from their eight-week junket to Europe, part business, part pleasure, to bring Jenny and Josh to their home in a tony part of Long Island. The day was beautiful and sunny.

As the car pulled up to the turn-around driveway in front of their home, a large, brick house that sat up on a rise a long way from the road behind a gated drive, they rushed from the doorway to hug Jenny and shake hands with Josh. Josh got the full tour of the grounds and the house as well, including a gift of a ball that was a replica of a real baseball from an earlier era that had won the World Series for the Yankees. Sparky's dad was a fan.

"Please call us George and Mary. We are very informal here." Sparky's mother rushed ahead of Jenny as she led them on to yet another room. This one a beautiful paneled study with a fireplace furnished with soft, leather chairs and a leather sofa. A vivid oriental rug gave color and design to the carefully polished original planked wooden floors.

On the sofa lay a dog lazily licking her whiskers. "Broomhilda, come meet Josh." Broomhilda refused to budge, staring at Josh as he ran toward her. Undeterred, Josh lifted his tiny hand to pet her. Broomhilda accepted the attention, eventually nudging Josh and licking his fingers. Josh laughed.

"Well, I guess they made friends. We got Hildy when Amanda left home. She's been a great comfort to us."

As they took tea on the sun porch, Manuel the all-round handyman showed Josh the grounds and roused Broomhilda to play ball with them both.

"How does Amanda take to farm life?"

"I think she likes it. She's never happier than when she's tending to her seedlings in spring and pulling in the harvest with her faithful, old tractor in the fall."

"Amanda was always a tomboy. She always preferred to play ball with George than to have tea with her dolls or dress for a charity ball. Her coming out party was almost a disaster. She hid in her room for hours."

Having tea on the sun porch of the beautiful home the previous owners had dubbed The Highlands, a facetious reference to the slight rise the home had been built on, and the few rolling hills behind it, the rest of the acreage being very flat, was a respite for Jenny. Never had she been in such a beautiful home, with such gracious hosts.

The time passed quickly. As the sun went down, they prepared for dinner. The meal was served in the most beautiful dining room Jenny had ever seen. The crystal chandelier sparkled in the candlelight and the artwork, most of it modern, melded into the walls, the reds, some bright, some soft, surrounded by hues designed to let that color, like a beautiful sunset, stand out.

Emilee, the cook, a refugee from the countryside of France, served the most exquisite roast duckling, complimented by a luscious port wine sauce and accompanied by a rice dish with morels her mother had shown her how to make. Josh was offered a peanut butter and jelly sandwich or a hotdog in deference to his age.

The after-dinner brandy was very expensive. Jenny basked in the glow, and the intensity of the after-dinner conversation. Politics, world affairs, and the differences in European cultures the Parkers had just experienced.

As Mary and George tucked them into the car for the return trip, Jenny thought of Aunt Gert. How she would have liked the recipe for the duck. How she would have enjoyed the intensity and smoothness of the very fine brandy. But, as they drove away, Josh asleep in her arms, Jenny couldn't think of Aunt Gert in any other place than where she was.

Chapter Thirty-Seven

J enny was enjoying her job at Mallory, Hollander and Wexler. The long commute was still a force in her morning routine, and she hadn't yet become as blasé as the other passengers in meeting her connections. But, once in the office she was ready for work, the sunbeams still dancing on her desk, ready for an assignment to be even a small part of a global deal. The thought always heightened her excitement.

Mallory, Hollander & Wexler concentrated on cementing the world through global trade. She had only read about that in her tenth grade social studies books. Mrs. Harper had glossed over that section. Here she could witness history in the making on a daily basis.

"Jennifer, Rich Morelli stat. He needs someone to take dictation on a pending deal."

"Going right now, Alma."

Jenny hurried down the hall, steno pad in hand, three carefully sharpened pencils, and new, fashionable loafers with a very slight heel which had replaced the high-heeled pumps. She waited outside the open door of Rich Morelli's office waiting to be summoned inside.

"Come in, Jennifer. This is Mr. Prolitov. From Moscow."

Jenny nodded slightly and slipped into a chair next to the Russian visitor. His expression remained humorless.

"Are we ready?" Rich looked over in her direction.

"Ready." Jenny sat poised with her pencil and steno pad on her lap.

Jenny tried to act invisible, but the Russian kept looking at her sidelong and shifting in his chair.

"She's clean, Boris. All our employees are subject to a rigorous investigation when they're hired."

That seemed to make the Russian relax, but not completely.

"We get the corn before we ship the vodka." The heavy accent did not disguise the toughness in tone.

"We can ship the corn as soon as we sign, but we need payment before we ship."

"I am authorized to give you full payment for the corn. Payment for the wheat will be delayed."

"Agreed."

"If your politicos block shipment, we cancel."

"We have only one senator dead-set against USSR trade. He's making it tough, but we're clear."

"Shipment must be immediate. We have problems in Russia as well."

"Will do. Let's get on with the contract."

Rich dictated as fast as he could. Jenny didn't try to understand the terms or the language, she just wrote fast and tried not to break her pencil point.

"We'll need four copies now. And, Jennifer, we'll need to see a finished copy for signing before Mr. Prolitov leaves the building. He should be finished with his tour in about an hour."

Jenny jumped up. She left without acknowledging Mr. Prolitov, figuring this was better protocol from the Russian viewpoint. She hastened down the hall.

Cathy's note for today's lunch greeted her from atop her typewriter. Jenny finished the contract and had it on Rich Morelli's desk by eleven. She hastened to meet Cathy at the front door by noon.

"How about a new New York experience?"

"Sure."

"Okay, we're headed for Mama Leone's. We'll need a cab. My treat."

Jenny admired the way Cathy hailed a cab. Public transportation was all she could afford, but she took note of Cathy's sophisticated ability. Someday, she might have to use it herself.

Jenny's calm was momentarily disrupted by the cab ride. Near hits and misses with the myriad of vehicles on the streets of New York forming the gridlock of The City lunch hour, and the strings of expletives from the mouth of the cab driver who barely spoke English, set her back a bit from the objectivity she had acquired in riding the train and the buses and trolleys. But, she recovered as soon as she and Cathy were settled at a table at Mama Leone's, surrounded by tourists and native New Yorkers all bent on finishing their lunch by one.

"How's the job so far at our fast paced import export?"

"Good. I had my first international experience this morning."

"Well, you've come up in the world. They don't usually allow that for at least six months."

"Rich Morelli needed someone. Some of the girls were out sick today, so I guess Alma had me fill in."

"Good for you. You either make it or buckle under the pressure. Rich is a good guy to start with."

"He wasn't the problem. It was the Russian on the other end."

"Well, they can be tough. They don't have the government or the countenance we have.

I can give you some books that might help. They're filled with the highlights of some of the cultures we deal with."

"I'd like that, Cath. It might take some of the fright out."

"If you can get smooth with some of the difficult cultures, they sometimes decide to take you on international trips. That means more money, and sometimes a raise."

"I'll study, Cathy. Right now I just want to collapse. It's all I can do to take care of Josh after I get back at night. He needs someone to be awake."

"It's tough, Jen. But, you'll get used to it. How is the little guy?"

"He's turning two on Saturday. Will you come to the party?"

"Of course. I wouldn't want to miss it."

"Thanks, Cath. And, thanks for the survivor tips."

"No problem. When I got here, there was no one to throw me a rope. I had to navigate this jungle by myself.

"Say, what about men, Jen? Are you interested?"

Jenny reddened. "I hadn't thought about it. It has been all I could do to get us both settled."

"Be wary. There are a lot of guys here ready to pounce and ruin your equilibrium."

"What about you, Cath? Do you date?"

Cathy laughed. "Oh, heavens, no. It's all I can do to study and get ahead in my job.

Before I came here, I had a boyfriend I went with for almost thirteen years. Juan Carlos. He was twelve when his father came to work on our farm and I was nine. We were a pair ever since. Then, two years ago, he left for Mexico to help his people and work on a ranch outside a poor village. He left me a note. He said he couldn't ask me to live a life of poverty."

"I'm sorry, Cath."

"Oh, I'm over it now, but it took a while. I studied and worked, with no time to think.

"What do you say we get out of here? Alma will have our jobs."

Cathy pulled out the right amount of cash and dropped it on the check. "Let's go!"

As Jenny followed as fast as she could, Cathy pushed boldly to the front. Jenny watched admiringly, but was certain she would never gain that extra expertise that transformed small town to experienced New Yorker. But, she continued to take mental notes. After all, she would soon be Josh's guide as soon as he was old enough to navigate these mysterious streets.

Chapter Thirty-Eight

Jenny's apartment was filled with parents and an under-five crowd. All of Josh's day care friends were there, plus a few siblings as well. Crayoning books and rounded scissors and construction paper lined the small table in the corner. Games were strewn about the floor.

Jenny had set out bowls of pretzels and chips, and an avocado dip that had been Aunt Gert's favorite. Juice glasses were everywhere.

She had chosen a red wine that was cheap but good, she thought. The jug had said table wine, but she thought it was close to a very good Pinot she had favored from a local winery back home. Everyone was busy and noisy.

The second-hand chairs and sofa she had slipcovered were standing the wear. Their oranges and yellows and paisleys and florals from the fabric shop down the street were holding their own. Dee's old but reliable Singer had helped with the transformation.

Jenny cooked the hotdogs with Dee's and Cathy's help. The other mothers set out the salads and baked beans they had brought.

Jenny, Cathy, and Dee squeezed around the only table with Josh in his high chair clearly enjoying a hotdog as finger food.

He banged his spoon on the paper plate in obvious enjoyment.

"Why the limp?"

Jenny looked mortified. Dee directed her gaze at Cathy. Cathy seemed not to mind.

"Country accident. Caught my leg in a thresher."

"We have city accidents, too. My friend lost her toe in a motorcycle accident when she was three. Her father was bringing her home from the grocery store.

"Do you miss the corn?"

"Sure. But, I like New York, too. Union Square market at 5 a.m. Central Park at dawn. A Village green grocer with so many heads of perfect lettuce it's hard to choose."

"Me, I'll take Brooklyn any day. Sitting on the front stoop on a summer's night. Mrs. Polimini shaking her fist into the air as she curses Maloney in the next apartment and swears she will call the cops if he gets drunk one more time. Kids fighting over the bats and balls and who will pitch."

Jenny stood up. "Time for cake." She marched to the refrigerator and pulled out a cake in the shape of a number two. She lit the candles and headed for Josh. His eyes grew big with excitement.

Cathy led "Happy Birthday" and Dee pulled the paper birthday plates from the corner cupboard. Jenny helped Josh blow and they all clapped.

Rosa helped him open his gifts and Jenny helped him to thank his guests.

As they sat, Jenny wished Aunt Gert could be here. And, Sarah and Sparky as well.

But, the one she missed most was Jake. She hadn't really thought about him since they had been in New York. But, now she was reminded of how they had shared every milestone together.

She hugged every mother as they left and thanked them for coming. She stuck an extra balloon or candy bag into the hand of every child.

Cathy and Dee stayed for the cleanup and left. Dee had to work an early shift in the morning.

Josh fell immediately to sleep as she laid him in his crib. As she looked around at the remains of the paper-laden party, she realized how tired she was as well.

Chapter Thirty-Nine

J enny pushed the button for the eighteenth floor as she arrived early for work on a Monday. She yawned and scanned the lobby. The display in the exhibit case in front of the first-floor deli had been changed from miniature cartons and cases displaying the products of the fourth floor manufacturing firm to brightly colored photos of cities and villages high in the mountains and barren but beautiful distant lands. Jenny was smitten.

"Change Your Life. Travel." boasted the small inked sign above the photos, announcing the birth of a travel magazine newly housed on the fourteenth floor. Jenny quickly changed her elevator request to fourteen. The elevator announced its arrival with its usual curt but pleasant ding.

The fourteenth floor differed from the eighteenth by a lot. The carpets were threadbare and the doors were made of pine or luan. The simple signs announcing the firms that did business within were often owner-created. Jenny knocked on the magazine's door.

"Hi, come in." A sleepy-eyed young woman with a pony-tail held the door open. Jenny stepped inside.

"Welcome. Would you like to look around?"

"Thanks. I'm early for work and I thought I would stop in." Jenny thought that a little lame, but wasn't certain that had come out of her mouth. She was too entranced by the brightly colored photos lying on the one desk and all around the floors, very helter-skelter.

"We're just getting started, so please excuse the mess. We've just finished our first issue, and we're trying to paint the walls at the same time. Feel free to look around."

Jenny took a tour of the only other rooms, two very small ones, that were presently occupied by ladders and a few people with paint brushes trying to change the drab and dingy formerly beige walls to a bright orange and yellow. The three other people nodded as they tried to keep a balance and wield a roller or paint brush at the same time.

"We're trying to start this on a shoestring, as you can see." Jenny's host had come out of the front room to fill her in. "We're four CCNY grads who love to travel. We've got our families' and some of our friends' backing, but it's a struggle. But, we're going to make it. We've got enough enthusiasm to make up for the lack of funding."

Jenny was entranced. The photos lying everywhere depicted so many parts of the world she had never seen. Small, cramped, dingy yellow quarters, with buildings stacked upon one another vied for space with modern office buildings and skyscrapers and centuries-old buildings with lots of stone and pillars and scrolls and huge, stone animals guarding the long flights of stairs that led to the pretentious entranceways. Barren hillsides and rocky mountains, all

210

without civilization as we know it, lay pristine though helter-skelter.

"Where do you get these photos?"

"These are all ours. But, soon, we'll have to start buying. As soon as we get a budget."

"I'd sure like to be able to take photos like that."

"You can. How good are you with a camera?"

"I'm just an amateur. I'm actually more of an artist."

"Well. Use your artist's eye. It's all the same thing."

"I haven't really traveled."

"You don't have to leave home to make it a destination. Lots of people who have never been here find New York fascinating."

"Thanks." Jenny glanced at her watch. "I better run. Don't want to be late."

Jenny's host stuck out her hand. "Edith Morris. Edie for short."

Jenny took Edie's hand. "Jenny Thompson. I'm up on the eighteenth floor. Import-export firm."

"Nice digs. We've been up there looking around."

"They do well. But, it's pressured up there."

"No doubt." Edie fished in her jeans for a card, coming up with a bent but readable one. "If you get good with a camera, give us a holler."

Jenny bolted for the door. She didn't want to risk Alma's wrath. "Thanks, Edie, will do."

She raced for the elevator as she pulled the door shut after her. The comfortable loafers with the sensible heel she had invested in were cooperating. She just made the elevator as she rounded the corner and heard it open to let off a fourteenth floor worker bound for the other direction. She quickly squeezed in before it closed.

As she reached her desk, the other stenos were just piling in, murmuring their "good mornings" in sleepy voices. She pulled her typewriter up from the drawer it was packed away in. The sunbeams danced across her desk. She was certain that was a good omen.

Chapter Forty

Cathy huddled in the corner of the booth at Lindy's. Lunch was short today. She had to pack. She needed to unearth all her woolens, because Russia and eastern Europe were at the height of their winter.

"I can't believe you're going, Cath. It sounds exciting."

"It's far from that, Jen. It's a lot of tough work with little equipment."

"You're lucky it's Rich Morelli you're going with. He's a pretty laid back guy."

"Yeah, maybe. But, he's bringing his wife and two children this trip. That means babysitting as well as working into the night to transcribe."

"I hope you get some sightseeing in. Gee, I wish I was going as well. I could get some photographs in if I worked it right."

"Not too much time for that. It's mostly meetings and meetings and trains and bad transportation."

"Just the same, maybe you'll get some good shots of the major sights."

"I'm not much of a photographer, Jen. I leave that to you.

"Mostly, I'll be cataloguing and cross-referencing. I'm ready to start my own firm. I can't wait. But, I don't have the resources yet. How does "Kusovich and Anderson" sound?"

"Oh, you're kidding, Cathy. What would you want me for? I don't have a head for business."

"You're good with people, Jen. And, the art of the deal often involves people a whole lot more than it does graphs and charts.

"I can just see us now. I do the number crunching, and check out the global politics and the razor-sharp stats of the trade, and you get the contract clinched in a dimly-lit restaurant over a fantastic dinner and drinks."

Cathy's determination moved Jenny. Despite a permanent limp and an inexplicitly lost love, Cathy pushed on, her perpetual loneliness buried beneath a cryptic exterior.

"I'll get the check. Here's to the future of Kusovich Import Export."

"I'll get it, Jen. You've got a kid."

"Thanks, Cathy. Put it on the tab. When we get rich, we'll leave a ten-spot, instead of fishing for change in our purses."

"You have that right, Jenny."

Cathy led them through the tangle of shabby tables and upholstery-torn booths to the front of the restaurant. Her slender figure was the envy of many, judging from the sidelong glances that followed them as they walked. She pushed the finger-smudged doors with a determination Jenny was used to seeing.

As they breathed the warm, summer air, slightly musty and mixed with the carbon-monoxide of the heavy New York traffic, Jenny glanced at her friend. She wondered if Cathy would achieve the ambition she so desperately sought. But, as she saw through the cynical mask Cathy wore almost as a trademark, she wondered how she could ever have doubted it for a moment.

Chapter Forty-One

Jenny walked the streets of her Brooklyn neighborhood, her SLR slung over her shoulder in a new black camera bag. She would photograph Brooklyn, and then the world.

Brownstones lined the streets, tall row houses made of brick stretched from corner to corner. Tricycles and roller skates punctuated the dirty grey cement of the sidewalks.

Drab front stoops were empty. Windows were open to let in the fresh air of a Sunday morning. The typical sounds of Sunday filled the air.

"Hey, Mabel, quit sittin' around on yer keester and get breakfast on the table."

"Quit yer bellyachin ya lazy drunk and mind yer own business."

Rosa tagged along, contentedly pushing Josh in the stroller. Dee was busy with her new main squeeze, Denny Houlihan, or her "big, Irish cop," as she called him. They had met at McGinnity's when Denny had stopped in for a couple of doughnuts and a hot, black coffee late at night on the midnight shift. They had been inseparable ever since.

"Birdie, birdie," screamed Josh, his chubby index finger pointing to a small, brown sparrow splashing in a puddle of yesterday's rain. The bird, oblivious to the rapture, continued his bath.

Jenny crouched for a shot. She framed the bird in the lens, setting the aperture as she had been taught in her ten-week class at the local high school.

The bird, now surrounded, took its last splash and flew to safety on the telephone wires above, taking its place in the long row of sparrows all alike. Josh squealed with delight. Jenny bent down to fix his sweater and pull a new toy from the bag hanging on the back of the stroller.

"Wanna take pictures," said Rosa.

"This is my camera. But, maybe you'll get one for your birthday and then you can take pictures. I bet Mommy would think you're old enough to get one of your own.

"Say, how about we go to the park. It looks like it would be fun to play on the swings and in the sandbox. I even took a few pails and shovels of our own for the occasion."

Rosa let go of the stroller handle and jumped up and down, the camera a thing of the past. Jenny headed for the nearby main drag, restaurants and shops looming in the distance. As they reached it, the shops closed and the weekday hustle replaced by the indolence of a Sunday afternoon, Jenny hailed one of the few cabs slowly trolling for fares on the other side of the street. The cabbie stopped, jumping out to fold up the stroller. Jenny climbed in the back, putting Josh on her lap and pulling in Rosa beside her.

"Where to, lady?"

"Prospect Park."

"Good call. The heat's rising."

"Thanks. Take us to a spot by the lake."

"Will do. How about where the carousel is?"

"Fine."

As they got out, and Jenny paid the cab driver, she looked round for a spot of shade. A family had just left a place under a large elm on top of the tree's gnarled roots. Jenny hurried, dragging Rosa and the stroller after her. She spread a very thin blanket over the roots.

"Can I play in the sandbox, Jenny?"

"Of course. That's what we came for. How about a new red and green pail and shovel?"

Rosa squealed with glee, grabbing the loot out of the bag Jenny was holding and running for the sandbox to carve out some territory. Jenny trailed after, putting Josh in the sand next to her.

As Jenny returned to the blanket, facing herself toward the lake and so she could keep an eye on the children, she looked about her. Families with picnic baskets were everywhere. Children in all kinds of dress tumbled about and chased each other across the sun-filled grasses.

Jenny wondered what she was doing here. Despite the wonder of the human-made lake she was facing, it didn't begin to give her the thrill she felt from her earliest memory when she gazed at the crooked lake the Native Americans had called Keuka. And, where were the meadows and farmlands?

And, the beautiful wildflowers flowing toward the horizon, depicting the season with the indigenous hues of their blossoms.

"A penny for your thoughts."

Jenny looked up to see a slender, well-dressed young man standing over her.

Startled, she blurted out a surprised "oh" without thinking.

"I didn't mean to startle you."

"That's all right. I should have been paying attention anyway."

"It looks like you've got the best seat in the house. Do you mind if I share some of that shade?"

"Of course not. After all, it's a public park."

As he settled his lanky frame on the roots of the large, old tree, she noticed a certain reserve about him despite his seemingly forward manner.

"Are you here to watch a young one?"

"I'm here with my niece. My sister is a widow. I try to help her out on weekends."

"Oh, I'm sorry. I mean, that's nice of you to do that."

"My name is Jeff. What's yours?"

"Jenny."

Jeff put out his hand. "Nice to meet you Jenny. Are you a native Brooklynite?"

"Oh, gosh no. I'm fairly newly planted here. From a little town along the southern tier of upstate New York."

"I'm from a little town, also. Lyndonville. But, it's plunk in the middle of Iowa. Corn and corn for miles."

"That's nice. I have a friend from Iowa."

"Where from?"

"Jessup."

"I know where that is. Maybe someday we'll meet. What brings you here to Brooklyn?"

"A divorce, cheaper digs than The City, and an in-law free environment."

"I see. Where do you spend your work days?"

"An import export firm on Madison. I'm a steno."

"Well, you picked a posh strip of the Big Apple."

"Yes, it's well-appointed. But, hectic. And, you?"

"I'm on Lexington. Harrington, Mueller, Harter and Seagrove. Real estate law firm, dealing mostly with the likes of big-time commercial entrepreneurs. But, I just do the ordinary homes on Long Island. No big movie stars."

"Well, it sounds interesting. How old is your niece?"

"She'll be five in October."

"I have a neighbor's five-year-old with me. Maybe they'd like to play together."

"That sounds fun. She's kind of isolated. Jill could only find a place way out. No kids."

As Jeff rose to find his niece, Jenny found herself thinking of Jake. How easy he was with the little ones, his brothers and sisters. How they had looked up to him. She wondered what he was doing now.

"Jenny, this is Delia. I found her hiding behind that tree over there. Maybe she'd like to play now."

"Hi, Delia. Maybe you'd like to meet Rosa. She's over in the sandbox. Do you like to play in the sand?"

Delia, dressed in nicely ironed blue cotton overalls and a pink tee shirt with ruffled sleeves nodded shyly, her finger still in her mouth. Jenny pulled out a new pail and shovel and headed for the sandbox, Delia dragging along behind her. Rosa, delighted to have a new playmate, pulled her in by the hand to sit next to her and the big pile of sand she had appropriated. Jenny returned to Jeff.

Chatting with Jeff was almost like chatting with Jake. But, not quite. Jeff was filled with a midwestern reserve that the wide-eyed ambitious young Mennonite farmer never knew. Jeff was satisfied to stay an associate in his high-powered firm, perhaps never making partner. But, his devotion to his sister moved Jenny. She decided to invite him to the mid-summer blast she and Dee had been planning for weeks.

"How about attending a mid-summer picnic in a sweltering Brooklyn apartment? Nothing fancy."

"Gee, I'd like that. Can I bring Jill and Delia?"

"Of course, I was hoping you would."

Inviting a complete stranger to join them was risky, she knew, but Denny Houlihan was very protective of Dee, and he was off that Sunday. Jenny knew she would find out more about Jeff than she probably wanted to know.

Jeff glanced at his watch. "Whoops. Gotta go. I promised Jill we'd be back for Sunday dinner. She's definite about family traditions."

He turned to Jenny. "Thanks for the invite." He pulled out his card hastily. "Here's my number in case you want to call with the details. Thanks for taking pity on a reclusive midwesterner. And, thanks for looking so lovely under that tree."

As Jeff scooped up Delia and wandered off to the parking lot, Delia's sand pail in hand, Jenny looked up at the sun, still fairly high in the sky, shining down on the mass of bodies taking refuge from the humdrum work week. Though there was an air of friendship, or at least an acceptance of human existence that flowed like electricity through the tumbling bodies of the children and the parents, the men now drowsy with drink and the women packing up the morsels of the leftover crumbs of a picnic lunch hard won with checking the parts on an assembly line or endless sewing in a clothing factory, Jenny knew this would never be home. She was part and parcel of the fields she knew since birth and still endlessly missed.

Jenny saw Rosa and Josh had migrated toward the swings. She hastened over to give them one last push, cautioning them to hold on tight to the heavy steel chains, the newly-painted battleship grey slat seats sending them skyward, as they had countless children before them. She bought them a quick dinner at the concession stand and hailed a cab. The ride back was swift, the cabbie wanting to scout extra fares before his shift was up on a very slow day. Both Josh and Rosa fell asleep on her lap.

PART TWO

Chapter Forty-Two

J enny put her feet up on the beautiful new cherry wood coffee table she had just purchased not even a week ago. She was weary of watching every footprint and fingerprint in an apartment she did not feel comfortable in yet. She had moved there to be closer to her work and to avoid the long commute to Brooklyn so she could spend more time with Josh. But, she had to admit she missed the shabby old apartment in Brooklyn and a landlady that didn't care whether she was a painter or a photographer and allowed her plenty of latitude to do both.

The new apartment was not far from Central Park. She and Josh could walk the ten blocks on a Sunday when Jenny was free. She had been able to quit her job at Mallory, Hollander & Wexler to work for the fledgling company of Kusovich Masters owned equally by Cathy and Jeff. They had become a couple almost from their first meeting at Jenny's apartment and business partners not long after.

Both Cathy and Jeff felt guilty since Jenny had seen him first. But, Jenny was only happy for them. Jeff tried to compensate by fixing her up with a steady stream of lawyers and acquaintances, but nothing had ever taken. Despite a few longer relationships which lasted the better part of a year, Jenny was happy as an independent.

Josh was twelve and growing very quickly. A gawky twelve, he spent most of his time at his studies. The only exception was basketball where as the tallest of his friends he excelled as center for his team.

Jenny was by now known in magazine circles for her excellent photography of faraway places and their cultures. She had travelled the world for import export and had combined photo shoots of the most interesting places as well. Some of her work had even appeared in *The New York Times*, most recently as a spread on the turmoil of politics in places like Kosovo, but mostly she preferred the slick beauty of the Italian countryside and the villages nestled into mountaintops or the stark green and brown of Wales, where she could envision the people of centuries ago inhabiting the same turf. It often reminded her of what she still considered home, where the Native Americans had navigated and fished the same waters she walked along, or had chased buffalo along the same fields that now sprouted wildflowers or bent to the plow of farmers like Father.

Josh was at Coney island with Dee and Denny and their brood which now numbered five plus Rosa. Jenny used the time to paint. A summer trip to Jerusalem had jogged her memory on her long ago determination to paint which somehow had gotten lost in her efforts to forge a life for herself and Josh in New York. She was determined to make up for lost time.

Josh had been disinherited by the Andersons when as an eight-year-old he had shown no interest in the car agency. Bud had not intervened. Josh's future was now solely up to Jenny.

"Hi, Mom." Josh burst through the door of the apartment, followed by Rosa and the rest of the gang. "Rosa made it through the roller coaster without screaming once. But, she turned white once we hit the ground."

"Well, Rosa's a young lady now. I'm not sure a roller coaster is going to scare her. How about it, Rosa?"

Rosa turned red and looked like she wanted to shrink under the carpet.

Jenny changed the subject. "When does school start, Rosa?"

"Two weeks."

"You're going to be in an upper class now. I bet you can hardly wait."

"I don't like school all that much. But, I'll be better than the freshmen. That'll give me an edge out on the baseball field."

Dee burst through the door, four small children in tow, Denny holding the fifth, a newborn infant all dressed in pink with ruffles on the sleeves and a pacifier to suck on. Dee threw her arms around Jenny.

"Long time no see. Fancy digs. You've come up in life."

"I don't know. I miss the earthiness of Brooklyn, the down

226

and dirty. But, this cuts out the commute. Time to paint, and more time to spend with Josh."

"We've got dibs on the first Brooklyn brownstone you paint."

"Well, I hadn't thought of it, but I'll consider it a commission."

"Great."

"How's your mom?"

"Mom's fine. She keeps trying to get me to get you out there for a spaghetti dinner. She says you've always been too thin."

"Well, I wish I could look as good as you after six kids."

"No problem. Chasing after six kids does keep a girl in shape."

"Hey, Denny, how's the job?'

"Great, Jen. I'm working more days. More time with Dee and the kids.

And, how's it going with you? Kinda lonely around here? I've got a great new guy on the force who's single."

"Thanks, Denny. But, I like it how it is for now. Time to paint, and time to look after Josh.

"Say, how about some coffee or tea or anything stronger? And, some soda for the kids?"

"Thanks, Jenny. I'll help you set the table."

As Jenny laid out the polka dotted paper napkins and the paper plates, she thought of the first times she entertained.

Sparky was her first guest, way back in Syracuse when Bud was at practice. They had attended the art show then at the Syracuse gallery.

Now Sparky was married to Cliff. A few years by now. The ceremony had been magnificent. Typical Sparky. It had been performed at dawn, symbolic of the new beginning. A seminary friend of Cliff's had flown in to perform the rites. Sparky had been radiant in a simple, long linen dress dyed in yellow, the color of the buttercups that filled her meadows and the fields behind her crops. Her hair was tied back with a length of yellow baby roses that made the gleams of sunlight that settled along it look like chunks of gold, and she held a beautiful bouquet of the wildflowers that dotted the countryside. Aunt Gert had provided the silky ribbons that held them together.

The reception was held in the evening under the sunset, the reds and the purples and the magenta had outdone themselves for the occasion. Sparky's parents, Mary and George, looked ecstatic. Sarah and Anne, now married to Sammy in an elopement to spare their parents the humiliation of an intermarriage, were there as well. Jenny was happy to see them, their well-being so very evident, their pride in their families so apparent, but she never asked about Jake.

The bubble of Jenny's daydream burst as Dee interrupted with a request for sugar.

"I'm not sure myself. Probably in that cupboard up there,"

she said, as she pointed to a cherry wood cabinet with exquisitely turned pewter doorknobs.

Jenny poured the soda into sturdy plastic cups. Rosa took over and put all the children around the heavy oak table Jenny had found in a Village antiques store. Dee and Denny and Jenny took the living room and talked until the toddlers fell asleep among their Legos. Dee put them in pajamas and prepared for the long ride home. Jenny hugged her as they left and promised a visit soon.

Josh retired to his newly appointed bedroom, complete with posters of Sting and Simon and Garfunkel. Jenny went to the small black and gilt chest she had placed behind the rocker in the living room. From it she pulled the book of Blake poems Jake had given her which had been nearly lost in the back of a closet for all the years she had lived in Brooklyn. She slipped it from its wrapping and opened it. The note he had written, now somewhat yellowed, fell out. "I hope you will read these poems when times are tough."

She skipped the poem "Jerusalem" she knew Jake had meant for her and found *Auguries of Innocence* where his plastic bookmark had been placed so long ago.

"To see a world in a grain of sand,
    And a heaven in a wildflower,
    Hold infinity in the palm of your hand,
    And eternity in an hour."

Jenny stared at the page. Blake's heavy-winged archangels with swords in their hands chased a multitude of never-ending demons, all with a different shape. Through it all Gabriel blew his horn.

Long ago Jenny had seen that heaven in a wildflower, but that vision had been replaced by the hustle and bustle of an environment of modern glass and steel.

Could she resurrect that feeling now that she had more time? Jenny would give it a try. She would turn the new, back bedroom into a studio where sunlight would pour through the large and airy windows like it had at Mallory, Hollander & Wexler and she would paint. The vision of the oils she would choose in the special hues she had always favored raised her excitement.

She dropped the book as she fell asleep in the easy chair.

Chapter Forty-Three

J enny stared at the photo of Jake which stood out at her from the front page of the *New York Times*. The bold typeface headline under it announced the news. "Lawyer Wins Unprecedented Case." She read the details. Jake had gone up against Saks Fifth Avenue and won. The suit involved a pair of shoes that had been advertised on sale but when the customer arrived they were gone and the store had refused to give a rain check. The plaintiff was listed as his fiancée.

Jake's title was listed as partner in a very large and prestigious New York law firm. The fiancée was cited as a socialite and member of one of New York's most wealthy families. Jenny sat down at her desk to take the strain off the sudden weakness she felt as her knees began to buckle. She stared out at the street from her window on the thirty-fifth floor in the well-appointed suite of Kusovich Masters.

"Hey, Jen, it looks like you've just seen the ghost of Christmas Past."

Cathy had just stuck her head in with a sheaf of papers in her hand outlining the specifics of the client they were supposed to meet that night.

"Well, not exactly a ghost. Just a long time no see old friend."

"If you need time off this afternoon to see someone that's fine with me and Jeff. We don't need to meet the Pulaskis until seven."

"Oh, I don't need to see him. It's just that he seems to have monopolized the entire front page of the *The New York Times.*"

"That lawyer who sued Saks and won? Gee, Jenny, that's unheard of in this town. He must be quite a powerhouse. Jeff was impressed."

"He is. But, Jake never meant to defend the rich. He always had his sights on helping the poor."

"Well, sometimes, the best laid plans, as they say. I thought I'd be back in Iowa by now."

Jenny stared out the large windows that faced the street as Cathy left. Somehow, she could not see the stack of papers on the desk or the map on the wall that signified the big deal that their evening guests the Pulaskis represented. Laslo Pulaski was an agent of the government of the Ukraine and as such could bring a huge windfall to the firm of Kusovich Masters with a trade the firm could broker for the United States.

All she could see was a young farm boy as earnest in his desire to help the poor as he was to help his father pull crops from a soil that was sometimes unyielding or pummeled by heavy rains or no rain at all or deprived of the very sunlight that would give them life.

Jenny's shock at the turn Jake's ambition had taken turned to industry as she began to look over the papers Cathy had brought on Laslo Pulaski. An eastern European as different from Jenny as anyone could be. An urban background, a repressive government, and a very heavy language difference. According to the reports, he spoke very little English. She searched the graphs and charts, the snippets of reports, for clues to find a common ground. She found none.

Well, she would try to find a restaurant that would please them. She knew nothing about Ukrainian cooking, so she searched the pages of the books she kept on the cultures of the countries they did business with. Perhaps a travel book with the recommendations of city restaurants for the travel weary. Or, a detailed description of the foods of the Ukraine in the new encyclopedia the firm had just purchased.

She chose the encyclopedia and turned to the section entitled "Foods of the Ukraine." "The traditional Ukrainian cooking takes in most of the tastes of the Ukraine's neighboring countries like Hungary, Poland, and Germany, as well as Russia."

Jenny stopped and thought. The Russian Tea Room. She dismissed that as too noisy and celebrity-conscious. She pulled her New York City restaurant guide from its hallowed place in the big, bottom drawer of her large , mahogany desk. Chez Kiev. 102nd Street. That sounded small enough and cozy. She called and booked it for seven.

Chez Kiev was all that Jenny had thought from the mini-description in her restaurant guide. It was homey, and seemed to draw only Ukrainians seeking a good meal reflective of their homeland, rather than celebrities waiting to be seen. The aroma from the kitchen of the tiny restaurant intrigued Jenny.

Jenny placed herself next to Raisa Pulaski, Laslo's very ample but pleasant wife. She ordered vodka for all, the drink she had read was the favored Russian quaff. The Ukrainians offered a toast to their American hosts.

Cathy waited to broach business until everyone had ordered dinner and the hot plates had been set before them. By then, everyone had been sated by many shots of vodka, especially their guests who seemed more immune to the effects of the alcohol than Jenny, Cathy and Jeff, who found it necessary to watch their intake accordingly.

The aroma from the family-style plates set in front of them was heavenly. It had been long since Jenny had enjoyed a home-cooked meal. The sausages, the meat and potato-filled dumplings, the sweet and sour red cabbage, and especially the beet borscht, which Jenny had never tasted, brought back memories of Aunt Gert's pot roast on a Saturday night.

Cathy began intently outlining the program she had designed to Laslo Pulaski. He was just as intent on presenting the Soviet side. They seemed oblivious of anyone else at the table as they threw out statistics and import export laws almost as fast as they could speak, despite Laslo's limited English.

Raisa turned to Jenny. "They are very, how do you say it, intense. Laslo loves his job. He was a professor for many years, and worked hard to get his present position with the government. He likes making deals that will benefit the agricultural economics for the Soviet Union."

"He seems well-suited to the task."

"I am an engineer. I love my job. People ask for me.

My job makes more money than my husband's. But, his job brings more privileges. We have one son, Dimitriy, who my mother takes care of during the day. Laslo was able to get him a place at a beautiful summer camp in Georgia."

"How nice. I have never sent Josh to camp."

"Dimitriy loved it. He was with all the sons of the highest members of the party."

Raisa's obvious pride in her husband and her son radiated from her rather plump face. She took her role seriously as a wife and mother in a society Jenny surmised was at least a generation behind the United States for women as homemakers (they did all the cooking and cleaning, as well as canning the very limited fruit rations, Raisa had explained) but were at least a generation ahead as bread winners. Jenny was awed by this very solid woman with no complaints. It was not until several days later that she came across some material that would lead her to believe that they had not been alone with the Pulaskis. It was common for the KGB to send spies along with traveling Soviet government officials.

As dessert was served, Jenny excused herself to call a cab for both the Pulaskis and herself. The deal was just about closed as she could tell by the look of flushed satisfaction on Cathy's face. All that would be necessary would be for Laslo Pulaski to show up in the morning and sign the necessary papers.

As Jenny rode the long way back to her apartment in the dark of the evening, she thought of Jake. Should she call him and be a visible reminder of his early hopes and dreams? She decided to let go of her feelings for Jake for now. He deserved to achieve in his own image. She dozed off, but not for long. The cabbie was shaking her. They had arrived at her brightly lit apartment building and Rinaldo the doorman was standing at full attention ready to let her in.

Chapter Forty-Four

J enny laid down her paint brush on the lip of the easel as Josh came into her studio. It was Sunday, and the sun was streaming into the third bedroom she had made over to suit the rush of enthusiasm she had felt returning to her first love of oil painting.

"Mom, why doesn't Grandma Anderson want to see me anymore?"

"The Andersons are busy traveling in the summer and your dad seems to take up all his time running the car agency. Some adults are too busy and too selfish to realize how lucky they are to have something wonderful."

"Is it something I did?"

Jenny felt a rush of sadness as she realized the impact on the psyche of a twelve-year-old from the irresponsible non-caring of selfish adults.

"Oh Josh, of course not. You have been nothing but a joy to everyone who knows you. You are growing into a young man, one who I'm so proud of. And, I know how proud Grandma and Grandpa Thompson are of you, and Aunt Gert, and Aunt Sparky and Uncle Cliff. And, I know how Shakespeare loves it when you come to play with him. I know he waits all year until you can come see him and throw a ball so he can catch it and play tag."

"Mom, could we take Petey Marshall with us when we go to visit in the summer?"

"Sure, Josh, if his Mom and Dad will let him."

Jenny was grateful for the Marshall family's friendship and caring for Josh, even though Gus Marshall was seen as the black sheep of his family. Born into a well-to-do family, he had always been a dreamer. But, none of his ideas ever seemed to take. Alice Marshall worked long hours at an accounting job she hated to support the family.

But, Gus had coached basketball for years, and always saw that the boys got ice cream after the games, or got support when they needed it, win or lose.

"Mom, why do you call me 'Josh' when my real name is 'Leland'?"

"Well, when I was in high school, way before I had you, I used to talk to a neighbor when we were finished with our chores. And, we used to think up names we liked, and the one we both liked was Josh."

"Who was your neighbor?"

"His name was Jake. Would you like to see a picture of him?'

"Sure."

Jenny pulled the clipping of Jake's win against Saks from the small cabinet in the corner.

Josh read the clipping. "Wow, Mom, he must be smart."

"Well, he is. But, I haven't seen him in a very long time."

"Does he ever go back home to Jerusalem?"

"I don't know. I don't think so."

"Why not?"

"Well, sometimes people get lost in time. They forget the things that once meant the most to them in trying to build what they think should be their future."

"I don't want that to happen to me. Petey's dad says you should always dream but never forget those dreams. He says to lose your dreams is to lose what life is all about."

"Well, everybody has different ideas on life. I'm sure Jake is accomplishing the goals he set out for himself."

"I suppose. Can I go to the movies with Petey this afternoon. His dad says he will take us."

"Why don't we give Petey's dad the day off. Would it be alright if I take you?"

"Oh, gosh, Mom, that would be great. I didn't want to ask because you never seem to have a lot of time."

"Well, maybe that should change. Have you finished your homework?"

"Almost."

"Well, okay then, whoever gets ready last does the dishes tonight."

Jenny assessed Josh as he hurried into his room to get dressed for the movie. A tall, lanky twelve-year-old, set with the features and build of his father but not his temperament. Josh was sensitive where Bud was not. Josh was humble as well. He had a strong appreciation of the world around him. Jenny reminded herself that she must help Josh to learn to protect himself from the soul-snatchers of the world. Those who would rather parasitically drain another, than build themselves up. She would at least give him the benefit of her experience. But, for now, he was too young and innocent. He needed room to grow and blossom.

"Ready, Mom, when you are."

"Okay, you got me beat. I guess I do the dishes again tonight."

"Well, I'll make sure I take out the garbage all week."

"Deal."

"Petey's dad will drop him off at the movies. That way we don't have to pick him up."

"If it wasn't for Gus Marshall, I don't know what we'd do. He's nothing if not thoughtful."

"He said a good coach keeps very good track of his players."

"Well, I guess he's doing that."

The movie they had chosen was of course an action-adventure, full of car chases and jumping from roofs of buildings. Jenny assured herself that it wouldn't affect the boys, since their buildings were pretty well watched. Both of them seemed to take it all fairly lightly, even laughing at the car chases which didn't seem real.

Dinner was a hamburger joint just around the corner from the movie theater. French fries and soda topped the burgers off. Not the healthiest, thought Jenny, but at the moment the most popular.

"Mrs. Anderson, do you think those cars in the movie were real?"

"Gee, I don't know, Petey, why don't you ask your dad? He seems to know about that stuff."

"I don't think they were real. Real cars couldn't go that fast on curves without crashing."

"Well, there are some pretty good stunt drivers around. But, I bet there are some pretty good engineers who can make some cars look real and go really fast."

"That's what I want to be. An engineer. Then, I can help my dad make all the things he wants to make."

"I bet he'd like that."

Jenny ordered a cab while the boys were chatting. She had given herself the day off from driving in the frenetic traffic of The City.

After they dropped Petey off, Jenny looked at the skyline. It was humbling, she had to admit, and looked particularly appealing in the twilight. But, she missed the hills and the trees of home. And, the fields of wildflowers that stretched as far as the eye could see, and the burst of color in autumn that seemed unrivaled by the human architecture about her.

241

As they entered the building, Rinaldo, still on duty, messed up Josh's hair and gave him a high five. Josh headed for his room and the TV as soon as they hit their apartment. Jenny curled up in the living room chair, the book on her lap her graduation gift from Jake. She had hardly opened it in all these years she had kept it with her.

Blake's engravings stunned her with their beauty. Their angels and demons, their figures of nature, so full of life. Could she ever duplicate that longing in her paintings?

She began to read. "I will not cease from mental fight/Nor shall my sword sleep in my hand,/Till we have built Jerusalem/In England's green and pleasant land."

Blake's Jerusalem was a dream, a dream to save England's "green and pleasant land" from the devastation of the "dark satanic mills." But, Jenny's Jerusalem was free and clear of that. Her home had always been there. It was she who had left it.

Jenny prepared for bed, scurrying about to relieve the pangs of homesickness and yearning she still felt after all these years. She decided to ask Cathy for a few extra weeks in the summer. She would take Josh back to his roots. She was stronger now, and the Andersons seemed less of a threat. She did need to keep Josh out of their hurtful and overbearing reach, but their pretenses and power-tripping seemed less of an obstacle, and the pull of the land much stronger.

Chapter Forty-Five

J enny daubed some cerise on the canvas that stood in front of her propped up on the new walnut easel she had just bought. She was standing on a manicured lawn used occasionally for croquet looking out on the vast and lovely cultivated gardens of the Parkers' immense estate. Sparky's parents had continued to invite her and Josh for long weekends, giving her Sparky's old room with its satin and lace to sleep in.

Both George and Mary had insisted she use their gardens to paint in, despite their long absences of travel in Europe and this year in the Amazon and Equator. Jenny surveyed the blues and the lilacs of the asters and the lupines, and the brilliant reds and oranges of zinnias. She looked at the ground covers in the rock garden which sported little white and purple flowers. It was almost too difficult to choose a subject from the varied and well-tended gardens. She chose a burst of clustered daisies. Common but elegant among the more exotic, imported blossoms which surrounded them.

The daisies were yellow and white and stood beside a cluster of magenta "painted' ones, no doubt a product of cross-breeding designed to make a more elegant daisy and pull the daisy out of the realm of common. But, Jenny missed the daisies that grew in abundance along the banks of Keuka

Lake and the fields of Jerusalem, all wild and untended. As a child she and her school chums would often pick them, using the petals to find out who they would marry, or making daisy chains to wear as a summer necklace.

"What you doing here, Miss Jenny? Why aren't you out on a date with some handsome young man? And, where is Mr. Josh?"

Jenny looked up to see Manuel, the all-round handy man, stopping the tractor he used to mow the estate. His brown work clothes made him practically invisible against the brown steel of the well-used tractor.

Jenny shaded her brow with her hand against the brilliant afternoon sun behind his back. "Josh is out with his friend practicing basketball, and I thought I better capture these beautiful flowers while they're at their height. You've made them look so perfect, Manuel."

"I like coaxing them, keeping the weeds away, loosen the dirt and feel it running through my fingers. Flowers favor the hand that tends them."

"Did you have gardens in Mexico?"

"We were too poor. We only have time to scratch for food. But, sometimes, if we were lucky, a flower would grow in the village square, its seed dropped by a bird, and people would tend it and worship it like a god."

"Sounds like you were pretty close to nature in your village. In my town, too. I miss it."

"Well. We were in one way. We could grow our own food. But, sometimes we were outnumbered by the bugs that ate it or the packs of wild dogs that would run through and destroy it. We managed to survive. But, it is much easier here. Mr. George is good to me. And, Miss Mary, too."

"Well, you take good care of this place, Manuel."

"I try. Say, Miss Jenny, why you not have a husband? You too young to be alone. My wife, we marry when she sixteen. She was beautiful. She still beautiful, but she chase after eight children now."

"I'll give it some thought."

As Manuel returned to his mowing, Jenny finished dabbing blues and purples, reds and oranges on the canvas that sat in front of her. The flowers grew fuller, and the slice of the garden she had staked out began to appear as a mirror image on her canvas, but with some strange twists. The colors seemed true, but the flowers seemed wilder than the gently tended flowers in front of her. Perhaps that was their true personality coming out. Or, perhaps it was hers. Anyway, they seemed far from the gardens that Monet depicted with his sense of calm and Madame Monet a picture of calm within them.

Jenny packed up her easel and her paints and took her canvas to the small greenhouse attached to the big house in the back to dry. It would be out of the way along with the new seedlings Manuel had planted just yesterday.

She took her leave of Manuel and got into her snazzy new BMW, a gift from Cathy and Jeff in honor of the huge contract she had helped them land. It was the only luxury she allowed herself. She didn't want to raise Josh coveting money. Despite her distance from Jerusalem, she wanted to instill in him the values she thought important.

As she drove along the empty back roads, in a car that could go 140 mph on a good day, she thought about what Manuel had said. Perhaps she was depriving Josh of a male figure by being so exclusive. But, she hadn't found anyone she really liked.

What had been stopping her? It was certainly not a lack of opportunity. Jeff had offered a number of times to fix her up with his clients and associates. Denny had found her a few who were part of the unit he worked in. And, there were many obviously eligible men who smiled at her on the elevators in her luxury high-rise apartment building.

No, she realized as she thought hard about it, it was Jake. Jake had been in her memory since she had left Jerusalem, and she had been measuring every man she met against him and they had all failed. But, it was the Jake she remembered, not the Jake looking triumphant on the front page of *The New York Times*. The Jake who had the dirt of the earth he had tilled and planted scattered about his coveralls. The Jake who had been so earnest in planning to help the poor. The Jake who had put his arm around her to keep her from the chill of an autumn evening.

She made a resolution to move on, to override the memory of a young, innocent girl. She had been raised to believe that Mennonites and Methodists didn't mix and she had complied. As she tooled about the streets of New York, the street lights coming on to cover for the twilight, the Sunday traffic sparse compared to the work week, she made another resolution to keep that philosophy out of the values she tried to instill in Josh. She must make him understand that it was character that counted in an individual, not some kind of restrictive background. She concentrated on the road until she pulled up in front of Rinaldo. The valet rushed out to open the door.

When she turned the lock of her apartment, she arrived to find Josh in the easy chair cheering on his favorite NBA team from the safe distance of a television set. She gave him a big hug and unpacked her paints. As she lay in bed in the later hours of the evening, she counted the stars in the well-lit sky, its natural light bolstered by the roof lights of the brick and steel skyline. Somehow they looked the same as those she had counted so often with Jake on an autumn evening over Jerusalem.

Chapter Forty-Six

Chip Everly stood in the middle of his gallery floor looking at Jenny.

"Have you brought me something new? I could use a large canvas. I just sold two last week."

"Congratulations! You are doing well."

"As well as I can. It was slow last month so I am trying to make up for it. Have you eaten at all? You look thin as a rail."

"If that is an invitation to lunch, I accept, only if I pay. We just closed a big deal last week and I am supposed to celebrate."

"Wow. Jenny the successful tycoon. I guess I will have to take you up on it."

"Well, I'm not the real tycoon. Cathy is. She works eighteen hours a day. But, she has been very generous."

Jenny surveyed Chip. Thin, somewhat balding, but pleasant underneath that brash exterior which still defined him, despite a big dose of humility thrown in since he had left the Brooklyn Museum and a steady paycheck for a modest, almost hole-in-the-wall gallery in Brooklyn.

They had become friends through a chance encounter in the diner where Dee had worked while Jenny was still a Brooklyn resident. Jenny had remembered him immediately, but it had taken a little prodding on her part to bring into focus their first meeting at the Everson in Syracuse where he had brought the Andy Warhol exhibit as curator and she and Sparky had attended thanks to Miss Lindstrom's gift of tickets.

They had immediately become friends in what could only be termed a symbiotic relationship. Chip urged her to paint, and she urged him to leave the museum where he was by her observations so highly underused. Both were successful. Jenny had begun to paint again and Chip set up in Brooklyn where he could afford the space instead of in the Village or in Soho where he would like to have been. Nevertheless, he had managed to lure those matrons who frequented those kitschy galleries to his place and Jenny's paintings were selling very well.

Not that she had considered what she really wanted to paint. She liked flowers, however, and she had great access to the Parkers' gardens, so the subject seemed a natural. She evolved into painting large canvases with the study of one flower against a stark, white background. That seemed to please Manhattan apartment dwellers and Long Island beach house aficionados as well. The subject went back to the Garden of Eden but the rendering was what sold. Modern enough to appeal to the decorators who furnished their assigned apartments in the very same style with a number of variations so the matrons who hired them could compete, but with enough flair so that a beach house resident could sit and quietly, secretly, share with the canvas a primal moment.

As they sat at lunch at a deli around the corner from Chip's gallery, Chip ordered the roast beef piled high on a thick slice of rye, along with their famous pickles. Jenny ordered the chicken, and picked at it.

"What's the matter, Jen? No man in your life?"

"Not really. But, Josh is on my mind a lot. Now that he's going to be a teen, I want to make sure I do right by him. His future is in the balance."

"I think you're doing fine, Jen. He's got a great mom, and he's got all your men friends to fill in the gap. He's got a great future."

"He wants to go to LaGuardia School of the Arts. I hope he can get in."

"He'll get in. He's got great grades, and a lot of extra-curricular stuff. Sports and the school paper. A great combination."

"He wants to be an international correspondent. It's a lot to ask. Too many wannabes and too few jobs."

"Well, he's got a good shot at it. He's a bright kid.

Say, Jenny, I know you're busy, but would you like to meet a guy who's as busy as you are? CEO of his own company, and an art lover. He likes your stuff a lot."

"I don't know, Chip, I'll give it some thought.

"I'd better go. Got to get back for Cathy's client from the Ukraine. Seems they have a great fruit deal she doesn't want to pass up."

"Thanks for coming to lunch, Jen. Give me a ring when you've got some more big canvases."

"Will do." She kissed Chip on the cheek and waved a hasty goodbye as she paid the bill on her way out.

As she sat on the train headed for Manhattan, she mused on Chip's enormous generosity. Not only did he keep his artists happy, he understood their angst. As a gay, he had experienced more than his share of loneliness, not to mention social scorn for his sexual persuasion. Nevertheless, he always kept good cheer and most often overrode his cryptic countenance with a steady dose of empathy. She must remember to relay his good wishes to Josh. Josh had practically enshrined the baseball Chip had given him won at a batting cage with a Yankee pitcher's autograph on it. It was the centerpiece of his room. As Jenny's mind began to wander almost all the way back to her high school art classes and the small-town atmosphere of Jerusalem, which she still missed, she almost passed her stop. But, the conductor's voice called her back to reality. She was, after all, a New Yorker.

Chapter Forty-Seven

S parky was playing croquet on the small patch of lawn behind her rambling farmhouse she had given up as a nod to civilization and her Long Island upbringing. Aunt Gert had joined her. Josh and Cliff were playing ball in the back field with Shakespeare catching the flies, and Sarah and Jesse were pushing their four little ones in turn on the tire swing Sparky had set up for the occasion. Sammy and Anne, pregnant with their first, were helping as needed, and Jenny was sitting on the porch on the creaking swing taking a much needed rest.

The drive home, despite a year's hiatus, had been the same. Different billboards, the same barns and fields, and towns on the edge of the thruway that looked dragged out of the 1930s. They had stopped at Dino's as always, just outside of Binghamton, where the burgers beat Manhattan's according to Josh, and the waitresses never stopped calling him 'honey' no matter how old he got.

As she mused from her perch on the porch swing, all was as Jenny remembered it. The fields that stretch for miles, the summer daisies, white and yellow, popping up everywhere, and Sparky's tractor named Alma after a former classmate who thought daily events revolved only around city life safely parked in the barn.

Some things had changed. Mother had given up her cranky ways toward Jenny's divorce, doting on Josh when the Andersons disowned him, despite her bitterness that she would never be connected to the high society she craved. "Mattie, he's your grandchild," Aunt Gert would say. In fact, she downright spoiled him as much as her stern nature would allow, plying him with his favorite lemon cupcakes whenever they visited, and knitting him scarves and mittens he would never need in the warmer climate of Manhattan.

Other things had changed as well. Most of Jenny's childhood friends had moved on and out of Jerusalem. Dotty Thatcher had gone to Boston to live, picking up with wealthy and well-connected men and landing the best office jobs in the city. Only Caroline Mackey had returned, a vet who had set up practice on the edge of town. But, despite their occasional get-togethers on Jenny's visits, they had little in common now. Caroline had never been to Brooklyn or The City and had no desire to do so. Jenny would never understand what it was like to be roused at 3 a.m. and face a farm family who was about to lose a whole herd of dairy cows to blackleg or Johne's disease.

What Jenny missed, she realized, as she reminisced, were the nighttime meetings with Jake and the call of the whippoorwill, their secret signal. The times in the hayloft where they shared their hopes and their dreams. But, Jake had never returned. Caught up in the excitement and challenge of a high-powered law practice, and the pull of a society new to a former farm boy, Jake had strayed far from his roots. Sarah and Anne rarely heard from the once adored big brother.

"Hey, Mom, watch out!" Josh called out, too late for Jenny to get out of the way. The ball just missed her by a hair, and Shakespeare diving to catch it, upset the precarious swing. Jenny laughed as she landed on the porch with Shakespeare's muddy feet all over her new jeans. No longer a puppy, the dog began to whimper, wondering what he had done.

"It's alright, Shakespeare," Jenny said firmly, as she rubbed his back. "Nothing a good bath won't cure." She laughed as he lay down at her feet begging forgiveness with his large brown eyes looking skyward.

Aunt Gert excused herself from the croquet game and headed for the kitchen to make the pot roast. Sparky joined the ball game, ever the tomboy. Josh was excited, since he and Sparky had had a special bond since his birth.

"How about some help, Jenny?"

"Love to, Aunt Gert. Soon as I wash up and shampoo Shakespeare."

As Jenny peeled carrots and onions in the kitchen that looked like it hadn't been changed in at least one hundred and fifty years, Aunt Gert pounded the chuck roast and floured it, starting up the oil in the cooker at the same time.

"How's New York?"

"About the same as you last saw it. It's hard to keep up with, but stimulating. No question."

"Have you ever thought of moving back?"

"Not really. Josh is thriving, and he needs that distance from the Andersons still. Their power seems never ending. But, it doesn't mean I don't miss here."

"You've done a good job with him, Jenny. He's grown into a fine, young man."

"Thanks, Aunt Gert. He's a handful sometimes, but he's such a great kid. I'm so very lucky. And, my friends have helped out when they could.

"I'm not sure I'd even fit in anymore if I moved back."

"You'd fit in Jenny. That's what home is all about. People still ask about you. Ned Baxter down at the dress shop still remembers your size. Edith, his wife, still remembers the pearls you coveted but Mattie wouldn't let you have. Too grown up, she insisted."

"I remember. And, when I was old enough to get them, I forgot all about them."

"Well they're still there. Ned doesn't change his stock or styles too often.

"Say, I'd better get to this pot roast. The oil is hot and sizzling. Just right."

As Aunt Gert tended the pot roast, Jenny looked round at the antique kitchen. What had happened to the painting dreams she had had? She was painting, but almost by formula. She knew what the matrons by the sea or the tenants of the posh buildings in Manhattan would want. And, she was turning it out.

What would Rafe Tewksbury have thought about that? His life cut short, she was the recipient of the scholarship his mother had put out in his memory. She no longer had the money, but she had the experience. Accepting that award had meant a lot. She knew it meant a lot to Aunt Gert as well. She knew that she, Jenny, had been the promise he could not fulfill.

Aunt Gert never mentioned it, but Jenny somehow felt the disappointment, even though she knew Aunt Gert would never express that feeling. Rafe lived in Aunt Gert, but he didn't live in Jenny. She had never known him. But, she must remember to show Josh the table Aunt Gert still had set up in his memory, and the parts of the planes he had flown still in her barn.

As Jenny tore the lettuce for salad, the odor of cooking pot roast permeated the room, as it had throughout Jenny's childhood. Mother's lemon pie, for which she was famous, had ended almost every family dinner.

Aunt Gert reached for the dishes in the cupboards above the sink. Chipped and mismatched, they were definitely bright and floral. Typical Sparky, mused Jenny. Sparky, who had wanted to change the world but ignore social convention. She smiled as she remembered their student days and their walks along the lakeshore. Sparky with her shoes off and her hair hanging braided along her back.

"I think we can call them all in." Aunt Gert took down the ricer to whip the potatoes.

"Will do, Aunt Gert. I can't wait to ring the old cowbell."

As they all straggled in, Jenny marveled at the patience of Anne and Sarah with the little ones. As they sat, Cliff said a short grace and they all dug in. Somehow, food here was savored in a way that didn't seem possible in a Manhattan restaurant. Long days in the field brought an appreciation no one could have after a day of hailing taxis and fighting the hustle and bustle of a busy and determined crowd.

"How's the job going, Sammy?"

"Not so well, Jenny. The Andersons have me going everywhere and working overtime. They refuse to hike my pay. And, with me and Annie expecting, it hurts."

"Why don't you go over to Nolan's in Dundee?"

"I wouldn't be able to help Ma and Pa and Bert out as much with drivin' that far."

"Maybe we can get you some weekend work. I've got an empty barn, and Anne could help me in the greenhouse."

"That would be nice, Miz Gert. Annie and I would be grateful."

"I'll look into it. I still roam the campus and I know a lot of professors looking for a good mechanic."

257

Talk turned to Josh's basketball and his schooling, both of which Cliff took a great interest in. Josh basked in the attention. As Josh regaled them with all that he was learning and the free rein at LaGuardia compared to New York City schools, Cliff promised him a basketball net installed by next visit.

"Father will probably challenge you to a game. He was on the team in high school."

"Mom's right, Josh. Your grandfather was a pretty good basketball player. All the girls were after him, but Mattie caught him."

"Jenny," said Anne, looking demurely up from her plate, "would you ever see Jake?"

Jenny paused, remembering the eager and ambitious farm boy. "I think probably not, Annie. He knows I'm in New York but he hasn't contacted me. I think he doesn't want any reminders of the early years. He's caught up in a high-powered career and a high-powered society. I think I would just be in the way of his ambitions."

"He doesn't write or call. Ma and Pa are sad but they try not to show it. Ma keeps the quilt from his bed she made him when he was ten in a special place above the sofa on the parlor wall."

"Sometimes life gets away from people, Annie. Maybe someday Jake will remember his roots."

Aunt Gert stood up. "Who's going to help me serve those beautiful desserts Sarah and Anne spent all those hours baking?"

"I will, Aunt Gert. Then I'll get first choice."

"Josh, that's true. Servers get first choice. But, it's hard to decide between cherry and peach pie. Especially since the fruit has come from the orchard back of Sarah and Jesse's fields."

"Okay, I'll have Rebecca choose."

Rebecca, Sarah's four-year-old, jumped up and smiled. "I choose one of each."

Everyone laughed as they cleared the table. Even the little ones pitched in, trained at an early age to lend a hand to chores around a homestead with no electricity and many long hours of labor for an income derived from the second poorest county in New York State.

Jenny watched as two-year-old Jeremiah trailed after Josh, a look of rapt admiration overcoming the toddler's countenance. Rebecca attempted to relieve him of the bowl he grasped with two very pudgy hands, setting up a howl of distinct possession.

She looked about the kitchen to memorize the scene. The memory would have to last a year. Josh would insist on Sparky skipping stones with him along Keuka Lake and Father letting him drive the tractor out into the carefully cultivated fields. Mother would insist on Josh purchasing his school supplies at the Windmill because they were cheaper than anywhere in Manhattan. And, Jenny herself would spend time in the hayloft, despite the dust on her new designer jeans.

But, they must be on the road promptly at seven on Sunday. Cathy was receiving a most important client from the USSR on Monday.

Chapter Forty-Eight

Chip's CEO friend was all that Chip had said he was. Charming, dashing, and very, very busy. But, he had taken time to call Jenny on a Sunday afternoon.

Mark Brigham wouldn't take "no" for an answer. Jenny found herself strolling through Central Park an hour later, munching a mustard and relish slathered hotdog purchased from a street vendor. The ride to the park had been swift, the sun roof open and the wind blowing through her hair in the fire red Porsche.

Jenny had forgotten how good a street vendor's hotdog could be. Especially strolling through the walks of the beautifully designed park, amid the lush maples and hawthorns and elms, the sun poking through the darkness of their dense green leaves. The arching branches of the dogwoods were at full bloom, sporting a remarkable number of lovely and pure white blossoms.

"It's nice to finally meet the artist of three of my favorite paintings. I really like your work, Jenny."

"Thanks. It keeps me busy."

"I'll bet. And, what else do you do?"

"I raise my son. He'll be fourteen next month."

"He seems like a nice kid, Jenny. You're doing a great job."

"Thanks. I try."

"So, does your painting support you, or do you do something else besides?"

"I work for an import export firm on the East side. A friend's firm. It's more fun than work."

"I see. You're lucky. My two businesses seem to be getting the better of me. Time for a break."

"What businesses do you have, Mark?"

"Two manufacturing firms. My facilities are in Brooklyn. That's how I met Chip. I have an office in Manhattan."

"What do you make?"

"We make an airplane part that only three companies in the world make. Small part, but it helps to keep planes up in the air. My other company makes gears for sports car motors. Very specific."

"Sounds like work. You must be brilliant."

"Not brilliant. Just persistent. But, I like the contribution to travel we make. When I was younger, traveling was one of my greatest joys."

"Do you travel now?"

"All the time. But, for work. I hardly get time to see where I am. How about you?"

"I travel also. It gives me a chance to photograph the world. The lure of Eastern Europe. It sells magazines."

"I bet. With your artistic eye, it's probably done wonders for tourism."

"I hope so."

"Where are you from, Jenny?"

"Jerusalem. Southern tier. About five hours drive from here. But, millions of miles away in sophistication."

"I'm from a small town, too. Indiana. Rows and rows of corn."

"What brought you here?"

"Well. Aeronautics is big on the west coast. But, I'm not the Hollywood type. So, New York it was."

Jenny looked toward the horizon and the setting sun. "I think those orange and red swatches in the sky are trying to tell us something. I promised Josh I'd be back for dinner."

"Will do. Spoken like a true artist. Thanks, Jenny, for taking the time to help a workaholic unwind. It's been fun."

"Same here, Mark. The weather and the company are about as pleasant as I can remember in a long time."

"Well, it's been especially nice to enjoy a tree and look at the summer blossoms and hear the song of a bird. It's been a long time since I breathed the air of the outdoors. Mostly it's been chasing planes and poring over blueprints."

"Well good. New Yorkers need a dose of the outdoors every now and then. Even if it's filled with taxis and smog."

"I'd race you to the car, but I think you'd win. Those look like serious sneakers."

"They are. Cathy has pointed out that when we're on the job overseas, time is money. So, our footwear reflects our company motto."

As Mark opened the door of his Porsche, Jenny breathed a sigh as she stepped in. It had been long since she had been treated as a woman valued for her femininity alone.

The ride through the New York streets, as deserted as they were for a Sunday, brought a musing Jenny hadn't entertained in a long, long time. She felt an interloper in a highly energized society. The City's melting pot reputation was highly deserved. Those walking the streets, she knew, were both "natives" and visitors. But, which were which?

In her mind, The City still belonged to the natives who had exchanged this island for a mere $24 in beads. Whether visitor or native, not one of the pedestrians looked comfortable in their environment.

"We're here. A penny for your thoughts."

Jenny remembered when a young farm boy had asked her that question. But, this time she was ready.

"I'm thinking that I had a very nice time this afternoon. Thanks for the excursion."

"I did too, Jenny. How about repeating it?"

"I'd like that, Mark."

"I'll call you when I get back from China."

Jenny used her key to open the door of the building. There was no doorman on Sunday afternoons. Mark put her hands in his. And then, with a quick farewell, he was off.

Chapter Forty-Nine

Mark's return from China marked the beginning of a whirlwind courtship. Jenny was swept off her feet. Mark was very persuasive.

Nights at the opera, posh restaurants, night clubs and Broadway plays, evenings walking the streets of New York turned into weekends in faraway lands. Thailand, Cambodia, the hinterlands of China. Mark was always on the lookout for new markets and cheaper labor, but most of all engineers who understood the aeronautical business. There were many with Ph.D.'s who could not find a job in their own country because there was no demand.

Josh managed. He often stayed with friends, or Dee who would take him in for the weekend with her loud and boisterous family. Rosa played the big sister, counseling Josh to save himself for the right girl and not be too hasty in falling for the wrong one too soon. Denny, when he was there, would take Josh off for "guy" stuff, letting the little ones tag along, mostly to the park for a game of softball, where Denny belonged to a Sunday league, or bowling, or for an action flick that would put the small ones to sleep during the requisite car chases.

Sometimes, the three of them, Jenny, Josh, and Mark, would spend the weekend together, soaking up a laziness that was rare for any of them. Josh would do his homework, or watch sports on the large TV Jenny had given in to buy, with Mark. Sometimes they would just sit around and play chess or checkers while Jenny cooked pot roast in the kitchen.

But, these occasions were rare. Mark was gone on business often, and most of his waking hours were spent abroad. Jenny was beginning to feel that they were almost having a long distance relationship though they lived in the same city. Between his travels and hers, they rarely saw each other.

Despite the absences, Jenny felt a connection to Mark she hadn't felt toward anyone since she had arrived in New York. Perhaps it was the easy demeanor they both displayed. Or, the extra sense of responsibility, independence and understanding they had both developed as strangers in the ultra modern culture of a city neither one of them understood. Or, perhaps, as Jenny began to feel, it was the strain of melancholy she sensed in them both.

"Mark, there's a sadness about you."

"I thought I hid that well."

It reminded her of Jake, of the talk in the hayloft between them when neither of them could see the future.

"Is it something I should know?"

"Not really, Jenny. An old love. An unattainable love."

"Why did you turn your back on it?"

"I didn't. I was simply run out of a Tanzanian village for falling for a chief's daughter when I was in the Peace Corps."

"She must have been very special."

"She was, Jenny. She was sixteen. Tall and graceful. A shadow of a memory to me now."

"Why have you never tried to find her?"

"I thought I could forget her. I didn't want to disturb her way of life. She was so much a part of Kilimanjaro and the bush country she was born in."

"Perhaps she thinks of you as well."

"I've thought of finding her, but by now she must be the wife of a highborn villager and the mother of six children."

"She also might be the sixth wife of a tribal elder and wanting a means to escape."

"Thanks, Jenny. I'll give it a try. But, now we should take a run in the park. We have to break in those new sneakers of yours."

Jenny was glad she had unearthed Mark's reason for melancholy. But, it made her question her own. She had suppressed her feelings of sadness and sexuality after her divorce in favor of a life of responsibility. But, they must be there and part of her soul as Mark's were.

As the sun went down over Central Park, and the endorphins took over to bring the most pleasant sensations of sunset, Jenny knew she was in for the first session of soul searching she would have since she arrived in New York.

Chapter Fifty

Mark's letters from Tanzania arrived sporadically, dependent on the political climate and the safe passage of mail. The Tanzania he had known had all but disappeared. In its place, the country had become a hotbed of political infighting, complete with multiple party factions and an ineptitude to move toward the "democratization" process which had eluded so many of its African neighbors. Uprisings and slaughter in nearby Burundi and Rwanda had taken their toll. The pastoral land tenure which had been the basis of their economy was in conflict with what they saw as progress. And, Dar-es-Salaam, their largest city and formerly the country's capital, a name in Arabic which meant the "house of peace," was full of bribery and sloth.

Mark's letters continued to be upbeat, but he had found no sign of his beloved Ajuba. He had continued to search, not certain where she might be found in the upheaval that was the Tanzania of the 90's. Jenny found comfort in his descriptions of the countryside, much of which was still left untouched despite the political upheaval.

Jenny found comfort as well in the now worn book of Blake poems Jake had left for her in the Thompson barn at graduation. Blake's vision of Jerusalem was what they had had in their own Jerusalem and she missed it now more than ever. "And did those feet in ancient time/Walk upon England's mountains green?/And was the holy Lamb of God/On England's pleasant pasture seen?"

Jenny closed the book and visualized the pastures and the fields with purple and pink and yellow wildflowers. She so much wanted to paint them. Jake's crumpled note was still in there. She reread it and noted his hope that she would read these when times were tough. Did Jake ever think of Jerusalem or their late afternoons in the barn or evenings out back when the sun went down and the whippoorwill called?

She decided to return the book to its drawer in the back of her favorite table. Jake would be so caught up in his society ways that he most likely never thought of her or Jerusalem. They must seem so provincial to him today. She sighed as she packed away the small volume.

"Hey, Mom, what's to eat?"

"How about the cookies I brought back from Brandanos yesterday?"

"Sounds good."

Jenny looked at Josh. Tall, slender, athletic build. A good kid. Eager to please, but watchful. A kid with dreams. She felt such unbridled pride. She only hoped she had done right by him.

She went into the kitchen and poured him a glass of milk. Then, she set the cookies out on a plate they had dragged from their Brooklyn apartment because Josh had dubbed it the cookie plate when he was only three. She set it down on the red checkered tablecloth and poured herself a glass of the iced coffee she kept for special occasions.

"Mmmm. Oatmeal raisin. How did you know?"

"You've packed away enough of those for me to guess. How's school going?"

"Good. We have a new girl in English class. She seems like she needs a friend."

"Well, you might want to go kind of slow with that. Your grades are good. You might want to limit the dating until summer. But, maybe she would like to go to the junior prom."

"Maybe. I'll think about it. But, first, I'd better get to know her.

"Say, Mom, have you heard from Mark?"

"I just got a letter yesterday. He says to say 'hello' to you and to tell you to be sure and keep an eye on Magic Johnson and Michael Jordan for him."

"I will. Is he there on business?"

"He's there to find someone he knew long ago."

"I see. He's been gone a long time."

"He's in a country with a lot of problems. Hard to get around."

Josh pushed back the chair and finished the last crumb on his plate. "I've got to go down and interview Rinaldo. We have to do a person piece. Mrs. Harrison says to think like we're working for the New Yorker."

"Well that should be fun. Be back in a half hour. Growing boys need to be in bed about now."

Jenny finished the dishes and settled back into the easy chair. She thought of Mark. Kind, generous, and thoughtful. He had brought out the womanhood she had suppressed for so many years.

But, their life together could never be complete if he didn't settle the question that had plagued him since youth. Her eyes became heavy as the weariness of the day settled over her. She woke to Josh's gentle shaking and prepared for bed.

Chapter Fifty-One

J enny awoke to the incessant ringing of her apartment phone. She reached for the receiver. It was Sarah. Jenny could hardly hear her through what sounded like a rush of tears and nervous chatter.

"Jenny, I'm sorry to wake you. But, Sammy's in jail and Anne's so upset we're afraid she's going to lose the baby."

"What happened, Sarah?"

"The Andersons told the police that Sammy's been taking money from their business. It's not true, Jenny. Sammy swears he's never taken a penny."

"I believe you, Sarah. Where's Anne?"

"She's here with me, but we're crowded."

"I'll call Sparky and see if she can take Anne in for now. What about Sammy?"

"He didn't do it, Jenny. Sammy is honest as the day is long. But, the Andersons have pull with the police. They give them coffee and doughnuts every day and as far as we know they remember them with large gifts at Christmas."

"I believe you, Sarah. What is Sammy's bail?"

"It's set at $3,000. But, Sammy doesn't have that much and no one in his family has it. Jesse and I don't have it. We barely make ends meet."

"I know, Sarah. I'll call the Penn Yan police and see if I can arrange bail."

"Thanks, Jenny. I know it would calm Anne."

There was a pause and then Sarah spoke again. "Jenny, it would mean a lot to us if you could rouse Jake. We've tried, but the telephone number he gave us is changed and the operator won't give it out. He's the only one who could help Sammy. All the cops here hate Mennonites and there are no lawyers we can afford."

Jenny stared at the phone. She hadn't seen Jake since she had been a newlywed expecting Josh.

"I'll do my best, Sarah. Meanwhile, tell Sammy to stay cool."

"I will, Jenny." Sarah hesitated. "Jenny, thanks for your help."

"I wouldn't do otherwise. Now, you make sure you take care of yourself and Jesse as well. I know this has been a strain on you both."

Jenny hung up and called Sparky. Her former roommate came to the phone with plenty of enthusiasm. She had just dodged a kick from the new cow she had acquired who wanted to knock over the milk pail. Sparky had barely rescued the morning's bounty.

"I'll get on it right away, Jen. Don't worry. I'll get Annie. That way her family can save face. And, I'll get some cookies to Sammy. Jeb Archer down at the jail owes Cliff. He'll let me smuggle them in."

Jenny hung up the phone grateful for the many long years of Sparky's friendship. She knew proving Sammy's innocence would be nearly impossible in a town corrupt with crooked lawyers and cops. She knew also that Jake was their only hope. He knew the corruption first hand. She put on the coffee pot. She would call Cathy as soon as the sun came up.

Chapter Fifty-Two

J enny looked at the imposing building a few doors away as she walked the pavement of Lexington Avenue. The street was filled with mid-morning traffic and the sidewalks filled with pedestrians. She had asked the cabbie to let her off a few buildings ahead so she could compose herself, but it wasn't working. She was as nervous as the first time she had ventured to Madison Avenue as a newbie to Manhattan and had found the offices of Mallory, Hollander & Wexler.

She had traced Jake through the Manhattan chapter of the ABA and the large, Manhattan yellow pages. The building his law firm took offices in was marble with a beautifully chiseled beige stone and large, black tinted windows. It rose twenty-four stories above the street.

She entered the foyer to a large sculpted display of the partners' names. Jake's was at the bottom, along with one other. The original, founding partners, no doubt retired or deceased by now, took the prominent three spaces at the top.

She rang the elevator button for the eighteenth floor, clearly spelled out in the gold plated directory next to the elevator bank in the reception area. Clients were asked to refrain from going above that level.

As she stepped off the elevator the silence seemed almost

eerie. The receptionist stared at her from behind a huge, mahogany desk.

"Can I help you?"

"I'm looking for Jake Martin."

"Mr. Martin is working at home for the next two weeks. Can I take a message?"

"I need to speak to him now. It's urgent."

"I'm sorry, but we can't give out personal phone numbers or addresses of our attorneys."

"Could you at least give him a call and ask him if he could see me?"

The secretary frowned. She hesitated. But, Jenny was used to watching Cathy negotiate a deal.

"Okay. I'll give him a call. But, you'll have to wait."

Jenny chose the leather sofa along the wall. She picked up a copy of *Newsweek* and leafed through it. Breaking world news. Reviews of theater and movies and even an interview with a chef who had concocted a fascinating dish for the president of France.

But, where was the real news? The news that was happening to people every day in every small town across the country and the world. In backwater places and even in cities where major magazines refused to consider their stories an item.

Jenny jumped when she heard her name. She rose from the

sofa with the same trepidation that had plagued her in the cab on the way over mid-morning.

"Mr. Martin said of course to give you his address. He has left instructions with the doorman to alert him as soon as you arrive."

The cab ride over seemed interminable. Lunch time traffic filled the streets and the address was in the poshest neighborhood in New York, its streets lined with private cars and chauffeurs waiting at a moment's notice to take off for the airport or an important business meeting or an equally important social gala. The cabbie stopped in front of the number Jenny had given him.

As Jenny stepped out, she gave her name to the doorman. She entered the lobby, one of the most wealthy and elegant she had seen. The potted palms fought for space with the statuary. The desk, unobtrusive and heavy mahogany, sat in the corner with an attendant who seemed to not be busy at all. She answered the muted ring of the elegant ivory telephone with a very soft voice that was nevertheless crisp and efficient.

Jenny stood behind a potted palm to look for Jake. In very short order the elevator opened to let out a man dressed in casual elegance with a coolly impervious air of authority. Jenny came out from behind her palm. Jake walked over.

"Jenny, it's so good to see you."

"It's good to see you too, Jake."

"Let's go up. I've canceled my afternoon calls. Can I get you lunch?"

"That would be nice."

"How about some cold salmon with some of that aspic thrown in? Does that sound good?"

"Sounds wonderful."

"I'll ring them as soon as we get up."

The ride up was fast and silent. Neither Jenny or Jake could think of anything to say.

The elevator stopped to let them out on the penthouse floor. The doors of Jake's apartment opened to a breathtaking view of Central Park. Jenny had never seen the maples and sycamores and oak trees from this height.

"Oh, Jake, it's beautiful."

"Thank you, Jenny. But, I never get to enjoy it, it seems. I'm either on a research trip in the rainforests of South America or here laboring over a pile of paperwork long after the sun goes down."

"The price of success."

"Maybe. How about you, Jenny? I've seen your work in the New York Times."

"I've had a few photographs there. My paintings are in a gallery in Brooklyn and I work for an import export firm."

"You're busy."

A knock on the door interrupted the awkward conversation. A waiter wheeled in the lunch on a silver cart and uncovered the dishes of salmon and Cumberland sauce, lifting the coffee urn and plate of petit fours to the sideboard.

"You can set that up over there, Jose."

"I'll be out of your way in a jiffy, Mr. Jake."

"Take your time, Jose. I'm entertaining a very special guest."

As Jake and Jenny stared at each other across the beautifully set table, candlelight flickering on either side of a crystal vase filled with three rare orchids, neither of them spoke. Then, Jake spoke up.

"Jenny, you must be here for a reason. I know you've been in New York but have never called me. You must have had your reasons."

"You never called me either, Jake. But, I didn't want to disturb your success. I thought a farm girl from your past might get in the way."

"I didn't call you Jenny because I was hurt. I felt that Mennonites were barely accepted at the Thompsons. I felt that so-called socialites like the Andersons had a better chance. And, Jenny, though you were kind to me, I never felt you changed that."

"Perhaps you're right, Jake. I'm truly sorry that a young girl had so little sense in her head."

"Well, that's water over the dam. Suppose you tell me what you came here for."

"Sammy's in jail, Jake. Falsely accused of theft at the Anderson agency."

Jake was silent. He took a moment to absorb the news. "I know I haven't been a good correspondent. It's been months since I called Ma and Pa or Sarah or Anne. How is Annie doing?"

"She's with Cliff and Sparky. They've given her a room with a place for a nursery if necessary."

"Jenny, I can't leave my practice. But, I'll see what I can do. I can find a pro bono in Penn Yan and open up all our resources to him. Or, I can pay the fees myself."

"Jake, you know as well as I do that the whole southern tier legal community is just about owned by the Andersons. And, they've set out to pick Sammy as a scapegoat for whatever wrongdoing they've incurred this time. Jake, you are Sammy's only hope."

"I'll lose my partnership and most likely the major part of my law practice if I leave now. I'm in the middle of some big, international cases which will bring in not only money but international fame to the firm. They've been waiting to go global and this is their big chance."

"Sammy never hesitated when you came to Penn Yan a gangling kid from Pennsylvania who didn't know how to stand up for himself. Sammy fought your battles for you and taught you how to defend yourself. And, for that, he lost his chance at football and a college scholarship."

Jake looked down. Then, without missing a beat, he stood. "Jenny, I suppose we'd better get back to work. It's been so good seeing you. I'll get back to you on this. I'll get the best minds in the firm working on it and we'll come up with a solution."

Jenny rose as well. "Thank you for seeing me, Jake. I'll see myself out."

As Jenny pushed the elevator button, she mused on the passing of time. She barely recognized Jake. And, what had time done to her?

She headed for home in a cab hailed by the doorman. In it, she looked around. Steel girders, tall buildings, some modern with tinted black windows, others preserved from a century before. People heading in all directions with a direct purpose of getting where they were going.

She had realized one of her dreams. She was selling to wealthy people on Long Island. But, why, she wondered now, had that been a dream so long ago in a hayloft set so far back on a farm in those pastoral lands?

She greeted Rinaldo and turned the key to her apartment. She headed for her bed without changing her clothes. When Josh arrived he found her peacefully asleep, her shoes still on and her Yves St. Laurent soft grey suit very wrinkled.

Chapter Fifty-Three

From her desk at the import export firm through the floor to ceiling windows Jenny could see the streets of Manhattan from thirty-five floors up. Miniature people scurrying. Traffic slowed to a crawl. A typical business day.

She fingered a letter she had just received from Mark. He had found his Ajuba, and needed Jenny to keep a line open to the US embassy in New York. Communication in Tanzania was primitive, and Ajuba, the fifth wife of a powerful chief in the backlands, who so much wanted out of her pitiful position, would be sorely missed by the other four wives who she had been a virtual slave to.

Cathy and Jeff had been married quietly in the city clerk's offices by a Justice of the Peace and were busy building a branch of the firm in Iowa. Jenny stared out of the window. She had been in a daze since her meeting with Jake a week ago. She hadn't recovered. She had called Sparky and talked to Sarah. She promised them she would do all she could to help Sammy. But, she didn't know what that was. She had money to contribute if necessary, but no legal skills. She felt helpless.

Josh asked her daily how Sammy was. Sparky was searching the Long Island area for a lawyer who would take the case but the answer was the same every time. They would be ousted or shunned by the "good old boy network" they knew existed there and it wouldn't be worth their time. They would lose and the case would be stacked against them.

Jenny's phone rang. She picked it up. "Ginny, can you hold the call?"

"I can't Jen. The caller's pretty insistent. He says it's urgent."

"Did he give his name?"

"Jake Martin."

"Okay, Ginny, put him on."

Jake's voice was brusque but authoritative. "Jenny, can you meet me at Lindy's, Seventh Avenue between 53rd and 54th, in about a half an hour?"

"I'll try, Jake."

"I'll see you then."

Jenny rushed in to the washroom to freshen up. She wanted to look good for Jake. It wouldn't do to be less than authoritative herself.

She put on a fresh blouse under her beige suit and applied new makeup. She would just have time to get a cab and get through the city in time to beat the lunchtime traffic.

She arrived at Lindy's, only a few minutes late. She paid the cabbie and rushed in the front door. Jake stood up, ushering her to a booth he had already reserved.

"Jenny, thanks for coming. Would you like coffee, a pastry, lunch?"

"Whatever you prefer. I'm flexible today."

"Then, how about lunch?"

"Sounds good."

They sat in the booth and for a moment Jake was silent. Jenny noticed he seemed flustered, perhaps unshaven as well, and the dark circles under his eyes pointed to a very sleepless night.

"Jenny, I've quit my job. Or, been fired. I'm not sure which.

"When I asked Dave Marchand, one of the three founders of the firm and my mentor since I came to New York, if I could have a few weeks off to go defend Sammy, he blew up. He accused me of being an ingrate, a hayseed from the sticks he molded into an attorney worthy of cases from Park Avenue. Now, at a crucial time for the firm, I was asking for time off.

I was stunned. I quit. Just like that. My voice and my delivery didn't even sound like me. All the years I spent learning how to argue in the courtroom suddenly seemed to evaporate in those few minutes."

"Jake, I'm sorry."

"No need, Jenny. It's not your problem. But, I'm asking for your help. I'll need someone to get into the Andersons' financials. I'm sure they're keeping two sets of books. And, we'll need to photograph the evidence. With your expertise in photography and your knowledge of the physical at the

Anderson agency, you would be a shoo-in. But, it's risky. So, I'm only asking."

"Of course I'll help."

"I'll be leaving today for Penn Yan. I have to pull out of the apartment before I set out. I lost my fiancée in the bargain."

"Oh, Jake. I'm sorry."

"She was Dave Marchand's daughter. She preferred to line up with the family code rather than stick with me. Social standing means more to Bitsy than life."

"I'll have to make arrangements for Josh before I go. I should be able to leave tomorrow."

"He must be quite a kid by now."

"He is, Jake. He's a great kid."

"I'm glad, Jenny."

"Thanks. I'll see you probably about tomorrow night in Penn Yan."

"I'll give you a chance to get settled in. Then, I'll give you a call on Thursday."

"Good. I'll be staying with Sparky or Aunt Gert. It's hard for Mother and Father right now to take any changes. Changes cramp their style and they don't cope."

"I'll be staying in my old room on the farm. Ma broke down when she heard. She's putting my old quilt back on the bed."

"I'll be there as soon as I get Josh settled. See you then."

Jenny rose to leave. She had to get back to the office. She put her hand in Jake's.

"Thanks for calling me, Jake."

"I didn't want to, Jenny. I didn't want to interrupt the life you've built for yourself here. But, I needed you."

"I would do anything for Sammy. He's the good in everyone's life."

"See you on Thursday."

As Jenny left Lindy's and hailed a cab, she wondered how she had gotten here. A woman at the height of her career, especially in the import export business. An artist whose patrons would draw the envy of her most accomplished peers.

But, the path to these accomplishments seemed shaky and almost dim. She wasn't certain what her goals had been or even if she ever had had any.

She decided to put the self-doubt on the back burner. Cathy was in the middle of a multi-million dollar deal and needed her. She paid the cabbie and took the stairs. She didn't have time to wait for the elevator or mill about in the lobby. Suddenly, the crowds and the din of mindless chatter seemed an unwelcome intrusion.

Chapter Fifty-Four

J enny woke to the jangling of Aunt Gert's old telephone which still hung on the wall of her bright yellow kitchen, its checkered gingham curtains drenched in the early morning sun. It was barely 8 a. m.

"Jenny, it's Jake Martin. Should I tell him to call back?"

"No, Aunt Gert. I'll take it."

She clambered down the back stairway, it's old treads creaking as she went. She was still hung over with sleep and the comfort of Aunt Gert's old feather bed and the warmth of the five-star quilt.

"Jen, can you get over here right away?"

"Where's that, Jake?"

"The old abandoned flour mill off 54A where we used to play as kids. Ethan Hawkins is letting me have it for as long as we need."

"Give me a half hour."

"Never mind breakfast. I've got coffee brewing and some Danish from Hartzel's."

"I'll be there."

She hung up the phone and looked at Aunt Gert. "Jake hasn't changed any. He's still as ambitious and impatient as he ever was."

"Folks don't change all that much, Jenny. Sometimes that's a good thing and sometimes it's not."

She gave Aunt Gert a kiss on the cheek. "We'll catch up, later. See you tonight."

"You take your time, Jenny. That's what you're here for. Shakespeare and I will be fine."

Jenny showered as quickly as she could and threw on an old pair of jeans she found in the bottom of her suitcase and an old sweat shirt she had left at Aunt Gert's years ago. She brushed her hair back into a ponytail and grabbed a ribbon from the dresser meant for a bouquet of greenhouse gardenias.

As she got behind the wheel of her BMW, she headed for the lake road. Somehow, as she saw the lake on her left, she saw in it the memories of her childhood. The evenings behind the barn in the moonlight, with the spring breezes blowing gently through her chestnut hair. Jake's arm around her to keep her from the chill of the evening. Their wishes on the moon which they were sure would all come true.

She parked in the gravel driveway of the old, abandoned mill and carefully opened the heavy, creaky door. "Hey," she called, testily.

"Hey," came the answer, loud and clear, from the farthest corner of the second story, reached only by an old, narrow flight of wooden stairs, their treads sorely in need of repair.

Jake motioned to the only other chair in the room, an old maple Windsor clearly left over from another era. He sat hunched over a large oak desk, its splinters the only drawback to its once majestic splendor.

"Sit down. That way we can get right to work." He motioned without looking up to the plate of Danish and the old coffee maker he had plugged in sitting on the floor.

"I've got an arrangement with one of my ex-partners. He'll feed us data and he's got us hooked into every legal website in the country. He'll keep backup on his own computer. But, we still have to work fast. If we're discovered we stand the chance of Andersons' goons confiscating everything we have."

Jake turned away from the only modern piece of equipment in the room, a laptop with a very large screen, and turned toward Jenny. He was dressed far differently than when she had seen him in Manhattan, a pair of old jeans replaced the expensive pseudo casual pants he had worn, and an old work shirt the carefully tailored shirt and cashmere cardigan he had used to complete his outfit.

"What I need you for is photography. And, if you can still remember them, your steno skills. The less of a paper trail we leave, the better."

"Will do. You just bark the orders and I'll follow."

"Well, we'll need to be careful. And, you will have to think things out on the spot. Time is important, but so is safety."

"Tell me what we need to do first."

"What you will need to do will be to get inside the Anderson agency and get at their books. If you discover their whereabouts, and can't get into them, I have a contact who can. He'll have to be flown from New York, but I've used him before. He's very good. We'll have to get the books out of wherever they are and get them photographed and put back all before the night is out."

"Sounds interesting. I know where they kept them before, but I don't know what they might have done with them in all these years."

"Let's hope habit and a false sense of security on the part of those wrongdoers will be on our side."

"What can I do for you now? I've freed up the day."

"Good. We can start by you taking dictation, if you remember how. There's volumes of information on these websites. It would take months to distill. If you can take my thoughts down as I pull them from these documents, we can do it in a few days. You can transcribe while I search the town for anyone who will talk."

"Great, Jake. Let's get to work."

The shorthand came back quickly. Though it had been only a tool to get her foot in the door in a town famous for being tough, she mused on its usage now. Perhaps she could believe in fate, though she had always discouraged that thought.

As she looked at Jake, she wondered how much he had really changed. True, he was much more polished. But the same ambition that burned in him as a youth seemed to be fueling him now as he pored over the laws and the precedents that he hoped might save Sammy.

"Good grief, it's two o'clock. We'll burn out. How about lunch?"

"Sure. Where?"

"I thought maybe the Seneca Dairy. The Andersons usually eat at the club."

"You seem to have everything covered for having only been here two days."

"I've been busy. I've found one cop who won't turn against us. Matt Johnson. An old friend of Sammy's, but he doesn't want that known. He'll cover for us here at the mill, but we can't leak that he's working with us."

"Will do. I think I remember him. A kind of shy boy."

"Well, he was younger than Sammy. His folks had a trailer nearby. Lots of kids. Sammy used to help out occasionally."

As Jenny looked at Jake over her burger and fries, she had forgotten how good it was to sit out under the pavilion in the back at the Seneca Dairy. Cars whizzed by on Route 54A and people streamed into the restaurant and around front to the ice cream counter. But they seemed not to be there. All she saw was the flyer stuck to one of the pavilion posts announcing an art show and a fiddlers' festival.

The trees in the neighbor's yard seemed like caricatures, rooted in centuries. Their thick, solid trunks held branches with leaves that barely moved, despite the winds of a threatening rain storm. Trucks lined the driveway.

"You look like a teenager, Jen. Being out of The City must agree with you."

"I could use the break."

"Well, this break comes with a little bit of stress. We'll have to hit the Andersons' books on Thursday evening, their night to be out-of-town entertaining prospects. It'll be an all-nighter for them, but we get only about two hours. Matt will cover for us, but he can only ditch his partner for about that length of time."

"Okay. I've got a special camera, small but speedy. That should work."

"Great. So, how did Josh take this?"

"He did fine. He wants Sammy to be freed, so he was all for my leaving so we could do this. He's a good student, so I know he'll pay attention to the books. He desperately wants to be a TV reporter so he can make a change in the world. He so detests the evils that wrack our planet."

"He sounds like a great kid, Jenny. I'd like to meet him sometime."

Jenny sensed there was more that Jake wasn't saying, but she sensed the rapport was over.

Jake picked up his empty paper plate and his plastic utensils. "Time to get back to work. Lose a minute, lose an opportunity on this project."

"Got it. Ready to roll."

Jake opened the door of the second-hand truck he had just purchased. Despite his wealth, he was never comfortable with the high-priced toys his law firm colleagues bought on a regular basis.

They drove in silence, memories crowding their thoughts as they watched the soft mist rise from the rain-filled lake. As they reached the mill, Jake pulled out the key to let them in. They climbed the stairs still silent, their thoughts lost on the pressing matters at hand.

Chapter Fifty-Five

Jenny sat in a rented car directly across from the Anderson agency. It was 3 a.m. With her was a man named Tango. Jake had described him as the best safecracker this side of the Mississippi. He was silent, his mind turning gears almost palpably.

"Around the back."

Jenny followed his instructions. He had cased the agency earlier in the day and Matt Johnson had turned the alarm off on one of his regular rounds about an hour ago. Jenny knew they had only about one hour. She drove around the back and parked the car among the trade-ins.

As they left the car, they closed the doors without shutting them completely, lest they arouse an insomniac neighbor. They crept toward the back door which Matt had left unlocked.

They spoke only in gestures and whispers. No sense feeding into a tape system the Andersons might have secretly installed to trip up their workers when they were not around.

Jenny led Tango to Leland Anderson's private office. Luckily, the door was unlocked. The safe was still behind a wall of Leland Anderson's favorite liquors which Whit had flown over regularly from his Hawaii headquarters at a very fancy price.

Jenny didn't even try the combination she thought she remembered. She motioned for Tango to begin his work. His slender fingers took over with a great deal of skill. It took less than ten minutes to open what they needed. Jenny reached for the books.

She was horrified to find much more in the safe. Travel itineraries on a regular basis for Grand Cayman with receipts from posh hotels and restaurants on the island. Clearly, the Andersons were laundering their take.

"Work as fast as you can," Tango whispered. "I'll hold the books and the flashlight while you shoot the pages. Then, you can shoot the rest of the stuff while I keep it in the same order we found it."

Jenny nodded. She pulled her camera from her bag and shot a test photo. She pushed the button that brought it up in the small window on the back of the tiny camera. It was legible!

Thanks to Tango's skill, they were finished in less than an hour. Jenny breathed a sigh of relief only when they reached the outskirts of the village and were headed for the mill.

"I couldn't have done this without you, Tango."

"No problem. I'm paid big bucks and I'd rather do it for a guy like Sammy than for a bunch of crooks."

Despite what she thought of Tango, he seemed to have a conscience, though it had been misplaced for a number of decades according to Jake while Tango spent most of his youth in and out of a number of hardscrabble jails.

Jake was waiting for them as they pulled into the grassy parking lot at the mill. He had doused the lights for safety.

Jenny handed him the camera.

"Good work! If we have enough, Tango, I'll have you on your way in no time."

"Thanks, Jake. No hurry."

As Jake downloaded the photos Jenny had taken, he stared at the computer. "They've been laundering for years! This ought to clear Sammy if we can find an honest judge."

Jake stopped. "Tango, I've got you leaving from Rochester. No sense taking the chance of running into the Andersons or their goons in Syracuse. You've got just enough time to return the rental and hop the plane. Everything's in this envelope, including your last payment."

"Thanks, Jake. And, thanks for talking to the guys at City Motors. They've been good to me. I work full time now and me and my woman are getting hitched next month."

"No problem, Tango. They said you've been reliable. Good luck on the wedding."

"We're just going to City Hall. But, it's special for her. Her sister's coming in from Kansas."

"Okay. Now, get out of here. Matt can only cover for us for one more hour."

As the two shook hands, Jenny saw a part of Jake she hadn't seen in Manhattan. But, she knew the moment was private between the two men. She stared out of the window at the stars she knew would soon fade as the dawn with its reds and oranges of sunrise rose across the skies of Jerusalem.

"Let's get some sleep. You did great, Jen."

"Thanks, Jake. Do you think you have enough to clear Sammy?"

"We'll know when I get the stuff back from New York. But, let's hope this will be enough to make a deal with the D.A. to get a change of venue."

As they left the makeshift office, Jenny noticed a change in Jake. He seemed more assured, more like his old self, though his demeanor seemed touched with a tinge of sadness. They turned out the lights and headed for sleep, Jake's truck rumbling ever so slightly as it made tracks for the Martin homestead.

Chapter Fifty-Six

J ake stood at the front of the Steuben county courtroom addressing his opening remarks in the trial of Anderson Motors, Inc. vs. Samuel Walker to a very attentive jury. He had had no problem getting a change of venue. Old Judge Wilson, the grizzled tough pol bought and paid for by the Andersons for eight consecutive terms in Penn Yan, had squirmed in his plush office chair as Jake had presented his evidence of Cayman trips and laundering.

The trial promised to be a fair one. The members of the jury had never heard of the Andersons, much less ever visited a Corvette dealership. The judge, Alexander Marinetti, who had a law practice in town, was known to be fair.

Although no juror in Steuben had ever seen a case more threatening than petty theft, the jury was intent upon delivering justice. They sat transfixed as Jake promised to prove to them the extent of the false accusations the Andersons had trumped up against Sammy, and to show where the money actually went.

The courtroom was filled. Sammy's relatives sat in the back with Annie up front hunkered down between Sparky and Jenny, a pillow behind her for comfort. The Andersons were missing, intent in the belief that the lies their team of lawyers had fed Bill McKay, the first-term D.A., would swiftly ace the case. Aunt Gert was home with the flu but had sent a white orchid for luck with Jenny to give to Annie.

McKay's opening remarks were sparse, calculated to give the jury an indication that only evidence gathered by himself and his assistants would be admissible. So far, all he had to go on were the papers the Andersons had pushed on him, but he promised to be thorough in cross-examination.

As he sat, the judge called the first witness. Burt Carlson, a ten-year veteran of Andersons, obviously ill at ease, came forward to take the oath. The court reporter sat erect in his seat, his fingers poised over the contraption he used to document as accurately as he could the entire court proceedings. As Burt was sworn in, he was reminded by the judge that he had been called as a hostile witness, the only way Jake had been able to get any of Andersons' workers to testify. He replied that he understood.

Burt huddled in the witness chair, sweat pouring down his forehead, fear visible in every wrinkle of his leathery, well-worn face, his grey hair smoothed back with hair gel, his suit an obvious discomfort.

"Mr. Carlson, can you tell us what your job is at Anderson Motors?"

"I'm a senior mechanic."

"And, how long have you worked for Anderson Motors?"

"Ten years."

"How long have you known the defendant, Samuel Walker?"

"I've worked with Sammy about ten years."

"What kind of a person would you say the defendant was?"

"Sammy? Sammy usually kept to himself. Quiet. But, if there was extra work to be done, he was always there. No foolin' or horsin' around like a lotta guys."

"So you would say he was a good worker?"

"Yeh."

"Would you say he was liked by the staff in general?"

"Oh, yeh. Everybody liked Sammy. Always willin' to do you a favor. Generous about his knowledge. If somebody was stuck, he would always help out. A guy needed a ride home, he was always there."

"In your opinion, do you think Sammy is the type to embezzle thousands of dollars from Anderson Motors?"

"Objection. Counsel is leading the witness."

"Objection sustained. Mr. Martin, please rephrase your question."

"Mr. Carlson, did Sammy have a key to Anderson Motors that you knew of?"

"Nah. The Andersons didn't give out keys to the mechanics. If anyone had to stay late there was always someone from the office there."

"Thank you, Mr. Carlson."

"Mr. McKay, you may now cross examine the witness."

"Thank you, your honor."

McKay stepped up, pausing as he assessed the witness. Burt squirmed in his chair, sensing a hostility he hadn't known in his job as boss to a squad of qualified mechanics.

"Mr. Carlson, how long have you been a senior mechanic?"

"Eight years."

"Didn't you think it was strange that you were promoted when the defendant Samuel Walker had been an employee of Andersons far longer than you and had never been promoted?"

"I didn't think about it. I thought that was the Andersons' business."

"Didn't you think that might create some jealousy with the defendant?"

"Sammy wasn't the jealous type."

"Please just answer the question, Mr. Carlson."

"Yeah, but I had a family to feed."

"Thank you. That's all, Mr. Carlson."

"You may step down, Mr. Carlson."

As Burt made his way to the back of the courtroom, Judge Marinetti cautioned him to remain for the rest of the proceedings in case he was needed. He then called a recess for lunch, advising the jury, which had been sequestered for the trial to keep them from Andersons' henchmen, to wait for his assistant to take them to their makeshift lunchroom.

"Let's get out of here."

"I'm with you."

Both Jenny and Sparky helped Annie up out of her chair at the very same time. Jake shuffled papers as he spoke to Sammy.

"Jake said to meet him at Jimbo's, the diner down the street. He'll bring Sammy with him."

"Let's go. We'll get Annie to eat. She's got to feed that baby. I'll call Cliff when we get there."

Jenny piled them into her BMW, parked at the back of the lot. They made tracks for Jimbo's, a popular spot, to beat the lunch crowd. They arrived in time to snag the back booth.

As they sat, Jake came in with Sammy.

"Hi, Babe, how you holdin' up?"

"I'm fine Sammy. How about you?"

"Okay, I guess. We've got Jake and Jenny and Sparky. We should be okay, Annie. We've got to be able to take care of this baby."

"We will, Sammy. I'm fine. Just hang in there."

Jake turned to Sammy. "I appreciate the faith, Sammy, but McKay's a good D.A. He'll give us a hard time. You've got to hang strong. If we let down now, McKay will slaughter us."

"I understand. I'll do my best."

"I know you will, Sammy."

Jenny looked at Jake and Sammy. Sammy was hardly different from the third-grader who had taken pity on Jake and helped him out on the playground. Jake was an outsider almost, just as he had been then, but not for the same reasons. He had been too long in the courts of Manhattan, where he had gotten used to the hardball they had played. Backwater justice was new to him, but he was determined to beat it.

"We've got one thing in our favor. The judge agreed to sequester the jury. That way they won't be out there for Andersons' goons to bribe or threaten.

"I'm not going to call you to the stand, Sammy. McKay would make chopped suey out of you. I know it's hard to stay silent, but that's the best way here."

"Okay, Jake." Sammy looked almost beaten, but he recovered when he looked at Annie. "I'll keep to myself like you told me."

"If we're ready to order, get something to really stoke your bellies. I'm paying."

"Thanks, Sparky. I'll get it next time."

"No problem, Jen. I'm fixed for life. I caught a flaw in a senior engineer's calculations that would have cost a company its job with the city of Brooklyn and probably set them up for a lawsuit. They were mega grateful.

"Jake, Cliff sends his best. If you need him, he'll be there."

"Thanks, Sparky. He can help by shoring up Sammy's folks. They're pretty down over this."

"Will do."

Lunch went all too fast and it was back to the courthouse. They rode in silence.

The afternoon saw a stream of witnesses, all Anderson Motors employees. The drift was the same. Sammy was a good worker who was always willing to help but pretty much kept to himself. The afternoon ended with the judge rapping his gavel on the bench and giving instructions to the sequestered jury while reminding everyone in the courtroom to be back at 8 a.m. the following day.

Jake packed up his papers and strolled out. Sammy found his family and Jenny and Sparky got Annie back to Sparky's house for a much needed rest.

Jenny drove back to Aunt Gert's. Aunt Gert was up but looked pale and wan. Jenny got her back to bed and made some chicken soup which Aunt Gert could only sip. Jake called. Their chat was brief. Despite their years in the sophisticated environs of Manhattan, the day had them beat. They could only look forward to a good night's sleep.

Chapter Fifty-Seven

Jenny stood in the windowless Steuben County courthouse as the bailiff announced the entrance of the judge. She sat at his instructions as well.

The jury was seated and the courtroom was packed. Bill McKay called his first witness, a Syracuse tax lawyer named Stanley Lee Bastian who took the oath with the calm of a courtroom veteran.

"Mr. Bastian, what is your relationship to Anderson Motors?"

"I am their lead tax lawyer."

"And, how long have you been in that position?"

"Twenty-five years."

"And, what are your qualifications."

"I am a certified public accountant and an attorney."

"Are you a solo practitioner?"

"No, I am a partner in the firm of Bastian, Piccolo, and McFee."

"How many people do you employ."

"Right now, we have somewhere in the neighborhood of sixty-five employees."

"And where is your firm located?"

"In Syracuse, New York."

"In all the time you have been working with the Andersons, have they ever found fault with your work?"

"No, sir."

"And, have you ever found fault with their method of record keeping?"

"No, I never have."

"And, would you say they are meticulous record keepers?"

"Yes, I would."

"What types of books do they keep?"

"The usual. A record of their sales, the money they bring in from repairs, and their expenses. It's a pretty straightforward method of bookkeeping."

"Have you ever noticed a deviation in this pattern in the twenty-five years you have been doing their books?"

"No."

"In your expert opinion, can you tell me what led you to believe someone was stealing money from Anderson Motors?"

"I started to notice a pattern. At first, it seemed that a small amount was unaccounted for and I put it to perhaps careless error in daily activities in their record keeping by one of the office workers who was tired or had personal problems. But, then, as time went on, the amounts were bigger and I notified Mr. Anderson and we started to investigate."

"And who did the investigation?"

"Blanchard Securities."

"And, what did they find?"

"They found an enormous amount of money missing. Hundreds of thousands."

At that point, McKay stopped his questioning and produced a thick, black-bindered report and approached the bench. "Your honor, this is the report which Mr. Bastian has referred to which I have labeled Exhibit A. I would like to pass this to the jury."

"You may do so Mr. McKay."

McKay returned to his questioning. "Mr. Bastian, how did you come to the conclusion that the defendant Samuel Walker was the one who took the money?"

"In their investigation, Blanchard was able to track a number of deposits to a specific bank account. They followed that lead to an account set up at Northeast Trust & Securities in Manlius."

"And, who did that account belong to?"

"It was in the name of Samuel Walker."

"And, why did you suspect the defendant Samuel Walker of embezzling the Andersons' funds?"

"Because the amounts of the deposits matched the missing moneys and the amounts were thousands of dollars over the salary Sammy made."

"Thank you, Mr. Bastian."

"Mr. Martin, you may cross examine."

"Thank you, your honor."

Jake walked to the front of the courtroom and faced the witness.

"Mr. Bastian, where did you generally meet with the Andersons to go over their books?"

"We went to Anderson Motors. With our bigger clients, we generally went to their place of business. It was a courtesy we showed all our large accounts."

"And, did you ever meet with them in the Cayman Islands?"

"Not to my knowledge. I may have run into them once or twice while they vacationed there. It's a popular spot."

"Mr. Bastian, it is well known in the financial world that Grand Cayman is the hub for laundering money, that is putting it into other equities and properties until it is no longer recognizable as to where it came from or who is actually getting it."

"Objection. Counsel is basing his observations on hearsay."

"I will be producing expert witnesses, your honor, who will be able to give credence to that statement. They will also be showing where the money went and how it was laundered."

"Objection overruled. Counsel may proceed."

"Mr. Bastian, how many times have you visited the island of Grand Cayman?"

"I don't know exactly. Maybe a few."

"As a matter of fact, you have visited Grand Cayman a

total of fifteen times in the past ten years. I have produced fifteen travel itineraries with your name on it paid for by Anderson Motors. And, according to Cayman records, your hotel accommodations were paid for by the Andersons as well.

"Your honor, I would like to show these receipts for Mr. Bastian's trips to Grand Cayman as Exhibit B and pass them to the jury."

"You may place that material in the hands of the bailiff."

"Thank you your honor. I am finished with my cross examination of Mr. Bastian."

"Thank you Mr. Bastian. You may now step down."

"The court now calls Mr. John Butterfield to the witness stand."

Jake returned to his table to file the papers he had used to question Bastian. There was buzz in the courtroom and buzz at McKay's table. Who was this Butterfield? McKay's staff had never heard of him.

Butterfield, a bespectacled, mild-mannered man in his middle forties, took the oath and sat. "You may now examine your witness, Mr. Martin."

"Thank you, your honor." Jake returned to the front of the courtroom.

"Mr. Butterfield, what job do you hold?"

"I am a bank officer at Chase Manhattan bank in Syracuse."

"And, what position did you hold two years ago?"

"I was a bank officer at Northeast Trust and Securities in Manlius, New York."

"And, why are you no longer employed there?"

"I quit. I couldn't take their policies."

"What do you mean by that?"

"The bank was started by a couple of local lawyers. Since they were a start-up, and that is very difficult in the banking business, they tended to relax a few banking laws or not abide by them. I have worked in the banking business for twenty-five years. And, I am not accustomed to doing that, nor do I think it's right."

"Which laws are you referring to?"

"Well, for instance, they didn't ask for proper ID when prospective customers applied to open an account. The laws are very specific on this."

"What happened when the account in the name of Samuel Walker was opened?"

"The same thing that happened with every other account. The officers were told to look the other way if the customer didn't produce the appropriate information."

"Was the appropriate information produced for the Samuel Walker account?"

"Not at all."

"Did you bring this to the attention of anyone at the bank?"

"Of course I did. I took it to the manager who told me that Mr. Blake, he was one of the owners, was very specific on that. We should look the other way because everybody was local and they were working hard to build up business."

"And, do you have any knowledge of who came in and applied for the account in the name of Samuel Walker?"

"Yes, I do. It is a very small bank, and at that time, had very few customers. I knew every one. That was part of our policy. To provide a friendly and neighborly atmosphere."

"Is that person in this courtroom?"

"Yes."

"Can you point him out?"

"That person there."

"Let the court reporter note that the witness pointed to Mr. Stanley Lee Bastian, the previous witness in this trial."

A collective gasp, though unheard, seemed to go up from the jury, who were now turned as one toward the witness.

"Do you remember any other transactions on this account?"

"Yes. There were periodic, sizable deposits."

"And, who made those?"

"The same person I just pointed out."

"Thank you, Mr. Butterfield. That completes my questions, your honor."

"Mr. McKay, you may now cross-examine the witness."

The surprise witness had knocked out McKay's panache for the moment. He merely mumbled he didn't choose to cross at this time.

The afternoon brought a number of expert witnesses, both for the defense and for the prosecution. The jury sat transfixed. McKay produced two very prominent Syracuse CPAs who had studied the Anderson books independently of Stanley Lee Bastian's firm and had never been connected to any of the accounts there. Jake had flown three forensic accountants in from Manhattan, the best The City had to offer. They were by far more knowledgeable in finding "lost" money and far more knowledgeable in finding where it went. Combined, they had put several New York racketeers behind bars and uncovered several white collar crimes worth millions.

The judge rapped the gavel at the end of the day. He cautioned everyone who needed to be there the following day to be there promptly at 8:00 a.m. The jury rose and the courtroom emptied. After a hasty goodbye to Sparky and Jake, Jenny left for Aunt Gert's. She would have lots to tell and a pot of chicken soup to make. Aunt Gert's health seemed still to be ebbing. She would call old Doc Masterson who Aunt Gert still seemed to rely on in the morning.

Chapter Fifty-Eight

"All rise for the honorable Judge Marinetti." Jenny stood as the judge entered the courtroom, his robe set for the early morning session. The jury was already seated in the jury box.

As the spectators sat, Judge Marinetti addressed the jury. The tension in the courtroom was palpable. A lot rode on the jury being free of Andersons' goons or being infiltrated or bribed. "The defendant will rise." Sammy stood up, his countenance pale and his hands which hung by his sides obviously shaking.

"Will the foreman of the jury please rise." A rather shy, middle-aged woman with mousy brown hair brushed and permed stood. "Madame foreman, has the jury reached a verdict in the case of Anderson Motors versus Samuel Walker on the charge of embezzlement?"

"It has, your honor."

"And how do you find the defendant? Guilty or not guilty?"

"Not guilty, your honor."

There was a moment where silence swept the courtroom. Sammy's mother, at the back of the courtroom, burst into tears. Annie breathed a sigh of relief and looked lovingly at Sammy. Sammy shook Jake's hand.

"Jake, I know I can never thank you."

"You already have. You have been a good husband to my sister and a good neighbor to all of us. I wish you the best of luck."

As Sammy rushed back to Annie, Jake looked at Bill McKay. McKay came over to shake hands. "Counselor, it's been a pleasure to be beaten by a pro."

"It's been a pleasure to go up against an honest and hard working D.A."

"If you're ever in the area, we could use a good member for our team."

"I'll keep it in mind. Until then, good luck in keeping the county safe."

Jenny stood. The courtroom had emptied, but her feet seemed rooted to the floor. She stared at Jake. His countenance seemed different than their days in the Thompsons' hayloft together, but despite the expensive haircut and the clothes that had replaced the heavy, denim overalls, there was a shred of the youth, a belief that the world was a place to make your mark, that you could make your mark. And, that the world would let you. If only you could just look straight ahead instead of roundabout.

"Hey, Jen." Jake smiled as he saw her standing there. "How about some lunch?"

"Sure, Jake. That would be great."

"How does Blimpy's sound. Or, would you like something more upscale?"

"That sounds fine to me."

Jake drove, finding a perfect spot in front of the neighborhood diner. He jumped out of his truck to let Jenny out. "I think we'll have the place to ourselves. The lunch crowd hasn't arrived yet."

As they sat, the far end booth being theirs without a struggle, they both breathed a sigh of relief. "You did good, Jen."

Jenny could barely answer. The relief she had felt for Sammy and his family had taken her words away. "Jake, you gave up a lot to do this."

"I didn't really, Jenny. It's where I should have been all along. It took you to waken me to that fact."

"You saved Sammy's life. Now, what will you do?"

"I think I'll shack up with Ma and Pa until I get my life back on track. I have a lot of catching up to do. How about you?'

"I'll be heading back to New York. There's not a lot of hurry. Cathy and Jeff gave me an open-ended leave and Josh is happy at the Marshall's. But, it seems I need to be busy."

"Okay. Let's celebrate. They even have champagne at this place. New York wine country's finest."

They clicked their glasses in celebration. Jake looked at

Jenny. "If you're going to be here awhile, maybe we can browse around some of our old haunts."

"That sounds fine, Jake. Aunt Gert needs looking after for a while."

Jenny felt the confusion of years taking root in the pit of her stomach. Jake, flushed with victory, single-mindedly following his overwhelming ambitions since he left the fields of Jerusalem for New York, seemed not to know where he was, or even what he had done. Jenny herself was stunned. Sitting in a diner along the southern tier of New York with pick-up trucks lining the streets seemed to bring her back to the days of hanging out at the The Captain's and shopping at a dry goods store for clothes. The woman who had climbed the ladder of success in one of the most competitive cities in the world seemed almost another person.

Jenny decided to put those thoughts on the back burner of life. After all, the effects of the champagne were beginning to take hold, and she would soon be back in New York where life was safe because people were too busy to contemplate much except elbowing out some poor tourist for a taxi.

Her thoughts began to swirl, her head drooped and her eyelids closed. Jake smiled and called for the check.

Chapter Fifty-Nine

Jenny sat at her oversized mahogany desk in her burgundy leather chair thirty-five stories above the streets of Manhattan. The sunbeams played over her black onyx pen stand and her multi-colored sticky notes. The work had piled up in her absence but Cathy had been generous about it. "Do it when you can, Jen. I know this has been hard."

Jenny could only stare at the street below, the miniature cars and taxis and buses and trolleys slowing to a crawl as lunchtime traffic crammed the avenues never wide enough for the antics of New Yorkers. Cathy stuck her head in the door. "How about lunch?"

"Sounds great. See you in about a half hour."

As Jenny studied what seemed like toy trucks and cars below, she thought of the month she had spent with Jake visiting their old haunts, eating ice cream from the Seneca Dairy with the carefree stroll of their youth, helping his folks sell their wares on Saturday at the Windmill Market in Penn Yan, walking the shores along the beautiful blue waters of the forked Keuka Lake, its name handed down from the native tribes who had lived there before them.

Suddenly, the city of eight million below seemed a lonely place without her childhood friend, someone who had shared the difficulties, the dreams, and the joys of a hard-scrabble

317

youth. Jenny put down her pencil. It was time to fight for space in one of the posh restaurants nearby.

As she and Cathy strode down the block toward the latest restaurant to brave the financial district competition it was almost like old times at Mallory, Hollander & Wexler. Cathy's step was more lively than it had been back then, and her confidence level had of course soared through the roof. And, she was happy. Jeff had been a perfect partner for her, helpful but not overbearing. And, he adored her. Jenny was happy for them both.

They managed to snag a corner table in the new restaurant, an upscale Italian affair with a menu that sported not only fresh pasta but a veal dish that nearly melted in your mouth. It was of course the talk of the office building.

"Jenny, you look like a fish out of water. Was the trial tough?"

"Not really. It turned out well. Sammy's free and he and Annie can have their baby in peace. They are so excited."

"I'm glad. And Jake. How does he feel about it?"

"He decided to stay. He's setting up a solo practice in Syracuse and a storefront in Penn Yan for pro bono. At least that was the word when I left."

"Nice. But, that means he won't grace the streets of Manhattan any longer. And, just when you found him."

"Well, he's fulfilling his dreams. I'm not sure about me."

"If you're going to pull a mid-life crisis on me, Jen, let me know in advance."

"Will do. It's just that Josh will graduate this year and I feel like an empty nester already."

"Well, I have a proposition for you that would fill a lot of your time. Jeff and I are going to start a branch of our firm in Iowa and we'd like you to run the New York office while we set it up."

"I'll think about it, Cathy. I'm pleased that you both trust me enough to ask, but I probably have to make some decisions on what I want to do with my life now that I'm about to be solo."

"Plenty of time to think it over, Jen. It won't happen for at least six months. Say, they aren't fooling about this veal. It's almost like a trip to Italy on your lunch hour."

As they returned to work, the rains of an early spring fell from the sky, turning all of New York and its skyscrapers into a misty grey pall. "Let's run, Jen. I don't want to get this expensive new cashmere wet and stretched out of shape."

Jenny tried to keep up with Cathy but Cathy was determined to save the latest addition to her expensive wardrobe which she was certain helped her clinch all those high-powered deals brokered in expensive restaurants. Cathy reached the dry, well-lit lobby before her.

"See you later, Jenny. Jeff and I can handle tonight with Mr.

Brezewski so you can take the night off. You deserve it. You've been working like five people since you got back."

"Thanks, Cath. I appreciate it. I don't think Josh has seen me for two weeks."

As Jenny settled at her desk the phone rang. Insistently. Jenny was surprised because Ginny kept a good check on her phone calls. She was surprised that Ginny had put this one through without checking with her first.

She picked up the phone a bit gingerly, succumbing to an eerie fear as she put it to her ear.

"Jennifer, are you sitting down?"

"Yes, Mother, I am."

"Your Aunt Gert passed away this morning. I thought you should know right away."

"Yes, Mother. How did it happen?"

"She was unconscious when we got there this morning. We called for the ambulance but it was too late. She died at the hospital. Doc Masterson said her heart just gave out."

"I'll be right home, Mother. As soon as I can get Josh."

"You better stay at Aunt Gert's. Your father and I can't handle company anymore."

Jenny overlooked the slight as she hung up the phone. As it nestled into its cradle, she put her head down on her desk and sobbed and sobbed. Aunt Gert was with Rafe, a comforting thought, but she would no longer be here with Jenny. As she lifted her head and stared at the grey fog enveloping the building across the avenue she realized how much she would miss her.

She picked up the phone and called Josh. They would need to be on their way as soon as she could get a cab to her apartment.

Chapter Sixty

A unt Gert's funeral had been confined to family and close friends. She had been laid to rest next to Rafe in a spot reserved for her long ago by the Tewksbury family at her request.

Mother was inconsolable since she had been certain that as the eldest she would go first. Father did his best to provide some comfort.

Jenny's tears had mingled with the mist of the rain at the outdoor service, but she had kept a close watch on Josh. She knew how dear he had been to Aunt Gert, and he had basked in the attention she had provided him.

The reading of the will took place on a dreary Wednesday afternoon in the ramshackle law offices of Andrew MacElbee in Dundee. He had been a close friend of Gert's since they had graduated together from Penn Yan Dundee Central.

There were no surprises except one. All of Gert's possessions and what little money she had saved had gone to Mother. A few special trinkets Josh had coveted had gone to him. But, what shocked everyone was that Aunt Gert had left the farmhouse to Jenny.

"You mind you take care of it, Jenny. Aunt Gert spent a lifetime tending it."

"Yes, Mother."

Jenny pondered the gift. What possessed Aunt Gert to make her the caretaker of an old farmhouse? She would sort it out on the way to the airport. Josh must return to school as soon as possible. She would stay and tend to a few loose ends and tidy up the farmhouse for the next few weeks.

The ride to the airport was treacherous and gloomy. Heavy rains beat down upon the roof of the BMW and the roads were slick.

"What will happen to Shakespeare?"

"He'll be okay, Josh. Sparky and Cliff will care for him, and all of Anne's and Sarah's children will be playing with him. He'll have plenty of farm dogs to run with."

"But, he'll miss Aunt Gert."

"Yes, he will, Josh. But, maybe he'll remember all the good times they had together. They were content to just be with each other. And, Aunt Gert always remembered to let Shakespeare play."

"Mom, will Gus Marshall meet me at the airport?"

"Yes, he will, Josh. But, Petey's in school so Gus said he would take you right there as soon as you arrive. I'll be along in a few weeks."

"I know you will, Mom. I promise I won't wreck the apartment."

"I know you won't Josh. You know I'll be calling every day to check. As long as that baseball Chip gave you doesn't go through the window and land on somebody's head below we'll be alright. Rinaldo will look in on you also."

"Okay, Mom. But, Petey and I will be studying most of the time. We've got to hit the books. Petey's aiming for SUNY at Stony Brook. I doubt we'll have time to even shoot a few hoops."

"Well, there'll be time for some fun. Dee's got Rosa looking in on you. She's getting married in a few months, but she's taking time off from her wedding shopping to do the job."

"Well, we might need to take a break there."

"Maybe not too much of one. Rosa's matured. She signed up for classes at community college in Brooklyn and has taken secretarial and business. Dee's very proud of her."

"We're here. Let's unload your bags."

As Jenny helped Josh with the details of boarding, she felt a rush of maternal pride. He had overcome so much of the unfair suffering he had thrown at him just for being born. To her, the gangling youth struggling with his duffel and his jacket was still the perfect infant she had held at birth. She held him as she said goodbye.

"Call me if you need me."

"Will do."

As he waved from the plane, she felt the loss she knew she would feel as he embarked on a life that would not include her. A life full of the hope of youth. She silently wished it to be filled with the wonders of this earth. But, she knew it was up to him now.

Jenny sighed as she left the airport. She must drive to Aunt Gert's to sort out her possessions. As she reached the farmhouse she climbed the stairs of the porch and nestled in the slats of the old swing now covered only with a coat of chipping paint. She swung softly, back and forth, mindless of the creak of the unoiled chain, as a strange numbness enveloped her. She barely heard the squealing of tires on an old farm truck as it braked or the footsteps that brought Jake to her side.

As they sat, Jake wrapped his arms around her as he once did so long ago to keep her from the chill of a late spring evening. She felt the strength of his arms he had once used to help till the fields of the Martin farm and for a moment her burdens seemed to vanish. They both looked up at the dark, clear sky and Jenny marveled at the moon that shared space in the skies with a host of bright, twinkling stars in the vastness of the universe.

Chapter Sixty-One

T he early afternoon sun was bright as Jenny set up her paints on the long, back veranda of Aunt Gert's farmhouse. She reached for her palette and began to mix the vibrant red she favored, the color of the tiny blossoms that bloomed for only two weeks on the miniature plants she had discovered beneath the stand of sycamores behind the barn.

She had returned to Jerusalem for good just one week after the will reading. Since that time, Jake had been her constant companion. They had strolled the shores and admired the clear, blue waters of Keuka Lake, they had eaten ice cream under the pavilion at the old picnic tables on a grassy spot behind the Seneca Dairy, they had helped the Martins pack up their vegetables for the Saturday market, and they had worked long hours in Jake's pro bono storefront in Penn Yan.

But, it was the land that had drawn them back. Flatlands filled with wildflower meadows, freshly tilled fields in spring, the scent of newly baled hay in autumn, and untamed patches that turned green every spring and nurtured the spirit. And, behind all this, the mist of a horizon that stretched forever.

There had been no formal courtship nor had there been a formal proposal. Their time together was as natural as the call of the whippoorwill they had used to summon each other on a cool spring evening after their chores were finished in their youth. They would be married in the early summer after the rains of spring subsided and the heavy work of planting was over.

"Hey, Jen. How's the canvas coming?"

"Hey, Sparks. I didn't hear your chariot pull up."

"Of course not. Sammy's been tuning it up. It's as quiet as a Rolls."

"How's Cliff?"

"Swamped. That's what I came to ask you. Would you take over the bake sale while I'm gone? I'll be back in a week."

"Will do."

"I think the patent will be wrapped up by Thursday. I'll spend the rest of the time with Mom and Dad."

"Give them my love."

"I will, Jen. They miss you and Josh."

"We miss them, too, Sparks. Josh expects to crash in on them for a weekend as soon as he's settled."

"I'll be off, then. Tell Jake I left the key to the plow with Cliff. He's welcome to add it to his collection. I have to delay spring planting till I get back."

"Thanks, Sparks."

Jenny listened as Sparky's latest Lexus squealed off, the only luxury she allowed herself in her quest to live off the land. Jenny smiled as she realized the contradiction.

She picked up her paint brush and began to mix the colors of the wildflowers she saw before her, the pale pink of the phlox, the brilliant blue of the lupines, the deep, golden yellow of the daisies, the soft oranges and reds of the brown-spotted meadow lilies, and thought of Josh. A newly settled freshman in the school of journalism at Columbia, he would follow the promise he had made her at thirteen. 'I'm going to be a TV reporter so you will always be able to see me.'

Jenny smiled as she thought of the earnestness of his youth. He had shared that trait with Jake and the two had bonded the moment they met. Jake took time off from his law practice to shoot hoops, toss a football, and teach Josh, along with Sarah's and Annie's broods, the benefits of wading in streams and skipping stones along the shoreline of the crooked lake.

As she mused, she heard the sound of little voices nearing the house, drifting in on the early afternoon spring breezes. She looked up to see Sarah with her latest addition, a three-month-old named Jacob, cradled in her arms, and four other little ones tagging behind. Their dress was modest and drab, but their obvious enthusiasm was not.

"Where's Uncle Jake?"

"He's out in the field getting ready for spring planting, Rebecca. How are your studies going?"

"Ma says we can take a break. We baked seven pies for the bake sale."

"That sounds like a lot."

"Where's Josh?"

"He's in New York. He'll be back to see us in the summer."

"Where's Shakespeare?"

"He's in the front. The barn cats chased him out of the hayloft. He could probably use some sympathy."

"Jesse will be along in a while to help Jake, Jenny."

"Thanks, Sarah. If you don't mind, you can just leave those pies in the kitchen. They smell fresh baked."

"They are. We picked the berries this morning."

As they left, she picked a canvas and placed it on the easel. She looked at the vista that stretched before her. The meadow filled with wildflowers, their pinks and purples, deep golds and oranges, swaying gently in the breezes of soft, spring winds, the fields newly tilled and ready to be sown with the seed of feed corn and beans and oats, stretching toward the mysterious mists and haze of an endless horizon. She would paint it as she saw it, no need to stylize it, its purity the essence of an artistic eye. She began to daub the canvas.

Contrary to popular belief, you can go home again, thought Jenny. No matter where you wander, no matter for how long or how far away, home is forever embedded in your spirit, and in your soul. But, there is a price to pay. Other worlds will leave their mark. No longer could she accept the strict tenets of a people unable to accept a single difference in the human condition when she had lived among eight million people who rubbed shoulders every day with as many cultural differences as existed on Earth.

She rose as the afternoon sun lowered in the sky, glancing at the sign she had pulled from the attic and Jake had nailed over the old, oversized barn doors, its red paint glistening as the sun's rays played about its timbers. "Windborne Acres." The sign Aunt Gert and Rafe had painted "one silly evening."

She packed up her paints and headed for the kitchen. She would lay out a light supper. Jake had eaten his heavy meal at noon.

She pulled from the fridge some cold, sliced chicken, the cheeses she had gotten at Laufler's dairy down the road, the sourdough bread she had pulled from the oven this morning, a bowl of slaw, Jake's favorite, made from an old Martin family recipe, and added some devilled eggs she had made the evening before.

She raced up the stairs. She would fetch Jake herself. Jesse would be gone and he would be forgetting the time.

She showered and scrubbed, removing the day's paint with difficulty. She slipped into a light cotton dress, its shades of mauve flattering her long, chestnut hair pulled back into a simple ponytail. She would run across the meadow barefoot as she had done so often in childhood.

As Jake saw her, he grinned. He jumped from the tractor, removed his boots and slung them over his shoulder, his gentle laughter mingling with the sounds of the crickets in the still of the evening.

As they headed for the farmhouse, its clapboards still sorely in need of paint, the sun setting above them, their toes digging into the rich, dark loam of newly turned earth, they were just two people on their way to an early supper.